Praise for
~ THE UNICORN QUEST ~

★ "Fans of magic and fantasy, especially those who love Madeleine
L'Engle's *A Wrinkle in Time* or . . . Neil Gaiman's *Coraline*,
can't miss this debut." —*Booklist*, starred review

"Hand to readers who love Narnia." —*School Library Journal*

"Rich worldbuilding and high stakes make this a quest worth taking
with a protagonist who grows by facing her fears." —*Kirkus Reviews*

"Enter and be transported to a lush land full of intrigue, danger, and
thrilling magic! Benko's sharp storytelling will keep readers madly
flipping the pages in this new, timeless adventure. Spectacular!"
—Jennifer Lynn Alvarez, author of the Guardian Herd
and Riders of the Realm series

"An adventure-quest brimming with magic and heart. Benko reaches
the child in all of us who secretly hopes that a door is never just a door.
Mesmerizing." —Roshani Chokshi, *New York Times* bestselling author

"*The Unicorn Quest* draws you into a richly imagined alternate world,
keeps you on edge with clever twists and turns, then leaves you
breathless as it gallops to its sensational climax!"
—Bruce Coville, author of the Unicorn Chronicles series

"Filled with wondrous surprises, fascinating magic, and appealing
characters, it hits all the right notes, and I loved every second of it!"
—Sarah Beth Durst, author of *Journey Across the Hidden Islands*
and *The Girl Who Could Not Dream*

"Utterly delightful! Taps into the wonderful childhood fantasy
of finding a secret door to another world."
—Jessica Day George, *New York Times* bestselling author

"As dazzling and richly imagined as anything I've read in years.
The Unicorn Quest promises to be a must-read."
—Peter Lerangis, *New York Times* bestselling author

THE UNICORN QUEST

KAMILLA BENKO

BLOOMSBURY

NEW YORK LONDON OXFORD NEW DELHI SYDNEY

First published in the United States of America in February 2018
by Bloomsbury Children's Books
www.bloomsbury.com

Bloomsbury is a registered trademark of Bloomsbury Publishing Plc

For information about permission to reproduce selections from this book, write to
Permissions, Bloomsbury Children's Books, 1385 Broadway, New York, New York 10018
Bloomsbury books may be purchased for business or promotional use. For information
on bulk purchases please contact Macmillan Corporate and Premium Sales Department at
specialmarkets@macmillan.com

Library of Congress Cataloging-in-Publication Data
Names: Benko, Kamilla, author.
Title: The unicorn quest / by Kamilla Benko.
Description: New York : Bloomsbury, 2018.
Summary: In an antique-filled mansion, sisters Claire and Sophie find a ladder
to the magical land of Arden, where wraiths roam freely, unicorns have disappeared,
and the guilds of magic no longer trust each other.
Identifiers: LCCN 2017022320 (print) • LCCN 2017038074 (e-book)
ISBN 978-1-68119-245-1 (hardcover) • ISBN 978-1-68119-246-8 (e-book)
Subjects: | CYAC: Sisters—Fiction. | Magic—Fiction. | Adventure and adventurers—
Fiction. | Unicorns—Fiction. | Fantasy.
Classification: LCC PZ7.1.B4537 Un 2018 (print) | LCC PZ7.1.B4537 (e-book) |
DDC [Fic]—dc23
LC record available at https://lccn.loc.gov/2017022320

Book design by Amanda Bartlett
Typeset by Westchester Publishing Services
Printed and bound in the U.S.A. by Berryville Graphics Inc., Berryville, Virginia
2 4 6 8 10 9 7 5 3 1

All papers used by Bloomsbury Publishing, Inc., are natural, recyclable products
made from wood grown in well-managed forests. The manufacturing processes
conform to the environmental regulations of the country of origin.

To Papa, who made me fairy wings,
and to Mama, who read me the world

THE UNICORN QUEST

The Queen and The Unicorn

In the light of a lavender moon,
The queen of Arden—
    The gracious queen,
    The crying queen,
    The last queen—
The queen of Arden stepped onto the plains.

Under the gaze of heartless stars,
The plains—
    The blackened plains,
    The sorrowful plains,
    The blood-soaked plains—
The plains trembled at her step.

"O Queen," they whispered,
"Turn away. Turn back."

"I cannot," said the queen.
"What I search for is here."

"What do you seek?"
(The plains knew what she sought.)

"I seek," said she,
    "The quickflame spirit,

The swiftness of grace,
The edge of courage."

"I seek," said she,
    "The star-forged horn,
    The cloud-woven mane,
    The moon-lit heart."

"I seek," the last queen said,
    "The last unicorn."

Excerpt from **The Queen and The Unicorn**,
*written by Spinner Glen Green of Arden
in celebration of the fiftieth anniversary
of the end of the Guild War, 1049 Craft Era*

CHAPTER
1

Claire had never seen a ladder in a fireplace before.

Of course, since moving to Great-Aunt Diana's mansion two weeks ago, she had seen many strange things: a castle in a bottle, a chair made entirely of antlers, and even the disembodied hand of a statue holding paper clips in the third-floor library.

But this ladder was different, somehow, and as she moved through the gallery toward it, she felt a slight jolt between her shoulder blades, as if lightning had pinched her.

Late-afternoon sunlight streaked in from the edges of the curtains as Claire wove among the sheet-covered pillars and sculptures scattered throughout the room. She ignored as best she could the statues pressing against the dust cloths, looking like stationary ghosts.

Claire's great-aunt Diana had been an art collector, and this, it seemed, was yet another gallery where she'd kept many of her treasures. She'd traveled all over the world seeking out strange and beautiful things, and because of that, Claire had only seen her great-aunt once, when she was a baby, which didn't really count.

So a few months ago when her father had solemnly told her and her older sister, Sophie, that their great-aunt had disappeared on one of her treasure-hunting trips, Claire didn't really know how to feel. She had given Dad a hug while Sophie remarked it was a spectacular way to die. And after that, Claire didn't think much about it—until, that is, they received notice that Great-Aunt Diana's house, Windemere Manor, and all its contents had been left to *them*. All those thousands of knickknacks and collectibles had to be sorted and cataloged for the estate sale scheduled at the end of August, right before school started again.

So now, all because of Great-Aunt Diana, Claire's last summer before middle school—the summer that was supposed to be full of late-night sleepovers with her best friend, Catherine, and two weeks of summer camp—had been canceled.

Dad and Mom had thought that moving into the house for the summer would be a good break from the humidity of the city. *Family bonding time*, they had announced, *with no distractions.*

Claire knew exactly what they meant: distractions like Dad's marketing meetings that ran into dinnertime because no one could agree which font was best, or the stack of essays waiting to be graded by Mom before next morning's classes.

In any case, Claire had to admit she was looking forward to this summer, too. Being in the country might mean bug bites and no cell phone reception, but it also meant time to hang out with Sophie again—just like they used to *before*.

While most girls their ages collected bracelets or pens, Sophie had collected Experiences. Directing neighborhood plays. Searching for fossils in the park. Researching the disappearance of a masterpiece as she tried to solve the mystery. They were all moments of excitement, and Claire always came along.

But after the diagnosis, Experiences stopped being fun. Sophie seemed more interested in stories about graveyards and doctors and other scary stuff that Claire hated.

Thankfully, now all that was in the past, along with the worry lines around Mom's mouth and the long hours in waiting rooms. Sophie was well again. Things were back to normal. Well, almost normal.

Sophie kept disappearing into the mansion's rooms, leaving Claire in a constant search. It was almost as if all her time away from Claire had marked her for places that Claire couldn't follow. In fact, she had been trying to find Sophie when she opened the door to this particular gallery.

Now, standing in the hearth's dusty mouth, Claire coughed as she studied the ladder. Of the many strange sights in Windemere Manor, this one stood out to her. Something about the ladder felt like an invitation. She looked up into the dizzying darkness. What was up there—spiders? Bats? Something else?

Claire heard a *creak* behind her.

She stiffened. This old house, with its dark corners and constant *hiss*es and *pop*s, had made her nervous since the very first time she'd stepped into the dimly lit foyer and seen the peeling wallpaper and crumbling trim.

Another *groan*, this time from the ceiling. Claire pulled her pencil out from behind her ear and lightly pressed her thumb against it. Its tip was sharp, and it made her feel slightly better. Sophie always said pencils were Claire's wooden thumb—that after she'd finally stopped sucking on her thumb, she'd replaced it with the equally annoying habit of nibbling her pencils. But it was much more than that. Pencils were what Claire used to draw and document the world around her; it was a way to understand.

Claire thought she heard someone exhale. A flicker of white caught her eye. She turned—

Hands suddenly gripped Claire's shoulders, and her scream drowned out the clatter of her pencil as it hit the floor.

"You should have seen your face," Sophie said, laughing as she brushed dark hair out of her eyes.

"Don't *do* that!" Claire said, crouching to her knees, partly to hide her burning face and partly to find her pencil, which seemed to have instantaneously disappeared. She felt around the marble floor beside the fireplace. The hard, cold rock stung her knees, but she didn't care. It was her best drawing pencil, and it had finally worn down to the perfect length. The next time she sharpened it, it would be too short.

"Sorry, Clairina, it was just too good to pass up!"

Claire kept her eyes on the floor. She was glad that Sophie, always fearless, couldn't hear her still-racing heartbeat. *There.* Her hand found her pencil, and she instantly felt better.

"Wow," she heard her sister say. Claire stood back up to see that Sophie had lifted the corner of a yellowing linen sheet and was peering under it. "Look at this!" She tugged the fabric, and it slipped loose from the display pedestal.

A beautiful ivory unicorn, slightly bigger than Claire's forearm, was revealed. Rearing, the unicorn arched its neck forward, its spiral horn ending in a perfect point. The sculptor must have been a master because the ivory mane seemed to ripple in a phantom wind. But though the unicorn was undoubtedly magnificent, somehow it looked sad, and the feeling pierced Claire's heart, sharp and certain. She tucked her pencil behind her ear and reached out to touch the flowing tail. One day, she wanted to draw something as wonderful as this.

But Sophie had already lost interest and was moving through the gallery, lifting the linens off more pedestals and inspecting the other pieces. Claire noticed she had pulled her hair back with the purple ribbon she always kept around her wrist.

When Sophie wore her hair in a high ponytail, she reminded Claire of a postcard they had received from Great-Aunt Diana.

It had a bust of an Egyptian queen on it, and Sophie had the same pointed features as the royal's profile, though the freckles on her cheeks were all her own. When Claire put her curly hair in a ponytail, she just looked like a squirrel had attached itself to the back of her head.

"Have you ever seen such a big fireplace?" Sophie asked, bored with sculptures, apparently, and returning to the hearth. Her voice echoed slightly as she looked up the chimney. "You could roast a moose in here."

"Or a sister," Claire said drily.

Sophie smiled her wild smile, showing all her teeth. Then she put a foot on the bottom rung.

"What are you doing?" Claire asked. "You can't climb that thing." She heard the waver in her voice and hated it, but there was something about the enormous dark fireplace, and the old ladder, and this whole *room*, that gave her a bad feeling.

"Don't be like that," Sophie said, putting her foot on the next rung. "Come on. Have a little fun."

There was really no choice. If Claire didn't climb, Sophie would never let her forget it, just like the time four years ago when Claire had stood frozen in fear at the top of the tallest waterslide, waiting for Dad to come get her, the sun umbrellas just candy-colored dots far below.

What her sister had never understood was that it wasn't the height she'd been afraid of, or the rush of water. It was the dark tunnel she had to pass through first, before the slide burst into sunlight. She had never liked the dark. As an artist, she understood the world by what it *looked* like. The dark was unknowable. And Claire hated not knowing things.

But there was one other thing she was beginning to hate more: Being left behind. Left alone.

"Let's go," Sophie said as Claire hesitated. "It'll be an Experience!"

The familiar word lit a match in Claire's heart, singeing— if not burning away—some of the strangeness of being in Great-Aunt Diana's house. Sophie was finally acting like herself again. She wanted Claire to come with her.

And so Claire took a deep breath and wrapped her hand around a wooden rung. Putting one foot on the ladder, she tested its strength. When it didn't snap, she took another step up. Then another.

One by one, she climbed, following the bright turquoise soles of Sophie's sneakers. Soon the darkness reached down around Claire's shoulders.

"Sophieee! Claaaire!"

Claire paused, her skin prickling as their names whispered up through the shaft as though from a great distance. A ghost?

"Sophieee! Claaaire!"

A rush of relief hit her. "Sophie!" she called. "I think Dad's looking for us!"

"Gah!" Sophie's sneakers were already so high above her, Claire could barely make them out. "Why does he always have to ruin everything?"

"Come on, Sophie," she said, scuttling down the ladder. Reluctantly, it seemed, Sophie began to follow.

Claire jumped the last several feet and landed just as the double doors swung open and Dad's head peeked around the corner. Above her, she heard the ladder creak as Sophie froze.

"There you are! It's time for dinner." Dad adjusted his glasses. "What are you doing in here?"

"I . . . um . . . I was exploring." Claire tried to keep her eyes fixed on him and not let them slide to the fireplace.

He nodded. "I don't blame you. Your great-aunt had a lot of cool stuff, huh?" He waited for her to nod obediently, then asked, "Do you know where Sophie is?"

There was a scuffling above, and Claire flinched. "Yeah. I can get her."

"Great." Dad smiled as he stepped back into the hallway. "Tell her to hurry!"

Claire counted to five before she called, "All clear!" She waited for the *squeak* of rubber sole against rung, but the chimney was oddly silent. "Sophie?"

Claire sucked her breath in tight. It was obvious what was happening. Sophie was going to scare her again. But this time, Claire was ready for it.

A few more seconds ticked by. Nothing.

Maybe Sophie had run into a family of raccoons. Maybe she'd gotten stuck, or—Claire suddenly felt as though she'd been kicked in the stomach—maybe she was about to collapse again. Like before.

Then she heard Sophie's voice, made tinny with the echo: "Claire?"

"Sophie!" Claire was so relieved she didn't know whether to cry or hug the ladder. Instead, she crossed her arms. "What were you thinking!? You're going to get us in trouble!"

"Calm down, I'm coming!" A second later Sophie's thin frame descended. "Sorry," she said, not looking sorry at all. "I climbed up a few more rungs to make sure Dad didn't see, but then I couldn't hear anything."

The ash had tinted Sophie's skin gray and left odd smudge marks all over her arms. For a second, Claire was reminded of how she'd looked in the hospital. Suddenly, she wanted to be as far away from sheet-draped statues as possible.

"Come on," Claire said. She took a few steps toward the double doors and glanced back. Sophie was still staring at the fireplace. For a moment, Claire thought Sophie would climb up again, but instead, her sister turned, her sundress swishing around her knees as she jogged to the door.

"I'm going to go wash my hands," she said. "Tell them I'll be there in a second." Claire was about to follow, but for some reason, she took one last look at the gallery behind her. The unicorn statuette looked like a snowflake against the black mouth of the fireplace, and again, sadness tinged her heart. She felt bad that something so pretty should have to stay hidden away in the cold, vast room.

Claire stepped into the hallway and carefully shut the doors behind her, then flicked the lock left. She checked the handle.

The doors stayed shut. She jiggled the knob a second time, and then a third. For good luck.

Mostly, the Martinsons ate together in the kitchen. But tonight they had set up in the dining room, which was the grandest room Claire had ever seen. The crystal chandelier looked like something that belonged in Cinderella's ballroom, and the tapestries hugging the walls added a hominess that was lacking in the rest of the manor. In the tide of arguments over which ice cream flavor was best and a funny story about one of Mom's students, Claire felt the long reach of the gallery unhook itself and burrow away.

As dinner neared its end, Claire watched Dad carefully, waiting for his signal. Finally, he looked at her across the table and pulled his ear.

Claire stood up, keeping her head down to hide her smile. Sophie always said Claire's smile was a billboard for I Have a Secret, and she didn't want Sophie to know until the last possible moment. Quickly, she gathered up some of the dirty dishes and followed her father to the kitchen.

Dad pulled a frosted cake out of a cupboard. "Do you have the presents ready?" he asked.

"Yes," she said, showing him the tote bag filled with gifts she had stuffed under the kitchen sink.

"Great," he said. "Now we just have to find where Auntie hid the candles . . ."

He began to open the pantry doors. Claire dutifully pulled out a drawer, but instead of candles, she found a geode the size of a dinosaur egg. She closed the drawer carefully. Great-Aunt Diana either had a complex organizational system, or she had been the messiest person in the world.

"Daddy?" Claire didn't usually call him that, but the coziness of the dinner had left her feeling wistful. The unicorn statuette flashed back into her mind.

"Yes?" He plucked out a bright box of birthday candles.

She took a deep breath. "Why didn't we visit Windemere when Great-Aunt Diana was alive?" To Claire, Great-Aunt Diana had been nothing more than the scrawled signature at the bottom of a birthday card. It had never occurred to Claire to ask much about her—all she knew was that Diana was Grandpa Leo's sister.

"Oh, that," Dad said. He tapped the box of candles against his palm and a bunch slid out. He stuck the first one in the cake before answering.

"Well, your great-aunt Diana traveled a lot. She loved her work, and she was obsessed with adding art to her collection. As I'm sure you've noticed," he said with a wry smile. "Besides, she could be . . . difficult. Your grandpa was never that close with her, so after he and your grandma died, we just didn't have much reason to visit. I suppose I always thought there'd be more time to reconnect someday. And then there wasn't."

Claire sensed something like regret shading her father's voice, like the softest pencil mark on paper. A tendril of guilt unfurled in her chest. She hadn't meant to bring up bad memories.

"Ready?" Dad asked, lighting the candles.

Claire picked up the bag of presents, double-checking to make sure her gift was there. "Ready."

She followed Dad and the birthday cake to the dining room. Because Dad was so tall, she couldn't see Sophie's face when he walked through the door, but she did hear her gasp of surprise.

"What's going on?" Sophie asked, and Claire was pleased to hear that her sister sounded genuinely astonished. "My birthday was months ago!"

"It's a *re*-birthday," Claire said as she dumped the packages onto the table. Dad presented the cake with a flourish and set it next to the mound of presents. There was plenty of room, as the large oak table could have easily fit half of Claire's fifth-grade class. "Mom came up with it."

"A what?" Sophie asked, sneaking a finger out to swipe a bit of frosting from the platter's edge.

"Hold your horses," Mom said, and shooed away Sophie's hand. "It's your re-birthday. You weren't able to leave the hospital on your actual birthday, but that doesn't mean you can't enjoy yourself now!"

"See?" Dad said. "We didn't forget you, um, what's your name again?"

Claire looked at Sophie and they both rolled their eyes at the same time. They were always in perfect harmony regarding Dad's jokes.

"A re-birthday," Sophie repeated softly. In the light of the thirteen candles, her cheeks were pink and her eyes sparkled. As Sophie smiled at her family, Claire thought she had never seen her sister look more beautiful.

Sophie blew out the candles, and even though it wasn't Claire's re-birthday, Claire made a quick, quiet wish. A wish so tender that it had cocooned itself deep inside her heart, only to flit out now. Little wisps of smoke hung over the table as the rest of the Martinsons clapped.

Mom cut slices of cake for everyone, and Dad snapped pictures on his big camera. Soon, there was gentle laughter as Sophie unwrapped gifts and held up the pink pom-pom sweater from Nana. Finally, there was one present left: Claire's.

"It's spectacular!" Sophie squealed once she untied the bow. Her sister smoothed out the curling ends, and Claire took in her own work. It was a charcoal drawing of Sophie sitting in the crook of the magnolia tree in their backyard, the knees of her jeans torn. Surrounded by leaves, her sister looked thoughtfully away into the distance. Instead of drawing the delicate blossoms that appeared each spring, Claire had filled the tree with all Sophie's favorite things—books, playbills, flutes, cupcakes, microphones, and ice skates.

Sophie stood up and wrapped her arms around Claire's shoulders.

"I'm glad you like it," Claire said.

Sophie gave her a quick squeeze. "I love it."

"We should get it framed," Dad suggested. "Then we can hang it in your room."

"Great idea," Mom said as she began to gather up the torn paper and ribbons.

Claire smiled and leaned against her sister. Her tiny, stolen birthday wish flitted back to her, and she hoped that maybe—just maybe—it had come true.

CHAPTER
2

The gargoyle's nose was giving Claire trouble again.

With a sigh, she used her thumb to smudge a shadow under it, trying to add depth. She'd been working on perspective this morning, and if she tilted her head, she could just see the profile of a stone gargoyle that roosted above an attic window. It snarled ferociously over Windemere's sprawling green grounds that stretched as far as the eye could see. Claire thought it was a bit weird to see so many uninterrupted trees, but in the countryside where the nearest neighbor was a ten-minute drive away, she guessed it was normal. At any rate, it wasn't weirder than the rest of Windemere.

Holding the paper at arm's length, Claire stared at her sketch. The shadow hadn't landed right—instead of making the nose pop, it just looked like she'd given the gargoyle a mustache. Rubbing the mistake away with an eraser, she tried again.

Claire had been drawing since she was tiny. There was something calming about dividing the world around her into small, knowable parts that could then be captured pencil line by pencil line.

"Have you seen Sophie?"

Looking up, Claire saw Mom framed in the attic doorway. A pair of earrings glinted in her hand. When Claire shook her head, Mom frowned. "Can you help me find her? We have to leave in half an hour."

"Where are you going?" Claire asked, not minding the interruption. Her drawing was looking more like a deranged koala than a gargoyle anyway.

Mom wiggled her earrings in. She seemed distracted. "Sophie has an appointment with a new doctor."

Worry hung itself on Claire like a wet towel. "Why does she have to go to the doctor if she's all better?"

"It's just routine," Mom said, holding the door open a bit wider for Claire. "Dr. Silva is a specialist, and we're very lucky that his offices are closer to Windemere than they are to home. We just need to get Sophie there." Mom tucked a few curls into the makeshift bun on top of her head. "Can you check the first floor?"

Claire nodded. Scooting past Mom, she padded down the threadbare Persian runners and to the back staircase. Once she reached the ground floor, she quickly started opening doors.

The first opened to a room filled to the ceiling with furniture. Wardrobes and tables and little poufs were balanced precariously in stacks, along with more unusual woodwork, like a love seat carved in the shape of a mermaid.

In the second room, the floor was clear, but the walls were covered in paintings of plants and bugs and butterflies . . . at least, Claire hoped they were paintings. She quickly closed the door. Sophie would never hang out in such a creepy-crawly room.

The third, fourth, and fifth rooms were more of the same— collections of jars, flocks of odd-looking musical instruments, jumbled suits of armor and riding boots . . . Claire had no idea why Great-Aunt Diana had wanted *three* sets of bagpipes.

And still no Sophie.

As she wound her way through the hall, Claire heard a cough come from behind a pair of double doors and she pushed them open.

"What are you doing?" Claire asked, finding herself once again in the unicorn gallery. And there, at the far end, perched on the ladder in the enormous fireplace, was Sophie. Her sister's hair shimmered as she turned around to look at Claire. Ash dusted the shoulders of her purple T-shirt.

"What does it look like I'm doing?"

"Mom wants you," Claire said, stepping farther inside. "You're supposed to go to the doctor's."

Sophie made a face. "There's still at least fifteen minutes before we need to leave."

"But—" Claire tried to think of something—anything— that would convince her to come down. The bad feeling the room had given her before was creeping back. "What if Mom and Dad find out?" she finished lamely.

"You're not going to tell, are you?" Sophie asked.

Reluctantly, Claire shook her head. The last time she'd made that mistake, Sophie had called a family meeting and made the case that Claire was now old enough to be a part of laundry rotation.

"Good. Sisters need to stick together." Sophie climbed up another few rungs so that Claire could only see the backs of her knees.

Vanishing point. The words popped into Claire's head. It was the term her art teacher used to describe the point in a drawing beyond which objects cease to exist. Her stomach turned. What was the vanishing point for her sister?

Then, suddenly, Sophie's sneakers stopped. They climbed back down and her sister's head reappeared. "Coming?"

From her sweaty palms to her racing pulse, everything in Claire screamed *No!* It was high! It was narrow! It was *dark*!

But . . . Sophie had asked her.

"Yeah," Claire said, a reluctant delight pushing aside her logical misgivings. "I am."

Sophie grinned, and scrambled up again, this time disappearing entirely. And so Claire began to climb.

She was faster than she'd been before, but she still wasn't as quick as Sophie, who was scrambling up like a squirrel. An occasional flake of ash fell into Claire's eyes, and the burned air tickled her nose. Soon, she couldn't see Sophie, but she could hear her feet thudding against the ladder.

Suddenly, loud coughs echoed down the shaft.

"Are you all right?" Claire called up to her sister.

"I'm fine!" Sophie said, her voice slightly muffled. "Hurry up!"

But the fizzy delight that had propelled Claire forward was now falling flat. She began to feel hot as she placed hand over hand, foot over foot. Her fingers twinged a bit, like they had fallen asleep.

Wondering how much longer it would be before they reached the top and got out of the dark, Claire tried to picture the outside of Great-Aunt Diana's mansion—the four stories of red brick, the many chimneys that reached past the attics' peaks.

How many rungs had they climbed . . . one hundred? Two hundred?

A chill curled in her chest. It was dangerous to play in chimneys. They could fall, they could get stuck, someone could light a fire . . .

Claire was sweating now, the air stiff and stale.

"Sophie!" she called. "Maybe we should turn back?"

Claire looked down—and immediately wished she hadn't. There was nothing below her but darkness. It was as if the gallery, the statues, the entire world below had all ceased to exist.

She wanted to turn around, but at this point, *surely* they were closer to the roof than the hearth. The tingling in her fingers intensified and the sensation spread to her arms and legs. It almost felt as though her bones were humming.

"Sophie?" she tried again. Claire paused, listening, and an awful knowing settled on her, heavy and suffocating: she was alone.

A scream clawed up from her belly and pushed out in one long word: "Sophieeee!"

She climbed faster, trying to outrace the blackness and unbearable hum that now rattled her lungs, making it difficult to breathe. Faster, *faster*!

And finally, there it was. A pinprick of light above her.

Claire gasped and hurled herself toward the bright dot. Suddenly the ladder ended, and her fingertips scraped against rock. Balancing precariously on the last rung, she hoisted herself up—and then she was tumbling, falling headfirst.

She squeezed her eyes shut, bracing for the ground that must be rushing up to meet her. But just as suddenly, she landed in a pile of sharp elbows, tangled hair, and rough denim.

"Ow! Get off me!"

A pair of hands shoved against her chest, and she rolled off Sophie onto damp grass.

Claire breathed in cool, sweet air. Stars twinkled above her, and the moon cast a buttery glow. *Wait.*

Moon. *Stars.* But it had just been morning!

Claire shot upright.

A garden of fluttering leaves and flowers encircled the sisters. Ivy crept along its edges, while squat fruit trees hunched forward, tired from years of neglect. The lingering scent of recent rain rose from the grass. Claire's throat constricted. Though it was beautiful, it was *wrong*.

They'd been climbing a chimney, but what they'd reached was not a roof. Chimneys always led to roofs, didn't they? And though the grounds at Windemere were pretty, there was certainly nothing like *this*. Even the air had changed. No longer heavy with summer's humidity, it felt brisk and springlike. It was almost as if they'd ended up in an entirely different world.

"Clairina," Sophie gasped, and pointed beyond the treetops, toward a dark shape that loomed against the night sky.

Claire squinted. It seemed to be something similar to a mansion, but larger. More like a school or a cathedral or a—

"A *castle*," Sophie breathed.

Claire rubbed her eyes and stared hard. "That's impossible."

"But it's there!" Sophie cried, and scrambled to her feet.

Claire couldn't deny its presence . . . but she couldn't explain it, either.

As her eyes adjusted, more and more details of the castle materialized from the dark: round towers, arched doors, and funny, ragged walls with the tops cut like a jack-o'-lantern's grin. In some places, stones had fallen, and entire portions of the gate had crumbled, making it look like a doomed sandcastle at high tide.

"But it *shouldn't* be there!" Claire protested. She gestured futilely to their surroundings. "Where's the roof? Where's the chimney? *That's* what's supposed to be here—not *this*!"

A grin bloomed across Sophie's face. "Oh, don't you see what's happened, Clairina? We're in another time! Maybe even another world!"

Claire's stomach lurched. "But that doesn't make sense,"

she insisted, despite the fact that she'd had the very same thought.

Sophie stooped and plucked a button daisy from the grass. Twirling the flower between thumb and forefinger, she asked, "Then what *would* make sense?"

Claire didn't have an answer.

From the castle and the cascade of stars unimpeded by electric lights, she knew they had definitely left Windemere Manor. She wished she'd paid better attention when Mom had pointed out the constellations to her and Sophie. Claire liked the stories of flying horses and queens trapped in chairs, but she could never find the shapes in that big mess of starlight. If she could, maybe she wouldn't be so lost now.

Turning from Sophie, Claire scanned the garden for the chimney, but all she saw was an old stone well.

She scrambled over to it and peered down. For a second, the air in the well rippled and glimmered like water. But then it stilled, and she could see that there was no water at all, only the wooden rungs of a ladder. The hairs along the back of her neck began to rise, one by one.

Claire looked up and realized Sophie had already left the clearing and was now making her way through rampant greenery in the direction of the towers.

Apprehension slammed into Claire's chest.

Even though a tiny part of her admitted that the ruined castle was beautiful, exactly like something a princess might have lived in once, they didn't know what this place was. There was no guarantee that a strange world with a chimney passage would be friendly—or even safe.

"Wait!" Claire called, running after her sister. The tall weeds whipped her bare legs. "We need to go back!"

"Just give me a second," Sophie said, pulling back a low branch as Claire caught up. "Have you ever seen anything so spectacular?" Still holding the branch, she gestured grandly with her other hand toward a newly revealed garden wall of broken pillars and lichen-covered arches. Through it, Claire could just make out a flagstone walkway that led to a doorway in the ruins of the castle.

"We need to go back," Claire repeated, but her words were less commanding than before. She drew in a breath as she looked at the moonlit walls. Slipping the pencil from behind her ear, she gripped it tightly, torn between an intense desire to draw what she was seeing, and the fear of being lost in a strange *other* world. Suddenly, she felt very cold

"How many times do you discover a castle?" Sophie asked, clearly exasperated. "I want to check it out."

A twig snapped loudly.

"Did you hear that?" Claire asked. Unease prickled her neck, and she shivered.

"What?" Sophie pushed past the low branch and continued to walk toward the collapsing wall. "I didn't hear anything."

"There was a snap," Claire insisted as she quickened her pace. "Like someone stepped on something." She looked around but the night was still, except for the drifting clouds.

Suddenly, she saw a shadow move along the ground, then dart behind a pillar.

"Sophie! Did you see that?" Claire grabbed Sophie's arm and twisted her around.

"See what?"

Before Claire could explain, Sophie's eyes became so wide that Claire could see twin reflections of the moon in them.

"Don't move!" Sophie whispered sharply. But Claire moved anyway, because she had to see for herself.

Only a few feet away, in the depths of the shadows, were the eyes of a monster.

CHAPTER
3

Perhaps "eyes" wasn't the right word for the two points of blackness that seemed to focus on Claire. Staring into them, she felt as though she were falling away from herself, as though she no longer knew up from down, no longer knew her own name.

Everything was erased—a terrifying blank.

Claire couldn't tell if the monster was more man or beast. It was human in shape, but overly long and stretched. A sticky darkness clung to it, like shadows melted onto a too-large skeleton. As it stepped toward them—knees bending oddly, hands dragging in the dirt—its eyes never left Claire's.

Suddenly, it threw back its head. For a split second, she had a clear glimpse of the monster's face: a human skull filled with fangs. Then the beast howled—a murderous cry that made Claire feel as though her insides had been wrenched out.

She screamed.

The sound of her own voice snapped the world back in place, and Claire was aware again of Sophie, who grabbed her hand roughly.

"*Claire!*" Sophie yelled. "*Run!*"

Claire moved. Stumbling over the uneven ground, half-sobbing, her sister pulled her toward a clearing. Sophie had had a growth spurt in the spring, and for each of her long strides, Claire was forced to take an extra half step to keep up.

Though she couldn't hear the creature behind them, Claire knew it was there. She could feel its coldness chasing them.

Hunting them.

Ice-cold air rushed into her lungs. As they burst into the clearing, Claire felt a long cold finger brush against her neck and tug the collar of her shirt.

She stumbled.

A dry hand latched around her ankle.

Claire sprawled onto grass and twigs. Trying to break the creature's grip, she rolled onto her back, kicking helplessly as she looked up at the looming figure.

"Sophie!" Her scream cut through her, slicing at her throat. Cold sunk into her bones and a pounding rush filled her ears, driving out all thought and reason.

The thing swooped down in a wave of indistinguishable shadows under the moon's glow, and Claire squeezed her eyes shut, not wanting to truly see it.

"Don't touch her!" Sophie's voice tore across the night. The creature roared.

Claire opened her eyes. Her sister had thrown herself onto the thing's back and was desperately pounding at its shoulder blades, her fists sinking into the shifting, smoky blackness that hung around it.

With another mind-ripping howl, the Shadow Thing jerked, trying to rid itself of the Sophie-sized pest. Claire's body flushed hot with panic.

"Get up!" Sophie shouted. Her hair whipped wildly as the beast lunged side to side.

Claire scooted away from the creature, but then there was another shriek—from Sophie this time—and Claire watched in horror as the beast's clawed hand reached behind and finally peeled Sophie off its back, throwing her to the ground.

"No!" Claire yelled. Without thinking, she leaped to her feet and grabbed her pencil from behind her ear. Clutching it in her fist, she charged the beast.

Something whizzed past her head—a bird? an insect?—but she kept running forward, desperate to help her sister. A second later, something else whistled by her cheek, and she saw a streak of white light arcing toward the Shadow Thing. The light hit it squarely in its shadowed face, and the air filled with the sound of a *hiss*, like steam from a radiator.

Claire skidded to a stop, bewildered, as the skeletal creature fell back from Sophie, clawing at its eyes. More streaks of light rained down on the beast, slicing away the shadows that surrounded it.

Claire gasped, and a sparkling bit of light fell into her mouth. Oddly, she tasted dirt. She looked around, trying to see where the light was coming from, and for a moment, as though illuminated by a shooting star, she could make out two figures running away through the garden.

The Shadow Thing screamed in rage, arms thrown over its head as it retreated into the bramble and disappeared.

Claire ran to Sophie. "Are you okay?" Tears sprang into her eyes as she pulled Sophie to her feet.

"I'm fine, but come on!" Her sister took a step, then winced. She flung her arm over Claire's shoulder, and they hobbled toward the yawning mouth of the well. Sophie hurled herself in. Quickly, Claire put her pencil between her teeth and hoisted herself up with arms that felt about as solid as sponges. Her feet hit the top rung. Scrambling, she skimmed down the well . . .

And then her foot crashed through a rung.

Screaming, Claire snatched the ladder. Her fingertips slammed against the wood of the next rung, but then slipped away before she could grab hold. The back of her head cracked against the stone shaft—

—She opened her eyes to find a blurry Sophie kneeling over her. As her face came into focus, Claire noticed that her sister's freckles stood out more than usual and that she seemed to be shaking Claire's shoulders. Either that, or Claire was experiencing a small earthquake in her head.

"Oww," Claire moaned.

"You're awake!" Sophie put cool hands to Claire's cheeks. "You're okay!"

Head pounding, Claire sat up on the soot-stained hearth of the fireplace. The whole world swayed for a moment, then righted itself. They were back in the unicorn gallery.

Sunlight trickled around the thick drapes, and from somewhere far away, a cuckoo clock chimed a quarter past. Claire's pencil lay a few inches away.

"What happened?" she asked, reaching for her pencil. The slight weight of the wood was comforting against her palm.

"You don't remember?" Sophie's eyes narrowed. "We climbed up the ladder."

The ladder. Images tumbled through Claire's mind. She was possessed by a desperate feeling that everything was about to come crashing down.

"The Shadow Thing!" she gasped. She began to shake uncontrollably and clenched her pencil, as though it were a knife.

A warm arm slipped around her shoulders. "Hey, hey," Sophie said softly as she pulled Claire into a hug. "It's all right. It was only a bat."

"A bat?" Claire heard herself repeat.

"A bat," Sophie confirmed. "We had just started to climb when it flew at us. Then, I don't know, you kind of lost your head for a second and started screaming. And you let go." Her arm tightened around Claire. "Luckily we weren't too high up."

Claire frowned—her head hurt so badly—could she have imagined the well and the sparkling light and the castle? A claw flashed across her mind.

"But bats don't have skeleton hands," Claire protested. "They don't make you feel *cold* inside." She pointed at a red stain blossoming a little above Sophie's knee, spreading across torn denim. "They don't leave you bleeding!"

Sophie glanced down. "My jeans got caught. It's just a scratch. You have a few yourself." She took Claire's hands and flipped them over. Her knuckles were scraped pink. "And I think you hit your head pretty hard."

A concussion could explain it all, but there was also another explanation . . .

"What about magic?" Claire blurted out.

Sophie frowned. "Claire—"

"No, listen," she insisted. "The hospital said your recovery was magic. Why can't other magical things happen?"

"Because magic isn't real," Sophie said shortly.

Claire's head throbbed. "But *you* said that we were in another world—"

"If you're going to be all weird," Sophie cut in, "I'm not sure we should have any more Experiences together. It's too much for you."

Her swift dismissal swung down, crunching Claire to two inches. "You're being unfair!" she cried.

"I'm not the one talking about magic," Sophie said. "But if you want to see for yourself, we can climb back up."

Claire's shoulders tensed, and her eyes flew to the ladder. A chill shuddered down her spine. "Promise me you'll never climb the ladder again."

"Claire—"

"*Promise* me."

Sophie let out a long, gusty sigh, the kind only an older sister can make when a younger sister is being silly, irrational, and *oh-so young*. "Okay," she said. "I promise."

"Swear it!"

Sophie made a fist with her right hand and stuck out her thumb. Claire quickly did the same. It had been their own special code ever since Sophie told Claire years ago that pinkie promises were for babies, and offered a thumb promise instead.

Pressing thumb to thumb, Sophie intoned, "I swear that I will never climb up the ladder again, even if the sun turns green and my eyes fall out. Feel better?"

"No," Claire said. Weariness settled over her. "Not really."

"Wait a second." Sophie stood up and began pulling sheets off more of the display stands, uncovering a polished hunting horn, a circlet of silver, and an alabaster vase. "That's not it," she murmured to herself.

"What are you doing?" Claire asked.

Sophie whipped off the next sheet with such force that dust exploded into the air. Underneath was a bookcase carved with flowers and vines.

"Perfect," Sophie declared, and Claire watched as Sophie threw her back against it, and the bookcase scraped forward a few inches. Claire tucked her pencil away and hurried to help. Together, they set the bookcase in front of the fireplace. It didn't block the hearth completely—there were about six inches on either side of the shelves, and Claire could still see the ladder extending above it.

Grabbing the alabaster vase, she stretched onto her tiptoes and placed it on top.

Now the ladder was obscured, too.

"Sophie?" The doors at the end of the gallery opened, and Mom's face peeked in. "There you are! We need to leave for Dr. Silva's. Bring a book."

Claire watched as Sophie turned slightly away from their mother, concealing the bloodstain. "Okay. Give me a second." She walked quickly from the room, limping slightly.

Mom dropped a kiss on the top of Claire's head. "There are leftovers in the fridge in case we get home late. Remind your father that you both need to eat dinner."

Claire spent the afternoon sketching in the field farthest from Windemere Manor. In the bright sun, she tried to draw the bat that had chased them down the chimney. A cute one, with fuzzy ears and wide eyes like the one she'd once seen in a picture book.

But when Dad found her later and asked what she was working on, she looked down at her sketch pad. In every single drawing, there were claws and shadows and burning black eyes.

Because she knew, deep down, that whatever it was that lived in the chimney hadn't been a bat at all.

It had been a monster.

CHAPTER 4

It had been raining for three days, ever since Claire and Sophie had *maybe* or *maybe not* climbed up the fireplace and been attacked by a skeleton wearing a cloak of shadows. And although Claire could see the reason in her sister's words—it was far more likely her imagination had created a world full of crumbling castles and terrifying creatures—that didn't stop her from thinking about it. Or from feeling the chimney's quiet tug, like a sweater's thread that has snagged and begun to unravel.

Luckily, there was a lot to keep her busy.

Claire shuddered when she opened another cardboard box and saw what Dad had called "bone china." He had explained that the plates were made of crushed animal bones that had been burned to ash and then melted together to create the dinner sets. They were often used for fancy parties, but Claire knew she didn't want to eat on bones in any form, no matter how pretty they were.

Using her pencil, she scrawled *Murder Plates* on a sticky note and put it on the box before writing on a yellow pad that the china was in box thirty-three. As an afterthought, she sketched a quick dog bone beside the entry. Then she scooted over to the next box in the billiards room: box number thirty-four out of a gazillion. August and the estate sale were still almost two whole months away, but Great-Aunt Diana's stuff seemed to overflow into every nook and cranny of Windemere.

From somewhere in the house, she heard loud voices. Probably Sophie and Mom, since Dad and Mom had only been talking in hushed tones lately.

Sighing, Claire looked out the diamond-paned windows onto the gray lawn under a gray sky in the gray rain. She knew cataloging all the artifacts in the house must be hard on Dad, especially since no one really knew what had happened to Great-Aunt Diana. That explained why *he* was acting different from normal, but it didn't explain why Sophie's personality had suddenly changed . . . again.

Because, for that brief moment before they climbed the ladder, Claire had thought the old Sophie was coming back, the fun Sophie. But after Claire had bumped her head, Sophie had become more sullen and grumpy than ever. And worse, she'd been avoiding Claire.

Claire opened box thirty-four and snorted when she saw

hundreds of earrings mixed together. It would take ages to sort and count.

"Hi kiddo."

Claire looked up to see Dad had entered the room carrying another box. He set it down. "I heard a snort and thought you might have come across a wild boar or something."

She scowled, in no mood for Dad's jokes. Not when he was bringing *another* box for her to sift through. "I think I'd rather be a wild boar," she said.

"No you wouldn't," Dad said. "Then you wouldn't be able to hold a pencil." He tugged one of her curls gently. "But you should take a break. Go see how your sister is doing."

Claire didn't particularly feel like going to find a moody Sophie who'd probably just snap at her, but she was glad for a break. Not having any particular place in mind, Claire wandered through the mansion, drifting into a room filled with portraits and another that was completely empty except for a giant vase in the corner.

Claire finally spotted Sophie in a hallway along the back wing of the manor, staring hard at a tapestry hanging on the wall. Claire recognized the same look of concentration on her face that Sophie had had when she was memorizing lines for her seventh-grade play.

Claire looked at the tapestry, but she didn't see anything special about the wall hanging. The piece of cloth, murky with age, was not even a full tapestry, only a fragment that seemed to have been ripped away from a larger picture.

"Where have you been?" Claire asked, secretly pleased when Sophie jumped a little. Clearly, she wasn't the only Martinson sister who didn't like to be spooked. "You weren't in your room when I went in this morning."

"Around," Sophie said, turning away from the wall. "What's up?"

If she squinted a little and tilted her head, Claire thought she could make out a creature on the tapestry. A white stag, maybe, drinking from a well.

She averted her eyes quickly. Wells and fireplaces littered her dreams lately, along with the memory of cold and dark. An uncomfortable thought wedged itself somewhere between her ribs and gut. She decided she could no longer hold it in.

Claire took a deep breath. "I saw a castle in the fireplace," she said, "and some kind of terrible beast. You saw it, too. So don't tell me any more stories about a bat."

Sophie turned back to the tapestry. "Claire," she said with a sigh. "Your imagination will get you in trouble someday."

"It wasn't my imagination," Claire said, growing angry. "I know what I saw."

Still, Sophie didn't look at her. Her profile was white and her mouth was a small dark slash. "Yeah, sure. You saw *magic*." She said the word like she was saying "dirty socks."

"So what if I did?" Claire said, matching Sophie's tone. "It's not the most impossible thing to happen to us. You got better, after all, even when—"

"Stop!" Sophie whirled around, grabbing Claire by the

shoulders and leaning in so close that Claire could see the tiny rainbows trapped in the four dangling moonstones of Sophie's necklace. Sophie had found it abandoned in a linen closet the first day they were in the house. Claire didn't know when she'd started wearing it, and for some reason this made her feel like crying.

"Magic. Does. Not. Exist. You have to grow up sometime!" The pressure lifted from Claire's shoulders as Sophie dropped her hands. "You need to face reality!"

Her sister's words wrapped around her like the tentacles of a jellyfish, squeezing and stinging.

"I *have* grown up," Claire said, each word getting louder. "You're the one who *told* me to climb the ladder!"

At one time, Sophie would have yelled back at her, shouting just as loudly. But now her voice was infuriatingly level as she said, "I wouldn't have if I had known what a baby you'd be about it."

Her calmness made Claire want to stomp her feet and stick out her tongue, but that would only prove that she really hadn't grown up at all. She opened her mouth, not sure what she was going to say next, but just then Dad appeared in the hallway, yet another box in hand.

"We need to take everything in the billiards room to your mom. She's in the sculpture gallery on the first floor," he said. "Grab a box and let's go."

Sophie rolled her eyes, but trudged toward the billiards room. Claire remained rooted in the hallway. No matter what had actually happened in that gallery, the dark cold had been *real*. She was sure of that, at least.

Claire quickly touched the pencil behind her ear for good luck and hurried into the billiards room to snatch a box of tarnished candlesticks. Then, squaring her shoulders, she walked toward the gallery, her eyes sweeping over every corner.

Mom was sitting in the middle of the floor, brown eyes pensive under the same loose curls that crowned Claire, as she haphazardly put a brass figurine into a box labeled *Clothing*.

"Thank you," Mom said when she saw the girls. Claire noted with worry that her mother's loose bun was now sitting directly on top of her head instead of at the base of her neck—a sure sign of stress. "Set those boxes against that wall, next to the fireplace, please."

A sucking sensation filled Claire. She had the sudden thought that if she got too close, the chimney would whoosh her away and she'd never return. Not wanting to look, but unable to stop herself, she glanced in the direction of the fireplace.

A spark shot through her body. The wooden rungs were clearly visible.

Though the bookcase was still there, someone, probably her mother, had removed the alabaster vase that had hidden the ladder from view.

Not real, Claire chanted, *Not real. Not real. Not real.* Knuckles white around the box, she slowly shuffled forward and dropped the candleholders where Mom had indicated.

It was then that she noticed the deep grooves in the wooden floor, right in front of the flagstone hearth. It looked as if someone had been shoving the wooden bookshelf out of the way, then returning it to its position. A slimy feeling like egg whites poured over Claire.

But Sophie had *promised* her.

Then she heard Dad say, "Sophie, what's that on your leg?"

Looking back, she saw him frowning at Sophie.

"Nothing." Sophie tugged her skirt lower.

"It looks like a Band-Aid," Claire said loudly before she could stop herself. It was as if someone were pulling the sentence out of her, knowing exactly how Claire could get back at her sister for lying to her. "What did you do?"

Sophie glared at Claire, but it was too late. The damage was done.

"What?" Mom asked, putting down her notebook. "You're hurt, Sophie?"

"It's nothing, Mom." Sophie tried to scoot past their mother to the double doors, but Mom put out her hand, barring an escape. Gently, Mom pulled the hem up a little and let out a gasp.

"Sophie! What happened?"

Claire could see that a mess of bandages went up Sophie's leg like a patchwork quilt. What had she done to need all of them? After exploring the chimney, she'd only had one cut above her knee.

"It's nothing," Sophie said, attempting to dodge her mother's accusing stare.

"Nothing?" Claire had never heard Mom's voice so sharp. "You have to be more careful, Sophie! You need to take care of yourself. You know what the doctor said."

"I'm done listening to doctors! I'm done listening to you!" Sophie had been dark and moody for days, but something seemed to snap inside her now. Claire watched in horror as her sister stormed at their parents. "I'm thirteen! I can take care of myself!"

"We're your family," Mom said. Her voice was steady, but it sounded thin to Claire's ears. "We take care of you."

"Oh, really?" Sophie crossed her arms. "It doesn't seem you've been doing such a great job of it!"

The silence was resounding.

Claire's stomach sank. She shouldn't have said anything. She shouldn't have tried to get Sophie in trouble. Without thinking, she pulled her pencil from her ear and began to nibble at it.

"Sophia Andrea Martinson," Mom said quietly, "go to your room."

Her sister's dark eyes met her mother's, and for a moment, Claire thought that Sophie would argue some more. But finally, she dropped her gaze.

"Fine," Sophie muttered under her breath before stomping past Claire and out of the gallery.

Sophie didn't come out of her room for the rest of the

afternoon, and during dinner, the entire family ate in frosty silence. The only thing that made Claire feel a tiny bit better was the fact that Dad had placed the unicorn sculpture—which, despite its delicate appearance, weighed a lot—on top of the bookcase. It was to keep it out of harm's way, he had said, but it had the added benefit of making the bookcase too heavy for anyone to scoot it away from the hearth. There was no way Sophie could move it now.

At least, Claire hoped.

Later that night, Claire was drifting off to sleep when her door opened with a quiet *creak*. She sat up straight as she fumbled for her emergency flashlight.

"Claire?"

"Sophie? You scared me!"

"Sorry," her sister whispered from across the dark room. "Can I come in?"

Then, without waiting for an answer, Sophie walked over and climbed under the covers beside Claire. She smelled like watermelon shampoo. A summertime smell. They didn't say anything for a moment, just lay side by side, looking up into the domed darkness of Claire's canopy, moonlight throwing scattered shadows around the room. She couldn't remember the last time her sister had crawled into bed with her. She stayed still, hoping the moment would last.

"Remember that time when we went camping"—Sophie's

voice finally floated to her—"and I convinced you that you could only use the outhouse at night if there were no clouds covering the moon?"

"I remember," Claire said. "You said the Toilet Ghoul would attack if the moon wasn't out."

"Ha, yeah! The Toilet Ghoul! That was so funny."

"Right, funny," Claire echoed. She had spent that rainy, cloudy weekend in terror, worried that she might wet her sleeping bag.

She waited a few seconds to see whether Sophie was going to say anything else. When she didn't, Claire asked, "What happened earlier?"

"It's nothing," Sophie replied. "It's just . . . Mom and Dad frustrate me sometimes, you know?"

"Yeah," Claire lied. "I do."

Sophie laughed. It wasn't a mean laugh, but it wasn't a happy one either. "No you don't, Clairina. You don't have to pretend." Sophie was silent again, and then turned on her side to face Claire. The night-light's glow glinted off the moonstones in the necklace that still hung around her neck. "Sometimes, I wish I were like you."

"Me?" Claire was baffled. "Why?" Sophie was the strong one. Everyone was always saying how brave she was.

Sophie brushed a piece of hair out of Claire's eye. "What I said in the hallway—I was wrong. It's good that you know how to make up stories. They're better than the real world."

Sophie turned onto her other side and snuggled deeper

under the covers. Claire quickly tucked the ends of the blanket around her feet before Sophie could hog the entire comforter.

Claire curled up next to her sister, back to back. For a brief moment, she thought about asking Sophie about the scratches on the gallery floor and the bandages on her leg, but her sister was already breathing deeply. She fell asleep remembering the times she would cling to Sophie's neck as her sister splashed and swam in the pool, pretending to be a mermaid saving Claire from sharks.

The cold light of dawn woke Claire, and an even colder certainty wrapped around her heart before she had opened her eyes.

Something was wrong.

Something was *missing*.

She sat up quickly. Sophie was no longer next to her—Claire was alone.

Shoving her feet into her slippers, she grabbed her pencil and sweater, and dashed into her sister's room.

It was empty, too.

Claire ran. With each stride, her dread increased, until she thought she would sink into the floor with the weight of her anxiety. Arriving at the double doors of the gallery, she flung them open. The doors hit the walls with a loud *thud*, drowning out her gasp.

No matter how many times Claire blinked, she still saw

the same thing: the bookcase shoved aside and shards of the beautiful unicorn statue littering the floor, leaving the entrance to the fireplace completely unobstructed.

And a pair of Sophie-sized footprints leading through the ash to the ladder, until they disappeared from view.

CHAPTER
5

Claire's footsteps echoed the *thump* of her heart as she ran through the gallery toward the fireplace.

I have to save her. The thought raced through her like a pulse. She tossed her sweater over her shoulders and tucked her pencil behind her ear for luck. Then she placed her foot on the first rung of the ladder and began to climb.

The smoke-tinged air stung her eyes, and her lungs burned from the loose ash that lined the chimney walls, but Claire barely noticed. She kept her face tilted up, ignoring the hum that entered her bones as she searched the darkness for the dime-sized spot of light.

Be brave. Be brave. Be brave.

Her fear stretched like a hairband on the brink of snapping. She could only focus on her next step, and then the next.

A draft brushed against her arms, bringing with it the smell of grass and rain. Light slowly bloomed from a tiny dot to a big, bright circle above her.

Almost there.

Confidence surged through her legs. She pumped them harder.

Finally, Claire reached the top. She cautiously balanced on the last rung. Bracing herself against the wall of the chimney, she stuck her head out of the well—into blinding sunlight.

Birds called softly to one another, and the distant chatter of a creek tickled her ears. Claire blinked away the dancing spots in front of her eyes and soon saw cream-colored ruins spiraling into a crystal sky.

It was real.

There could be no doubt now. This world through the chimney was an entirely *new* world, different from what she had left behind.

The truth—the majesty—of it thundered through her.

The castle, the sparks, the Shadow Thing, they all existed. They had all *happened*. There'd never been any bat, like Sophie had claimed.

Sometimes when Claire had the itch to draw, she felt her fingertips tingling. She had that exact feeling now as she gazed at her surroundings. But this time it was more than just the urge to have a pencil and pad in hand. It was the urge to understand. To know more. What was this place? And why had Sophie lied? And what would the world look like from the top of that crumbling tower? She decided she would climb it, and from there, she might be able to spot her sister.

Claire pushed down on the well's ledge and launched herself out. Dropping onto the grass, she felt dew soak through her slippers. In her hurry to find Sophie, she hadn't changed out of them.

Putting her pencil in her sweater pocket, Claire followed a path of trampled grass and flowers through the wild garden and toward the broken archways. When she and Sophie had first arrived, at night, the grounds had been gilded in starlight, but now late-afternoon sun poured color onto the forgotten garden.

Claire's curiosity blossomed inside her, big and lush as the vibrant flowers that bowed and swayed. Around her, leaves dappled the grass with fairy-sized shadows while remnants of fountains peeked out from among the foliage.

Of course, she thought. Of course Sophie would come back here. It was too beautiful, too wonderful to stay away.

But why hadn't she told Claire the truth?

Claire thought again of the Shadow Thing that had chased them, its cold breath at her neck. Its skeletal fingers reached out from her memory to stroke her spine.

"There's no one here but me," she said aloud to reassure herself. "Just me and Sophie, and *not* a horrible mon—oof!"

The air whooshed out of Claire as something—some*one*—tackled her from behind.

She felt a knee land firmly on her lower back, pinning her

to the ground. Pain ripped through her shoulders as her arms were yanked behind her. She tried to scream, but her lungs felt trapped by the weight on her back, and what came out was more of a whimper. She kicked.

"Nett, grab her legs!" a girl's voice ordered.

On hearing this, Claire kicked even harder. Finally, her foot connected with something squishy.

"Ow! Dee god my dose!" a new voice exclaimed. It sounded as if the speaker was pinching his nose.

The girl spoke again, "Stay back!"

The world suddenly tilted, and Claire found herself rolled onto her back, looking up into the scowling face of a girl with a heavy auburn braid twisted around her head like a crown. She wore a long red shirt that was cinched with a belt, and leggings.

Over the girl's shoulder, Claire could see a boy about her age dressed in a similar outfit, but with a green shirt and loose trousers. He was cupping his hands around his nose.

Claire coughed, spitting out the soil that coated her mouth from the fall. Something cold and hard suddenly pressed at her throat: the edge of a knife.

She gasped and clenched her eyes shut. She lay absolutely still, suppressing the next cough.

"Don't hurd her!" the boy protested.

The girl snarled. "If she talks, she won't be hurt."

Claire thought she felt the knife bob a little, and opened her eyes. She noticed her attacker's hand was trembling. The girl leaned forward, coming so close that Claire could see sweat beading at her hairline and flecks of brown in her amber-colored eyes.

"Where. Is. She," the girl growled. It wasn't a question, but a demand.

Claire's heart skipped. "Who?"

"Sophie."

Claire didn't know what she had expected the girl to say, but it certainly wasn't that. It was as though they were in a play, but their lines had accidentally been switched. *Claire* was the one who should be asking about Sophie.

"How—how do you know my sister?" she stammered.

The boy frowned. "Dister?"

"Look." The girl pointed at Claire's feet with her chin. "She's wearing the same kind of slippers Sophie had when we first met her. And if she's Sophie's sister, then she must know where Sophie is." The blade pressed a little harder against Claire's neck.

"Yes!" Claire wheezed out. "I mean no! I mean, Sophie *is* my sister, but I don't know where she is!"

The girl shot the boy a triumphant smile. "See? Told you we'd find a lead out here." She turned her attention back to Claire. "Don't try to protect her. I know you're lying."

"I'm not!" Claire gasped out. Tears of unfairness, pain, and terror stung her eyes, but she blinked them back. "I'm trying to find her, too!"

"Sena, come on," the boy said. His voice sounded less

funny now, and Claire could see that he had let go of his nose, which looked red and swollen. "I think she's telling the truth."

The girl, Sena, studied Claire for a moment, then sighed. She adjusted her weight and moved off Claire's chest. For the first time, Claire could see what the blade in the girl's hand actually was: a butter knife.

"Why are you sneaking around Hilltop Palace?" Sena asked, her voice as cold as the ocean in January. "Who were you speaking to?"

"Myself." Claire took a moment to breathe in, letting her ribs stretch to their fullest. Relief filtered through her. "I thought you were the Shadow Thing."

Sena frowned. "What shadow thing?"

"I think she means a wraith," the boy volunteered, digging in the dirt with his fingers.

"Wraiths can't come out into the sunlight," Sena said casually, as though she were pointing out that the sky is blue, or that chocolate chip cookies are better with milk. She narrowed her eyes. "What did this 'shadow thing' look like?"

Claire felt like she'd swallowed an ice cube, but she tried to explain. "I'm not really sure—it all happened so fast—but it was big and dark and cold. It kind of looked like a skeleton wrapped in shadows."

"She's definitely talking about a wraith." The boy straightened, and Claire could see a flower bulb now in his hand. Taking a pocketknife from his rucksack, he peeled away some of the bulb's skin and held the exposed side to his nose. "She doesn't even know wraiths can't stand sunlight," he continued. "She doesn't know anything."

Claire was indignant. She might be tired and confused, but she knew lots of things—she knew the oldest paintings in the world were forty thousand years old and how to draw ears so they didn't look like they belonged to an alien.

She opened her mouth to retort, then blinked. The boy had moved the bulb away from his face, and she now saw that his nose no longer looked like a ripe tomato, but was rapidly returning to a color that matched the rest of his light brown face. How was that possible? When Tony Rook fell off the slide in third grade, he'd gotten a black eye that hadn't gone away for more than a week!

Claire blinked again. With the boy's nose shrinking back to a normal size, she could see that he had inquisitive brown eyes framed by brush-bristle lashes. She tried to focus on this detail and how she would draw it, rather than on the utter strangeness of what had just happened. Of *everything* that was happening . . .

"Nett, we can't let her go," Sena said, still holding her butter knife toward Claire. "What if she's working with Sophie?" Claire saw the girl's jaw twitch. It was a movement Claire knew all too well. Was this knife-wielding girl *scared*? Of *her?* That didn't make sense.

But then again, nothing made any sense here. Wherever here was.

"Where am I?" The question exploded out of Claire. "What is this place?"

"This is Arden, of course," Nett said, not really paying attention. "We're less than a mile outside Greenwood Village."

Arden. So the chimney world had a name.

"But—*who* are you?" Claire asked, desperate to understand. "How do you know Sophie? *Where's* Sophie?"

"Quiet," Sena ordered. "I can't think with all your questions!"

Nett peered at Claire. "Bringing her to the Hearing Hall isn't really an option. It'd look so bad if the only Forger in a village of Tillers showed up with Sophie's sister. We're trying to find clues that will prove you're innocent—not make you guiltier!"

"Hearing Hall? Clues?" Claire asked. "Guilty of what?"

Sena pressed her free hand to her forehead, as if she were trying to keep millions of thoughts from flying away. "If I bring them someone who knows where Sophie is, maybe the council will stop questioning *me.*"

Claire tried again. "Who's questioning—"

"Get up," Sena said, ignoring Nett's look of protest. She flicked her amber eyes back to Claire. "And don't take your time about it."

Claire kept one eye on the butter knife's dull edge as she slowly got to her feet. Sena seemed a little too eager to point it in her direction. Claire would go to this Hearing Hall, whatever it was, if it meant that they'd start answering her questions.

Arden. Greenwood Village. Council. What did it all mean? And more important, what kind of trouble had Sophie gotten herself into?

Claire tried to brush the dirt off her pajama bottoms, but Sena grabbed her arm roughly. She mentally added her dirty pants to the list of things she'd have to hide from her parents when she got home.

Her chest tightened.

If she got home.

"Rope," Sena said, and Nett hesitated, but then he crouched down and pulled a vial out from his bulging rucksack. Carefully, he let a drop of something green tumble onto a blade of grass. With his thumb and forefinger, he pinched the blade and gave it a twist. For a moment, he was totally quiet, his excited energy concentrated on the little plant in front of him. Then he began to pull . . .

and pull . . .

and pull.

The blade of grass was growing longer and larger, going from the length of some floss to shoelace size in a matter of seconds.

Claire gasped in wonder. "How are you doing that?"

"I added a drop of Mile High Potion." The boy kept tugging, but his eyes darted toward her. "It's not *quite* as strong as my last batch, though. I'll need to add more redwood bark to set an example for the other plants, but it's a fine line. Too much redwood, and the grass will be as inflexible as a trunk, but too little, and it won't grow tall enough."

He concentrated on the grass, as if his explanation of Mile High Potion and example-setting bark had made any sense.

"What?" Claire asked. "I don't understand."

Nett frowned. "It's just basic Tilling. What don't you get?"

Claire stared at him. "Basic *what*?"

"Ah, I forgot," Nett said, his air of puzzlement lifting. "Sophie didn't know anything either. I'm a Tiller and I Till. It means I work with all that grows from the earth. I can shape the magic within plants."

"Magic?!" Claire's mouth dropped open, even though Sophie always told her it made her look like a hippo. A boy her age had just spoken about magic as though it were something as normal as making toast.

She stared hard at Nett. He stared back, unfazed.

"Can everyone do that here?" she asked faintly.

"Anyone in the Tiller Guild can do what I do," Nett said. "But the magic in the other three guilds is different, of course."

"*Other* guilds?"

Nett sighed. "There are four guilds of magic," he said as he continued to pull the grass like taffy. "Sena's a Forger, and she can do the same kinds of things I can, but with metal. Gemmers work with rocks and gems, and Spinners weave magic from thread—"

"That's long enough," Sena interrupted. "We're going to be late!"

Claire's mind was a whirl of confusion as Nett gave a last

yank, and the grass blade—now as long and thick as a jump rope—tore from the ground.

Soon, the grass rope bound Claire's wrists together in front of her, as if she were a prisoner. Which, apparently, she was.

Sandwiched between Sena and Nett, Claire was maneuvered out of the walled garden. For the first time, she could see that the ruins and its sprawling grounds were on the top of a high hill that overlooked a meadow.

Across the meadow, yellow rooftops clustered in the middle of carefully maintained fields that stretched to a black line of forest. Claire guessed that this must be Greenwood, and from what Nett had said, it sounded like the village was just one of many places in Arden.

Panic fluttered in Claire's chest. The world up the chimney was not only real, but it was much bigger than a castle ruin and an old stone well. How was she ever going to find Sophie?

The grass rope cut into her wrists, and she felt her temper rise.

"Why are you tying me up? All I did was climb a ladder to find my sister," Claire said, trying to sound calm even though Sena's glare frightened her. "That's not illegal—so just tell me what happened to Sophie, and let me go!"

"We don't know what happened to her because we don't know where she is," Nett said, tugging the ends of his shaggy black hair. "She disappeared last night. The entire village has been looking for her since dawn, and no one's found her yet."

Fear rang through Claire's whole body now.

No one could find her sister.

She shook her head, trying to concentrate. "The entire village is looking for her? Why?"

"Don't tell her anything," Sena ordered Nett. "She's our prisoner!"

Nett glowered. "It's not like I was going to say anything about the Unicorn Harp."

"Nett!" Sena yelled.

"The what?" Claire asked.

Sena groaned. "You may as well tell her *now*," she said grudgingly.

"The Unicorn Harp," Nett said, ignoring Sena's eye roll, "is one of the few unicorn artifacts left in Arden. It's carved from mahogany and strung with hairs from the mane of a unicorn. And no one was supposed to know that we had it here in Greenwood Village."

"'Mane of a . . . ,'" Claire repeated, astounded. The conversation was sliding around like a slab of butter in a frying pan—she couldn't grasp anything they were saying. "Are there *unicorns* here?" She thought of the statue in Great-Aunt Diana's gallery.

"Well, once," Nett said, adjusting the rucksack on his shoulder, "they used to be common in Arden, but then about three hundred years ago, they began to die out. It was during the Guild War, so no one really noticed until it was too late to do anything about it. In *Records of Arden and Its Territories*, Timor the Verbose had several interesting theories about—"

"No one's interested in what Tim*bore* thinks," Sena interrupted. "Stop showing off."

Claire's head spun. This place not only had ruins, and guilds, and magic, but it had a *history*. A history complete with its own records and wars. And unicorns.

Nett made a face at Sena. "Anyway, the harp is made with unicorn mane, and that's what matters. That's what makes the magic."

"I don't get it," Claire said, frustrated. "What do you mean it 'makes the magic'?"

Sena sighed. "Well, it doesn't make it, exactly . . ."

"Our magic, guild magic, only extends to what's around us," Nett interjected. "The magic doesn't come from within us, but from the things around us—plants, rocks, thread, metal. All we do is encourage the magic that naturally exists in those things, to make plants grow bigger and faster and stronger, for instance."

"Or," Sena cut in, "if you're a Forger like me, then to help make mirrors so shiny that they can reflect the future, or forge swords that will never lose a fight." She sounded like she was bragging.

In a way, it was lucky Claire was sandwiched between the two kids. If she wasn't being supported, she might have had to sit down.

Nett nodded. "But the unicorns, they were *pure* magic. They made every kind of guild magic stronger. With the unicorns gone, we depend on the unicorn artifacts to increase our own abilities."

"Please," Claire said, completely overwhelmed, "what does any of this have to do with Sophie?"

"I'll tell you what it has to do with Sophie," Sena replied. "Your sister came as a guest and how did she repay us? She *stole* the Unicorn Harp."

CHAPTER 6

There had to be a mistake.

"Sophie wouldn't steal," Claire protested, nearly tripping as Sena pulled her along. They were nearing the village now. "She doesn't even know how to play a harp!"

Sena pursed her lips. "People don't usually want the Unicorn Harp for music," she said. "And besides, it's too much of a coincidence. What are the chances Sophie *and* the harp disappeared at the same time?"

"Maybe it's exactly that," Claire argued. "A terrible coincidence!"

Sena and Nett exchanged an uneasy glance. Their silence was as frustrating for Claire as a pencil line she couldn't get right. She was opening her mouth to argue again, when a loud, rhythmic beat resonated from somewhere inside the village.

"Slug soot!" Sena swore. "The drums—we're late!" She broke into a run, forcing Claire and Nett to lurch after her.

By the time they stumbled into the yellow-roofed village, Claire's slippered feet ached, and her head rattled with words she'd only just learned: *Forgers, Tillers, guilds of magic.* She tried to take deep, calming breaths as she took in the squat wooden houses on either side of the road. Each structure had a plot of land in front of it, with vegetable gardens so green it almost looked like someone had taken a marker and colored them in.

But even though Claire saw signs of life everywhere— shovels on the ground, carts next to houses, footprints in the dust—she saw only one other person. A blond-haired boy hunched over as he weeded an herb patch.

"The hearing must have already started," Nett murmured. They turned a corner, entering the village's cobbled square. Claire gasped.

In front of her was the most wondrous building she could ever have imagined—a building that looked more *grown* than built.

It was as though a small forest had come together to form a cathedral. Towering trees with silvery bark grew side by side, forming thick walls of trunks and roots, then somewhere far above Claire's head, they leaned inward, their branches inter-twining to form a roof. As Claire stared up in wonder, a wood-pecker alighted on one of the many circular windows and began to peck at the treewall.

Sophie would love this. The thought came to Claire quickly, and with it her fear returned. Claire didn't believe that her sister had stolen anything, but what had she done to make everyone suspect her?

Sena was walking them quickly toward the entrance when Nett stopped short.

"Wait, you can't go in looking that," he said disapprovingly. It had gotten warm as they hurried to the village. Sweat sheened Sena's face and tendrils of her red braid had come loose, frizzing around her forehead. Still in her sweater, Claire could feel the shirt underneath begin to stick to her back. It was much hotter than when she'd climbed with Sophie. Then, it had felt like early spring, but now, just a few days later, the heat was the kind only found at the height of August.

"You don't look that great yourself," Sena retorted, eyeing Nett's dirty knees with distaste. "But we're late, so we don't have a choice."

Claire had only a second to take in the intricately carved flowers and trees on the door before Sena cracked it open and slipped through, tugging Claire after her and into a gigantic space full of patchy sunlight, birdsong—and people.

The entire village must have been there, from the youngest, baldest baby to the oldest woman with a few faint whiskers on her chin. They all sat on benches, facing a sort of stage at the front, where a group of four men and women sat in highbacked chairs behind a long table. It looked, Claire thought, like one of those courtrooms she'd seen on TV. The people in the chairs even wore robes similar to judges' clothes, but they were emerald instead of black.

Sena motioned Claire and Nett to follow her to a bench in

the back. No one in the crowd paid any attention to the three latecomers, as they were all too busy listening to a man in an apron who was standing before the judges. He was stammering something, while off to one side of the platform, a boy frantically took notes with a feathered quill.

"It had just chimed four bells," the man in the apron said, "when I first noticed the harp was gone. I remember because—"

"A moment, Baker Seedling." The woman in the center of the stage held up her hand and the man stopped talking. Claire could practically feel the woman's eyes land on her. "It seems that Nettle Green and Sena Steele have finally decided to arrive. Along with a guest."

Claire heard the wooden benches creak and shift as the villagers craned to see what was going on. Her neck flushed.

The woman's white hair, cropped close to her head, was in sharp contrast to her dark brown skin, and her eyes almost exactly matched the color of her robes, which were solid emerald, except for four white stripes that circled her sleeves—two on her right, two on her left. She pressed her finger pads against one another and peered down the aisle. "You're late."

"Grandmaster Iris, it's my fault—" Nett started.

"Enough, Nettle," Iris said sternly. "Your loyalty to your friend is admirable, but *you* weren't the one requested to report before the drums. You weren't the one to show the harp to Sophie." Iris gestured toward the hall and continued, "Take your place with the others. Sena, however, must be questioned by the council."

Nett shot the girls an apologetic glance before hurrying to a bench. Claire locked her jaw, trying to keep it from trembling. Without Nett by her side, Claire felt even more exposed.

Sena shifted her feet. "I'm sorry, Grandmaster."

But Iris didn't seem to have heard Sena's apology. Instead, she looked pointedly at Claire. "And who is *she*?"

Sena pushed Claire slightly in front of her. "This is someone you will want to question even more than me. This is the thief's sister."

The crowd broke out into loud exclamations. People stood up from their benches to get a better look, and even the other judges—*councillors*, Claire supposed—whose faces had been impassive until then, leaned forward in their chairs. Claire wanted to shrink, to hide—it was hard to be brave in your pajamas.

"Order, please," Iris commanded, and nodded to the girls. "Sena, approach."

Sena placed a heavy hand on Claire's shoulder and propelled her down the grass-carpeted aisle.

As they neared the stage, the four members of Greenwood's council came into sharper focus. There was a man with hair like a skunk—part white, part silvery black. He scowled at Claire with such ferocity that she quickly looked away. Another councillor had a pair of half-moon spectacles twinkling on his nose. Next to him, a paper-white woman with a wreath of feathers on her head leaned over to whisper something in his ear. His eyes narrowed as he glanced at Claire's slippered feet.

And in the middle sat Grandmaster Iris. Sena stopped them directly in front of her, and Claire was strongly reminded of her third-grade teacher, a severe woman who had drilled the class in multiplication tables and insisted that all her students be able to rattle off the five longest rivers in the world and locate the highest mountain on each continent.

"You may sit," Grandmaster Iris said to Sena. Her eyes turned toward Claire like a spotlight. "What is your name?"

"Claire," Claire said—or rather, squeaked. She felt very alone and small without Sena next to her. Clearing her throat, she tried again. "Claire Martinson."

"Sophia Martinson is your sister?"

"Y-yes. That's why I'm here. I need to find her," she stuttered. Iris's expression did not change, but she lowered her voice and began to confer with the other council members.

The longer they whispered, the louder the crowd's murmurs grew. Claire stared down at her feet, unable to appreciate the tiny violets that punctuated the grass carpet of the Hearing Hall. Finally, there was a rap on the table.

Claire looked up to see that the councillors had leaned back in their chairs. None looked particularly friendly, but the skunk-haired man looked positively predatory as he glared down at Claire like an owl marking a mouse.

"Silence, please," Iris called. Immediately the room quieted, except for the occasional bird chirp coming from the leafy ceiling. Then the grandmaster addressed the hall. "Greenwood Council will question Claire Martinson first, and then we shall speak again to Sena Steele. If Claire chooses not to speak, then she will be arrested as an accomplice to the theft."

Claire gaped at the woman. She was only eleven! Could someone her age even *be* arrested? But almost immediately four men, all wielding large wooden staffs and dressed in olive uniforms, silently appeared around her.

"Claire Martinson," Iris said, her voice grave and deep, "our village's most important treasure has gone missing. If word spreads to the other guilds that a Tiller village has not registered a unicorn artifact, we will *all* face the consequences."

There was a muttering in the room, and though most of the words were unintelligible, there was one that Claire could clearly make out: "war."

"Knowing this, do you agree to be heard?" the grandmaster asked, her eyes boring into Claire's.

Claire didn't trust her voice, so she just nodded.

"Very good, then," Iris said. Reaching into the wide sleeves of her robe, she pulled out a small satchel. "Fetch my tray," she said to the scribe who'd been taking notes.

The scribe quickly delivered a wooden tray with a tea set on it. Steam came from the bright pink teapot, and the boy carefully placed it in front of Iris. Benches creaked as everyone leaned forward, paying close attention as Iris poured the tea. Then she stood and stepped off the stage to stand in front of Claire. Tall and slender in her robes of green and white, she reminded Claire of a pine tree with snow on its boughs.

"Hold out your hand," Iris commanded, after removing the grass rope from Claire's wrists.

Though her skin smarted slightly, Claire did as she was told. Iris placed a wooden mug into Claire's palms.

"This is Sinceri Tea," the grandmaster said. "Distilled from forget-me-not petals for recollection, sunflower seeds for openness, and a blade of hedgehog grass from the beaches of the Sunrise Isles. It will ensure that you cannot lie when you answer. Do you willingly agree to drink this tea?"

Claire peered cautiously into the cup. Steam swirled up in the shape of a question mark, before dissolving into the air. The tea looked harmless enough. It was as clear as water, and smelled like the soap her father used when he washed the hardwood floors—clean, with a hint of lemon.

But could she trust these people? What if the tea was poisoned?

Then again, if she didn't drink the tea, it would be like admitting that Sophie was guilty, and that she herself was guilty, too.

She had to depend on the truth to save her. She'd have to take the risk.

Claire took a deep breath. "Yes. I will drink the tea." She lifted the cup to her lips and drank.

CHAPTER
7

After just one sip Claire knew she had drunk something stronger than water and lemon. The Sinceri Tea made her tongue thick and slippery, and the back of her throat grew hot.

Iris, who had returned to her chair, looked at Claire expectantly. "Tell me that my robes are red," she said.

Claire was startled by the command. "But they're green." The truth fell easily from her lips.

Iris shook her head. "I did not ask what color they were. I told you to tell me they are red."

Claire tried to obey. She formed the words in her mind, but before she could speak, she began to cough. It felt like a hard crust of bread had lodged in her throat.

"Good," Iris said as Claire hastily took another sip of

Sinceri to clear her throat. "We can begin. Claire Martinson, did you help steal the Unicorn Harp?"

"No," Claire said, the answer smooth and slippery as vanilla pudding on her tongue.

The councillor wearing the feathered wreath raised her hand next, and Iris nodded at her. "Did you know of your sister's plot to take the harp?"

"No," Claire said, a little more loudly than she intended. "My sister did not take the harp."

The council members looked at one another. The woman who'd asked the question pursed her lips, while the spectacled councillor whispered something to the table.

"I should remind the council, and everyone here, that the tea does not drag answers from thin air!" the skunk-haired councillor burst out. Claire jumped, and Sinceri sloshed in her cup.

"Claire might *believe* that Sophie did not take the harp," he said, standing up, "but that does not mean Sophie is innocent."

"My sister would never steal," Claire insisted, confidence burning inside her chest. Or maybe that was the tea, she couldn't be sure.

"Grandmaster," the skunk-haired man said. "May I question the girl?"

Iris tapped her long fingers on her armrest. "Proceed, Councillor Ragweed."

He nodded, then turned to Claire. "How can you be sure Sophie would never steal?" he asked. His words felt sharp and pointed. "How well *do* you know your sister?"

Claire opened her mouth to respond, but as his words sunk in, she bit her lip.

"Speak up," Ragweed demanded. "Is your sister a willful girl?"

Claire felt lost, adrift in her uncertainty. She knew her sister (*Do you? Do you really?* a treacherous part of her mind whispered) and Sophie *was* willful—but did Sophie seek Experiences or did Experiences just happen to find her?

Again, Claire opened her mouth, ready to defend her sister, but as she took a breath, she could feel her throat tighten, stopping the words from flying out.

As she choked, the entire hall burst into sound.

Cries of "Guilty!" and "This proves Sophie's the thief!" filled the space, and Claire was forced to let go of the answer that might have saved her sister.

She quickly took another sip of tea and tried to concentrate. "Sophie *is* adventurous," she carefully admitted, speaking loudly to be heard over the crowd. Slowly, the babble died down. "But she is definitely not a thief."

There. That much was true. It had to be if the tea let her say it. But did they believe her? Claire looked at the stern faces of the council members seated on the platform before her, and they stared back, expressions unreadable.

"Sophie has a temper," Claire continued. She turned to face the rest of the assembly. Her eyes immediately landed on Sena, who stood out in her red tunic, so different from the browns and greens that the rest wore. Next to Sena sat Nett, who managed to stop chewing his nails long enough to give

Claire a weak wave. It was the only friendly gesture in the entire hall. Keeping her eyes on him, Claire stumbled for what to say next.

"Sophie's forgetful," Claire said. "And stubborn. But she is also loyal and—and good."

An old man sitting on the other side of Sena looked at Claire thoughtfully. His eyebrows were so bushy they seemed to have knitted together across his brow to form one long caterpillar. She noticed a few of the others nodding along. Hope rustled in Claire's heart. Maybe she *could* convince these people that Sophie was innocent, and then they would help her find her sister in this strange, terrifying land.

"Who else would speak?" Iris asked.

The caterpillar-browed man raised a hand, and Iris motioned him to stand. Claire had never known either of her grandfathers, but she thought now that this man looked like the kind of grandfather who would take you to the beach and wouldn't mind if you got sand in the backseat of the car.

"Many things take root in soil," the man said once he'd gotten to his feet. Even his voice was relaxing. "The earth does not reject a plant if it is a flower or vegetable or tree. Iris's Sinceri Tea is strong—the most powerful Sinceri that I have seen in all my time in Greenwood. Therefore, I think we must believe the girl—that both she and her sister *and* Sena are completely innocent of stealing the Unicorn Harp."

"You're just saying that to protect the Forger girl." The feather-wreathed councillor scowled from the high table.

"Sena has already confessed that she showed Sophie the location of the harp!"

The old man frowned, his one eyebrow resting low over his nose. "But Sena never admitted to helping Sophie *steal* it. Sena is a Greenwood villager just like you, Miranda—and as such, you should believe that her word is as sound as oak."

"Then you're a fool, Francis," Miranda barked out. "Everyone knows the saying: *A Forger rusted can't be trusted.* If anything, if Sophie didn't take the harp, then *Sena* probably did!"

Opinions began to flood the room all at once.

"Shameful!"

"Lock her up!"

"Give them to the wraiths—that'll make 'em talk!"

"I'm not protecting anyone," Francis said loudly. "I am simply saying what I believe is best for Greenwood!"

Claire's head throbbed, and she could no longer follow the swirling conversation. Instead, she focused on what she knew. The kind old man—Francis—was on her side, and Sena's, too. Though the people here didn't seem to like Sena much.

And then, Iris had called the Unicorn Harp an "unregistered unicorn artifact." Claire wasn't exactly sure what that meant, but she knew enough to guess that the people of Greenwood had been hiding the powerful harp, and that the rest of Arden didn't know about it. Which was why they were so desperate to figure out who had stolen it.

To figure out if *Sophie* had stolen it.

The strange thing was, everyone seemed to know a lot about Sophie. When had Sophie first come back here on her own? When had she met Sena? Or Nett?

Sophie had disappeared into Windemere's many rooms on various occasions over the last few weeks, but there was no way she could have visited Arden long enough to upset an *entire* village . . . Was it possible Sophie had already climbed the ladder before they went up together?

Claire mulled over the little she knew until a *clink clink clink* cut through the web of noise.

Iris was clanging a small spoon against the teapot. "The sun sets in an hour, and with the harp still missing, our crafting will be weakened. We must double the Wraith Watch tonight," she ordered. "We shall adjourn for dinner, and when the drums strike eight, all villagers must meet to secure the protective wards. Both girls can spend the night in the cage."

Claire's eyes widened. Cage?

"But Sena's done nothing wrong!" Francis sputtered.

I didn't either! Claire wanted to cry out, but she was too afraid.

"The council has made its decision," Iris said sharply, rising from the table, the other members following her lead. "We can't have possible accomplices disappearing like Sophie did."

Tiller guards bearing staffs hustled Claire and Sena outside, while a handful of people from the Hearing Hall followed them to the town square. There, Councillor Ragweed was waiting for them next to what looked like an enormous metal birdcage with dark, leafy vines entwined around each of its bars. In the dimming sun, the leaves looked as black as iron.

"In you go," Ragweed said, swinging the door open. Although Claire didn't want to, she knew she had no choice. Reluctantly, she stepped inside, keeping her chin high, as she knew Sophie would have done. Almost immediately she heard a strange rustle and turned.

Claire realized the leaves didn't just *look* as black as iron—they were *made* of iron. And the vines did not just wrap around the bars, they *were* the bars of the cage. As she stared at them, the wrought-iron vines thickened as they moved closer together, like metal snakes.

Claire breathed in sharply and sat before her legs gave way. More magic, and this time, it wasn't just plant—*Tiller*—magic. Metal was involved, too. Sena walked into the cage next, her mouth as thin as a paper cut. Claire scooted over to make room, but Sena sat down in the opposite corner.

The door shut, and Ragweed jiggled it a bit to make sure it was secured. He ruffled the metal plants, like they were his favorite dog, and the creaking sound intensified as the vines wound themselves closer and became more and more impenetrable.

"That's that," he said, turning his back on the cage and facing the crowd of curious spectators that had trickled out from the Hearing Hall. "It will hold."

A few of the spectators stepped forward, blatantly staring at the girls. Uncomfortable, Claire dropped her gaze.

"You're sure it's locked?" a woman asked. "You never know with Forgers."

"Oh for pine's sake," a familiar voice said, and Claire looked up. Nett stood next to the cage, glaring furiously at the woman. "This cage has stood since before even the Guild War, when the guilds were allowed to jumble magics. It is both Tiller-crafted *and* Forger-made, reinforced with fire and thousand-year-old heartwood. There's no way just Sena could escape."

"Stand back from there," Ragweed barked at Nett. "You're her friend and not to be trusted."

Nett threw back his shoulders, trying, Claire guessed, to stand as tall as he could . . . which wasn't very tall at all. "The Greens are one of the oldest families in Greenwood!" he said heatedly. "How *dare* you—"

"Nettle." Francis, the kind old Tiller who'd spoken up for Claire, suddenly appeared beside Nett. "You've made your point. Come along."

"You step back, too, Francis," another Tiller snarled at the old man. "You're growing rot-weak in your old age. That girl doesn't belong here!"

Francis's hand darted toward the pouch that hung on his belt while a Tiller guard raised his staff. But before anything could happen, Ragweed stepped forward.

"That's enough," he drawled, looking at the girls with distaste. He turned toward the woman: "It's as the sprout said—it's impossible to escape. Those ash-covered Forgers are useful for *something*. See for yourself." He gestured toward the bars.

Muttering under her breath, the woman gave the bars a hard shake, but when the vines started growing so rapidly they almost trapped her hand inside, she seemed to be satisfied.

Ragweed raised his voice and addressed the crowd: "Come, it'll be dark soon. All must help raise the wards. Francis, Nett— you lead the way."

Claire's heart dipped as she watched Nett's shaggy head bob into the village along with Francis and the others. He didn't look back.

Claire thought she heard a whimper from the far side of the cage.

"Are you okay?" she asked tentatively.

"Leave. Me. Alone." Sena's voice was harsh as ever, but Claire was sure she heard a sniffle.

"Fine," Claire said, wrapping her arms around her knees. She wished she were as small as she felt, because then she could slip between the bars and start looking for Sophie. But she was stuck here, with a girl who obviously hated her, with the eyes of an entire village watching, in a world she did not understand.

Claire shuddered as she held back her tears. Brave people didn't cry. Sophie wouldn't cry. Guilt mixed with homesickness, forming a strange ache that settled in her abdomen. She wanted Mom and Dad. What would happen when they realized both their daughters were gone?

Fear and wonder twined around her heart. Part of her wanted to break out of the cage so she could run back down the chimney-well to safety. Another part of her wanted to see more of this terrifying and beautiful thing: magic. But she knew that, most important of all, Sophie needed her.

Claire reached out a tentative finger and stroked a hard leaf. It curled away from her, thickening as it blocked out the indigo twilight. Maybe there was a way she could rip the leaves, or trick them somehow. She pulled her pencil from behind her ear. If she nudged the bars with her pencil instead of her hand, would the vines still respond?

Sena shifted in her corner. "Don't even think about it."

Claire started. "Don't even think about what?" she asked, hastily slipping her pencil into her sweater pocket.

The girl rolled her yellow eyes. "Escaping. We're stuck here and tomorrow night we'll be lucky if we're even *in* this cage, because if we're not, we'll be chained outside of Greenwood for the wraiths to find us."

"But I didn't do anything wrong," Claire said, her voice catching on a rising lump. "It isn't fair."

"Don't talk to me about fairness," Sena retorted. She turned her back on Claire again, and didn't say anything for the rest of the evening—not when a guard slipped them stale crackers, not even when some village children came to mock them.

As the shadows lengthened and melted with the night, Claire lay on her back and looked up to the sliver of moon she could see through the bars. Sena's sniffles had long ago turned into soft snores, but Claire's thoughts wouldn't let her sleep so quickly. In the shared cage, she felt as lonely as the empty sky between the stars. Her sister was out there, but she didn't know where, or how to find her.

CHAPTER
8

Whispers, dark and smoky, filled Claire's dreams and yanked her from sleep. She sat upright, breathing heavily. Night folded around her, and the metal vines and leaves still arched overhead. Sena snored, an unmoving lump in the corner.

But the whispers hadn't been a dream. They were real.

Her stomach somersaulted. Had the guards come to feed her to the wraiths?

"Careful, not too much . . . ," said a boy's voice.

Pearly light suddenly spilled out, illuminating Nett's round face beyond the bars, as well as Francis's white beard. Claire let out a huge sigh of relief, just as Sena leaped up, suddenly wide awake.

"You came!" Sena whispered.

"Of course we did!" Nett said indignantly. "I told you—I

said it was 'both Tiller-crafted *and* Forger-made.' Didn't you get my hint?"

"What's happening?" Claire asked before Sena could reply. Nett and Francis were carefully brushing a reddish goop onto the leaves of the cage.

"Shh," Francis answered, and wiped his forehead. "We must all be quiet."

"Hi, Claire," Nett whispered between the vines. He handed a brush to Sena, and she began to help. "We're here to get you out! Even though the cage is mostly metal, Grandpa thinks that we can wilt the bars—"

"Nettle, 'quiet' applies to you, too," Francis said. "The Watch could come back any moment. Light, please?"

Nett hurried to hold up a ball of moss that glowed like a small sun.

"Nice to meet you, Claire," the old man said very quietly, still carefully daubing the leaves with the red substance—the same color as the rust around some of Windemere Manor's pipes. Was it rust?

"Nice to meet you, too," she whispered back. Claire liked the way Francis had wrinkles around his eyes. She thought it must mean he laughed a lot, even though his face was currently all concentration.

He let out a low cough. "All right. Nett, Sena. It's ready," Francis said, and gave the brush one last flourish before stepping aside.

Claire didn't understand what was supposed to happen, but

then the metal leaves began to clink together like wind chimes. Looking at them, Claire saw one start to shrink, curling up at the edges and unwinding itself from the others.

She gasped. The cage was . . . *withering.* The vines were softening, collapsing in on themselves like wet noodles as orange began to speckle the black iron.

Magic again—a thrill raced through Claire. She watched in amazement as Sena put her hands between two of the vines and easily pushed them aside, then slid out the gap.

"Come, Claire," Francis said from somewhere in the dark. "The effect won't last very long."

Taking a deep breath, Claire carefully pushed away the vines, trying not to think of them hardening again and crushing her. She clambered through, wincing as the rusty leaves moaned like a sick dog.

Then she was free.

"Let's move," Sena whispered. "Francis, we—wait. Francis?" The girl's voice wobbled with uncertainty.

Claire looked around, and saw that the old man was supporting himself against the withered vines. He was breathing heavily. Sena hurried over to him. "Are you all right?" she asked him. "You should have let Nett do most of the Tilling."

"I'm fine," Francis said, straightening up, though his voice sounded hoarse to Claire. "Just not as young as I used to be. To the cottage, first. Hurry!"

Nett covered the glowing ball with one hand, allowing only the faintest of light to trickle through his fingers. Claire saw that the ball had a feathery texture to it. But before she could get a closer look, Nett, Sena, and Francis walked swiftly across the expanse of cobblestone and disappeared into the shadows of the bordering buildings. With her heart beating faster than hummingbird wings, she ran after them.

Under the cover of night, the four of them padded down the road. The white light in Nett's hand bobbed in front of them as they headed toward a small house on the edge of the village. It looked cozy, and Claire was hoping there was food inside, when Francis cut a sharp right and went into the cultivated field *behind* the house. There were no more houses here, only one tiny cottage that straddled the border of tame and wild at the edge of the forest.

Nett hurried inside, and the others followed. Claire's nose immediately caught the scent of damp soil, fresh spices, and a comforting smell she associated with the small bookstore where she bought all her art supplies. Embers glowed dimly under a cast-iron pot in the fireplace, and two straw pallets lay next to it.

"Double the curtains!" Francis hissed as he covered the windows with woven hangings that looked more like place mats than drapes.

Nett and Sena quickly followed him, draping thick furs from pegs above the windows to seal them completely. Only then did Francis strike a match and light the candles on a long wooden table. Nett stirred the embers in the hearth, feeding twigs to the hungry coals, and soon a cozy light bathed the cottage, revealing Francis's home.

Two entire walls of the one-room cottage were just shelves—shelves of strange books with titles like *Mushrooms and Their Mysteries* or *Alistair Sprout's Composting Essential: A Classic*, glass jars with neat labels, and plants tumbling out of pots, either hanging down to the ground or clambering up the bookshelves to spread leafy arms onto the wood-beam ceiling above them. There was even a tiny bush pruned into the shape of a lion that stood proudly on the windowsill.

Bundles of dried plants hung on hooks all around the cottage, leaving enough space on the floor for the two straw pallets, a bed frame covered in a thick quilt, and the large wooden dining table. Or maybe it was a worktable, because instead of plates and spoons, there were pots of seedlings and little spades lying on it, surrounded by dirt.

In the flickering amber light, Sena began pulling dried meats and cheeses down from a shelf and placing them into a leather satchel.

Francis looked at her curiously. "Are you hungry? I can prepare—"

Sena shook her head, not looking back at any of them. "Nett, hand me your rucksack. We'll need tools . . ."

"Sena," Nett said suspiciously, "What are you doing?"

"Packing, obviously."

"Sena, no, it's not safe," Francis said, touching the girl's arm. "We don't know what happened to Sophie. We don't know what dangers lurk beyond Greenwood."

Sena stopped what she was doing and turned back to face

the three of them. "I need to get—I need to find her. I'll never be safe *here* until the truth is out."

Claire's heart leaped. She could hardly believe her ears. "You're going to help me?"

Sena sighed and looked up at the ceiling. "If that's how you want to look at it, then yes."

Francis leaned back on his heels, frowning. "You can't just set off into the wraith-filled night without some idea of where Sophie has gone. You need a plan, Sena."

"But I do have a plan," Sena said. "I spent all night thinking about it."

Both Francis and Nett looked at her, clearly surprised. Claire couldn't blame them. Even though she'd only just met the Forger, Sena didn't seem like someone who thought things through—she just did them.

"There's an easy way to find the harp—and Sophie," Sena said. "We just need a Looking Glass."

There was a clatter as Nett yelped and dropped the fire iron. "First frost," he said. "You have to be joking!" But Claire didn't see anything humorous about the set of Sena's jaw.

"Not at all. I know the theory." Sena tried to tie her ruck-sack shut; by now it was bulging with all sorts of strange supplies. "A Looking Glass can show you the location of whatever it is you've lost. In this case, we've lost Sophie. And if we find Sophie, we'll find the harp."

"Sophie didn't steal—" Claire began, but stopped when Francis held up his hand.

"And where are you going to get the Forger tools you need?" he asked Sena. "Where will you find a forge to melt metal?"

Sena's chin jutted out farther. "At a smith's workshop. In Fyrton."

Nett no longer seemed startled by what Sena was saying. Instead, he was staring at her with a look of suspicion. But Francis was clearly shocked by Sena's plan. He moved so he was standing in front of the door, blocking it.

"I'm afraid I cannot allow that." There was a warning in the grain of his voice that gave Claire a chill.

"Why not?" Claire asked. "Mr. Francis, if this Looking Glass can lead me to Sophie, then Sena and I *need* to go to Fyrton."

"Because," Francis said, turning grim eyes on her, "as Sena knows perfectly well, going to Fyrton would mean certain death."

CHAPTER
9

Certain death.

The words hung suspended in the air, before clattering down around Claire like hail. She'd been afraid many times in her life, but this particular moment had a distinct feeling to it. It was the same feeling she'd had when they'd learned the doctors didn't have a name for Sophie's illness, and that, without a name, they didn't know a definite cure.

Claire shuddered, throwing off the memory and reminding herself that Sophie was better now.

"But . . . *why*?" Claire whispered. "Why is Fire Town so dangerous?"

"Fyrton," Francis corrected. "And there are many reasons." With a grunt, he stepped back from the door and then, with effort, lowered himself into a rocking chair. Now that he was next to the fire, Claire could clearly see how his leather jerkin strained over his belly and how thin blue veins spidered his hands. He was old, she realized. Very old.

"Hundreds of years ago," Francis began, "in Arden's Golden Age, when unicorns roamed freely, people could travel anywhere they wanted. All the guilds were welcome to work together and combine their magic. Cities with grand buildings rose up and large universities welcomed everyone to study and exchange new and brave ideas."

"But then the war came," Nett said, his voice low, his eyes shadowed in the flickering light of the hearth.

"That's right," Francis went on. "The guilds began to compete with one another. Each felt their magic was stronger and better than the others'. The Gemmers came to power and tried to enslave the Forgers."

Claire gasped and looked at Sena. The Forger was still standing in a corner of the cottage, clutching the rucksack to her chest tensely, like a cat about to spring.

"The Forgers, naturally, rose up against the Gemmers and rebelled. All the guilds eventually got involved, and a terrible war was waged. And here we come to our point."

Francis shifted slightly. "When the Guild War finally ended, new laws were made. Since then, each guild is to remain separate. No member from one guild may travel to another guild's town or city, unless given explicit permission to trade. In addition to that, each guild has exactly the same number of unicorn artifacts, and any new discoveries must be reported to the capital. It's the only way to stop one guild from becoming more powerful than the other three. It's the only way to keep the peace."

He glanced back at Claire. "That's one of the reasons why Grandmaster Iris is so concerned about the Unicorn Harp. It was never reported to the capital. Greenwood has broken one of the laws."

"But . . ." Claire's mind was turning. "If the guilds aren't meant to mingle, then why does Sena live here, among the Tillers? Isn't she—aren't you," she said, trying to catch Sena's eye, "a Forger?"

"That's private," Sena said harshly. "I don't ask you why Sophie didn't tell you about us, and *you* stay out of my business."

Claire's heart twisted. Sena had hit on something painful. Sophie *hadn't* told Claire she'd been coming back to Arden. She hadn't trusted Claire with her Experiences. Claire's eyes stung, and she didn't know what to say.

"Enough," Francis said firmly, frowning at Sena. "Sena's an exception, Claire. Which leads me to another point. Sena, you know that you have been *exiled* from the Forger Guild. And though it seems you've forgotten, that includes Forger cities like Fyrton."

Claire studied Sena, wondering what awful thing she had done to be kicked out of her own guild at such a young age. Sena couldn't be more than thirteen.

Sena's eyes hardened, glittering like gold coins. "A Looking

Glass is the only way we'll be able to find Sophie and clear my name!"

"Arden is strict about guild interactions," Francis warned. "And the Forgers of Fyrton are the strictest of all."

"But *Francis*"—if Sena had been anyone else, Claire would have said she was pleading—"if we don't find the harp, Greenwood and the rest of the Tillers will blame *me*." She crossed her arms around herself, a movement that was somehow at once both defiant and helpless. "I have to go *somewhere*."

"Yes," Francis said, sounding surprisingly fierce. "You will go somewhere, but *not* Fyrton. You and Claire will go to the old cabin and lay low for a week. In the meantime, I will talk with Iris and make her see reason. And"—he raised his voice over Sena and Claire's sounds of protest—"I will send word to my Tiller friends throughout Arden asking them to keep a lookout for a girl of Sophie's description. Agreed?"

Sena walked over and knelt down beside Francis's rocking chair. "All of Greenwood knows about your old cabin," she said softly. "It'll be the first place they look." For a moment, Claire thought their roles were reversed, as though Sena were the adult and Francis the child.

"Young lady—"

"Oh Francis, don't you see?" Sena said. Her voice trembled like a tear about to fall. "I can't get *you* in trouble, too. I can't let *more* people be hurt because of me. Because of my mistake."

Claire almost took a step back at the current of guilt in

Sena's voice. Again, she wondered what exactly Sena had done to have been exiled.

Francis grew very, very still. And for once, Nett seemed to have nothing to say. The fire crackled in the silence.

The old man seemed to be at war with himself. He ran his hands through his hair until it looked as fierce as the mane on the little green lion. But just when Claire thought he was about to roar his disapproval, Francis let out a soft sigh. And with the sound, something inside him seemed to wilt. When he lifted his eyes to look at Sena, Claire saw that they were full of sadness.

"If you must," he said quietly, "take a village horse."

There was another long pause as Sena squeezed his hand. "Thank you," she said, and she actually sounded like she meant it. "I promise we'll be careful and—"

"You will return in one week," Francis interrupted, his voice once again firm. "*One week. Do you understand?*"

And as Sena nodded, Claire realized how truly dangerous it must be to stay in Greenwood if Francis was willing to let them risk this journey. Her heart began to beat rapidly.

Sena stood and swung the bulging rucksack onto her back, while Francis cleared his throat, then got up and went to a cupboard, from which he pulled out a pair of boots in soft gray leather.

"For you," he said, handing them to Claire. "You don't want to be traveling in thin slippers."

Claire hesitated a moment. By accepting the boots, she was

agreeing to a trip that would end in *certain death*. But if she didn't, she'd never find her sister. She reached for the boots.

"Thank you."

"They're a bit big, but I've got some long laces, and we'll tie them tight," Francis said. "Nett, one of your tunics might fit Claire."

Nett nodded, and rummaged in a nearby trunk. A moment later, he returned with a small bundle of clothes.

"Here you go," he said. "You can change behind the screen."

Claire took the squishy armful and looked down. *Nettle Green* was embroidered in orange thread on the inside of the green collar. Suddenly, Claire felt almost hopeful. Wraiths might exist here, but it was good to know that kind people did, too. Nett and Francis might not know what happened to Sophie, but they still wanted to help her. Even grumpy Sena was ready to assist.

"Don't just stand there," Sena barked, as if to disprove that last thought. "Change!"

Claire quickly walked over to a screen made of tall reeds. She slipped on the soft moss-green shirt. The wide trousers were slightly too big for her, but they cinched in around the ankle so she wasn't in danger of tripping. She laced her boots tightly.

Before Claire came out from behind the screen, she carefully pulled her pencil from her sweater pocket and pressed her thumb to its tip. It was a reminder of home. She didn't want to leave it behind. She stuck it behind her ear, securing it with a few thick curls.

Stepping out from behind the screen, she saw Sena standing with two packs now slung over her shoulder. She handed one to Claire, who was surprised by its heaviness.

"And here's a cloak."

Claire automatically took the slate-blue cloak with the soft hood that Sena was holding out to her. She thought that when she tied it around her shoulders she would feel silly, as though she were playing dress up, but as the cloth settled comfortably around her, she suddenly felt the weight of what she was doing. For the first time, she realized what was happening: she was going on a quest.

What would her parents think? *Her parents.*

"How long do you think it'll take to get there?" Claire asked anxiously. "I don't want my mom and dad to worry."

"Calm your heart," Francis said, coming up behind her and dropping a few more wrapped parcels into her pack. "Time seems to run differently between your home and Arden. Sophie insisted she visited one night after the other, but sometimes there were several days between her visits. Months, even. There didn't seem to be any discernable pattern, Sophie said, except that time always seemed to run faster here."

Buckling down a final strap, Francis gave Claire's rucksack a last pat. "You should be home before your parents even notice you're gone," he continued. "The Greenwood Council, though, that's a different matter. You two better hurry."

"Not two, *three*," Nett said, stepping out from behind a shelf where he had been cramming more things into his own rucksack. "I'm going with them."

"No, Nett!" Sena said before Claire had a chance to open her mouth. "This isn't your fight!"

"I'm coming," Nett insisted stubbornly. "I know magic better than you—"

"Only because you've been trained!" Sena cut in.

"I know that," Nett said. "But I can help! And Claire has no magic, and she probably doesn't even know the difference between a yew berry and a rose hip—do you?" he asked Claire.

"No?" she said.

"One's poisonous," he said promptly. "See? You need me."

Arms crossed, Sena turned to the old man. "As soon as they see we've escaped, they'll know you helped us. They'll come after you."

The furrows on Francis's face deepened, mapping out worry, concern, and love.

"My dear girl," he said to Sena. "I'm an experienced craftsman. I can take care of myself."

"Ha!" Nett stuck his tongue out at Sena.

Francis handed a small pouch to Sena. By its tinkling, Claire thought it must be full of coins. "Out the back entrance," he said. Then he looked down at Sena.

"May the silver sing sweet—" she said gruffly.

"—until again we meet," Francis finished.

Sena nodded her head in acknowledgment, then she flung her arms around him.

"Be safe," she mumbled into his leather vest.

"You, too."

Sena broke the embrace and turned toward Claire. "What are you waiting for?" she snapped irritably. "Open the door!"

Claire swung the door open, and Sena marched into the night, Nett hurrying after her.

"Claire?" Francis said.

She looked back at him. His eyes were dark, the color of the ivy that concealed Windemere's red brick.

"Do not tell people where you've traveled from—it could be dangerous for you," he whispered. "If anyone asks, say you're a Tiller. And once you've found Sophie, you both must leave Arden as fast as you can."

"We will," she said quickly. "Thank you for—for everything, Francis."

"You're very welcome. It's the least I can do, as this is partly my fault."

Surprised, Claire frowned. "What do you mean?"

Francis's eyebrow dipped. "Sena and Nett don't have many friends in Greenwood. It was nice to see them with Sophie, and I'm afraid I . . . encouraged her to come back."

"Sophie would have come back anyway," Claire said, not needing any Sinceri Tea to know that what she said was true.

A sad smile appeared on Francis's face. "Then I thank you for your comforting words. Now go."

Claire nodded and stepped into the blue darkness, leaving the glow of Francis's cottage behind.

CHAPTER
10

This way!"

Claire followed Sena's whisper to the tree line. Clouds skittered across the moon, making its glow dim while shadows quivered in the grass.

"Put your hood up," Sena instructed, and Claire slipped her cloak's hood over her hair. It was slightly too big, and came down low over her forehead, framing her vision on all sides so she could only see what was directly in front of her.

Sena nodded her approval. "Keep your head down, and you shouldn't be recognized." She paused. "Not that people are out tonight. No one wants to risk running into a wraith with the harp gone."

"But," Nett rushed to add, "we don't have too far to go. The sun will rise soon enough, and then the wraiths will retreat. Just stay close—and no sudden movements."

The three of them snaked their way along the forest's edge, Sena in the lead. Without a light, Claire tripped often. The darkness had a tangible quality to it, as though she were trying to wade through sand instead of air. It forced her to move slowly even though she was desperate to run.

After several minutes, they arrived at a long, low building that was just beyond the faint glow of neatly lined cottages. Carefully, Sena slid open a well-oiled door and disappeared inside, Claire and Nett following close behind.

The smell of manure and the sound of soft munching filled the space. From somewhere near her, Claire heard Nett fumble, and then the moss's light spilled from his hands, washing over the velvety muzzles of a dozen horses in their stalls.

Claire suddenly had a very bad feeling. She had only been on a horse once before, when Sophie had begged their parents for a trail ride through a state park. It had taken some convincing for Claire to get on, but when the park ranger had offered to hold on to her rope, she'd been okay.

Somehow, she didn't think Sena would be so patient.

"Keep up," Sena said as she marched them through a small door.

Stacked from floor to ceiling, golden bales of hay circled the room like the edges of a nest. Only one small corner had been brushed clear—a space just big enough to hold a pair of boots slumped next to a trunk, and a pile of blankets.

Sena froze. "I thought this was where the saddles were kept. Who's living here?"

"No one that I know of," Nett whispered back.

"State yourselves!"

Claire jumped at the new voice. Heart beating rapidly, she turned to see a tall boy emerge from behind a wall of hay. In his hand was a pitchfork, and it was pointed directly at them.

"Thorn! It's just us!" Nett whispered. "See?" He held up the ball of moss and its circle of light spread. The boy squinted in the brightness, then his eyes widened.

"Nett? *Sena*!?" The pitchfork dipped in surprise. Then, if possible, his eyes grew even wider as they landed on Claire. "And you—Sophie's sister! How did you get out of the cage?"

Claire hesitated—the pitchfork was uncomfortably close.

Sena crossed her arms. "Put the pitchfork down, and we'll think about telling you."

The pitchfork lowered a little, but not completely. "What are you doing here?"

"We could ask you the same thing," Nett retorted.

The boy shifted. "With a thief on the loose, Grandmaster Iris said she'd pay a few extra coins if I guarded the village horses tonight."

As though he had just remembered his purpose, the pitchfork lifted again. "And it looks like she was right to worry," he added grimly.

"Thorn, we need your help," Nett said—rather bravely, Claire thought. "You can't give us away. We're going to find Sophie!"

The pitchfork stayed level at their chests.

"Why would I care about Sophie? I've never even seen her," Thorn replied. "And I'm pretty sure I can't let you go."

"Can't or won't?" Sena spoke up. "There's a difference, you know."

Thorn's eyes flicked to Claire. "If anyone finds out I've seen you—any of you . . . It's nothing personal—"

"Nothing personal!" Sena whisper-shrieked. "*Who* made sure you could stay in Greenwood after your grandmother died? *Who vouched for you at the council?*"

Thorn flushed. "Technically, Francis did, but I—"

"Technically? Why you—!"

"Wait," Nett interrupted. He tilted his head at Thorn. "How did you know Claire was Sophie's sister?"

"What? I mean"—Thorn looked confused—"I just assumed!"

"You weren't at the Hearing Hall," Nett accused.

"I was!" Thorn protested. "You just didn't see me."

"I *did* see you," Nett said grimly. "I saw you outside Baker Seedling's house after the start of the meeting—not in the hall. If you've never seen Sophie, *then how did you know that this girl was her sister?*"

Claire looked again at Thorn. This time, she recognized him as the hunched blond boy she'd seen weeding a garden as they ran toward the Hearing Hall. What was Nett getting at?

"Come on, Nett. Everyone knows that she and Sena were locked up together," Thorn said defensively. "If Sena's free, it only makes sense that *she's* Clairina Martinson."

Nett's face fell. "Oh. I guess that explains—"

"Wait," Claire said, mouth suddenly dry. "Clairina isn't my full name. It's a nickname that only Sophie calls me."

Nett shot her a triumphant grin, while Sena gave a small yelp.

"Do you know my sister?" Claire pushed on. "Do you know where she went?"

For a second, she thought Thorn was going to do something drastic—like pierce them with the pitchfork and run—but instead, he folded up like an umbrella, his shoulders almost touching his ears.

"I know her," he said miserably.

"You liar!" Sena shouted. "What do you know? Tell us the truth!"

If possible, Thorn seemed to shrink even more. "I was trying to protect Sophie," he mumbled.

"Protect her from *what*?" Sena asked.

Thorn leaned the pitchfork against the wall and plopped onto a hay bale near them. This close to him, Claire could see that he was very handsome—or that he would have been, if his ears weren't so big.

"For the last few weeks, I've seen a Forger at Greenwood's boundaries," Thorn said. "He was asking questions about Sophie."

"But Forgers—" Nett blurted.

"Aren't allowed in Greenwood," Thorn finished. "I know."

Nett and Sena stared at Thorn in shock.

"What kind of questions was he asking?" Sena demanded.

"Nothing too specific. Just which guild did she belong to, where was she from, when would she visit again. Things like that."

The light wavered as Nett squeezed the glowing moss ball. His knuckles were white. "Why didn't you report him?" he asked tightly.

"I didn't want Sophie to get in trouble," Thorn said. "If the council knew there was a Forger asking about Sophie, they'd start asking questions about her, too. I didn't want her to be banned from Greenwood, seeing as she's not actually a Tiller and all." He coughed and a blush crept up his neck.

An incredible idea came to Claire.

Thorn liked her sister.

As in, *like*-liked her.

Claire studied him, and wondered if Sophie *like* liked him, too. And if she did . . . why hadn't Sophie told her about him? She used to always tell Claire about her crushes. As Claire looked at Thorn, she realized that his eyes were actually too small for his face and his chin was a little too square for him to be considered handsome at all.

Sena leaned forward. "Do you know who the Forger was?"

Thorn shook his head. "I know he's a master Forger since he had three red rings, one on his right sleeve, two on his left. He's taller than any of the Tillers here, and his hair is shaved close to his head."

"That could be *any* master Forger," Sena said. "Anything else?"

Thorn nodded. "Yes. He wore a double-headed ax slung across his back. The blades were made to look like the wings of a bat."

Sena blanched. "Anvil Malchain," she whispered. "*Anvil Malchain* is looking for Sophie?"

The name meant nothing to Claire, of course, and Thorn looked as confused as she felt, but Nett recoiled, as though the name had fangs.

"Who?" Claire asked.

"He's the best treasure hunter in all of Arden," Sena said grimly. "Anything he sets out to find, he finds. And he's known for doing whatever it takes to get the job done."

Whatever it takes.

For the millionth time that day, Claire asked the same question: "*Why*? Why is someone hunting Sophie?"

Thorn opened his mouth, then closed it, his face twisting before he finally replied. "I don't know. But yesterday, I saw Malchain's horse again in the woods. When Sophie arrived last night, I told her about him and asked if she knew him. She said she didn't, but it kind of seemed like she was lying."

"What do you mean?" Claire asked.

Thorn bit his lip, thinking. "She seemed upset—you know how she can get kind of distant when she's mad? Well, when I asked her what was wrong, she said everything was fine, but I could tell it wasn't. And I've been thinking," Thorn paused, seeming to need a moment to sort through his words. "I've been thinking that Sophie wouldn't steal—but that Malchain seems suspicious. Maybe *he's* the thief. And if Malchain stole the harp, then the only reason I can imagine he'd want Sophie is because Sophie knows something about the crime. Maybe she *saw* him do it."

Thorn looked up, and his blue eyes met Claire's. "I thought Sophie returned home. I only realized that she hadn't when I heard Sophie's sister had been on trial and was in the cage with Sena. And now I'm afraid . . ." His voice cracked, and he cleared his throat. "I'm afraid that maybe Malchain kidnapped Sophie. To keep her quiet about the harp."

They were silent as the words sank in. Only the soft snuffling of the horses filled the stable, but Claire could barely hear them with her pulse beating loudly in her ears. Her sister . . . *kidnapped?*

Sena shifted her weight uncomfortably. "Or," she offered, "maybe whatever Sophie saw, or knew, made her run. Maybe she's safe, at least for now, but felt she couldn't stay here because Malchain would come back for her."

Claire nodded. What Sena said made sense. Sophie had always been good at escaping trouble. If she thought this man, this Malchain, was looking for her, she wouldn't have just let herself get captured. Sophie was smart. Sophie was brave. But that word—"brave"—gave Claire a new reason to worry.

"What if Sophie isn't running from Malchain . . . ," she

said to the others, an idea slowly forming. "What if . . . what if she went after him to try to get the harp *back*? To be a hero?"

To have, Claire thought, *an Experience.*

"Whether Malchain's after Sophie or Sophie's after Malchain," Nett said in a hushed tone, "we need to get to her first. She may not realize how dangerous he really is, or that war between guilds is at stake." He looked at Thorn. "Can we count on you to stay quiet?"

Thorn grimaced. "If you steal a village horse they'll know I let you get away. And the Greenwood Council barely tolerates me as it is. I heard Ragweed call me 'lackie' under his breath just the other day, when he thought I couldn't hear."

" 'Lackie'?" Claire asked.

"As in, 'lacking in magic,' " Nett clarified in a murmur.

Claire saw Thorn's flinch, but then he shrugged. "I've never been good at Tilling, but that doesn't mean I—"

"Just stop! You're a coward is what you are, Thorn Barley!" Sena cut in. "You've got to let us have a horse, or else I'll—"

"What, Sena? You're an escaped prisoner!"

"I'll make you sorry!"

As Sena and Thorn argued, Claire felt something ugly rising in her chest, trying to claw its way out of her.

"Please," she said, in what was nearly a shout. "Sophie doesn't have time for this!"

Sena sputtered, but Thorn immediately fell silent. He studied Claire, his eyes the same blue as her favorite colored pencil. He puffed his cheeks and slowly let out his breath. "Where are you trying to go?"

"Fyrton," Nett said. "We need to make a Looking Glass."

Thorn laughed, but when no one else smiled, he quickly fell silent.

"I could get in so much trouble," he finally said, running his fingers through his hair. "And so could you."

He picked up the pitchfork. "But I have an idea."

CHAPTER
11

The wind-tossed clouds drowned the nearly full moon as Thorn led the other three to the river. Claire hurried to keep up. She wished she'd brought a flashlight with her, but immediately realized how silly that was. If wishes could be granted, she would have wished that Sophie were found. That they'd never climbed the ladder. That they'd never moved into Windemere Manor for the summer.

As they neared the riverbanks, the moon broke through the ocean of clouds, and a ghostly light illuminated a train of houseboats. They were long and narrow, with windows like flute holes. The boats, about twenty of them, were all linked together, each connected to the next by two or three rafts that floated low in the water under the weight of the large crates of vegetables set on top. A thin moonbeam fell on the name of one of the boats: *Thread Cutter.*

"Slug soot," Sena hissed as they paused in a thicket. "Thorn, you didn't tell me these were *Spinner* boats!"

"I thought you knew," Thorn protested. "The Water Bobbin Fleet always comes the week of the full moon to replenish their food supplies. But the last narrowboat will be empty. It belongs to a storyteller who's spending her summer in the capital."

"But we're not allowed on Spinner boats," Nett whispered.

Claire peeked out from behind the grove to take in the boats again. "Why not? Aren't *they* the ones in Tiller territory?"

"You've been listening, haven't you," Sena said, and for a second, Claire thought she saw a flicker of something like approval cross the girl's face. Sena was impressed, but Claire couldn't help but feel annoyed.

She might not have been the tallest or the bravest, but she was a good listener—she had to be, if she wanted to learn important things. From experience, Claire knew that the biggest bits of news were often told in the quietest of voices.

"Merchants are the only ones who really travel between guilds," Nett explained, keeping his voice low. "That's how the Forger cities, Spinner communities, and Gemmer settlements get food, and in exchange, the Tillers receive non-magical tools and clothes."

He sidled up to join Claire behind the tree. "Tiller merchants are only supposed to travel with other Tiller merchants," he went on, "and Spinner merchants with Spinner merchants."

Claire pushed aside a branch and began to walk forward.

"Well, if this is the fastest way to Fyrton, then I'm getting on a boat."

"Claire—" Sena said.

"No!" she said, almost forgetting to whisper. "Haven't *you* been listening? I need to find Sophie. She doesn't belong here. *We* don't belong here. If you want to leave, just leave!"

Instead of responding, Sena tackled Claire to the ground.

A second later, sparks shot into the night above them.

Squinting, Claire could just make out the figure of a man standing on the riverbank. In the light of the last spark, she saw he had a white stripe of hair. It was the skunk-haired man, Councillor Ragweed.

"Wraith Watch," Thorn said, his voice barely louder than the crickets.

Claire's mouth suddenly felt dry. "Are the wraiths here?"

Nett shook his head. "Probably not—they tend to gather around places where something terrible has happened, like an old battlefield. But Greenwood always has a watch at the village's outer boundaries, just in case."

For a second, it looked like Ragweed was juggling stars. Fragments of light arced into the air and then went out as quickly as a camera's flash. It reminded Claire of the sparkling light that had scared away the Shadow Thing who attacked her and Sophie, the light that had fallen into her mouth and tasted of dirt . . .

"I think I've seen those sparks before," Claire said, squinting.

"Of course you have," Nett said. "I distracted the wraith that night before you disappeared into the well."

Claire and Thorn looked at him, astonished.

"Sophie was chased by a wraith?" Thorn asked. "She jumped into a *well*?"

"*You're* the one who made the dirt glow!" Claire said. "You scared away the wraiths!"

Nett grinned at her. "Neat trick, right? It actually wasn't dirt—it was leaf mulch. Plants drink the sun's rays in order to grow, but even when the leaves die, they still hold some sunlight in them. All I had to do was release the spark of sun trapped in them. It's not very bright, but it was enough sunlight to scare the wraith away. Understand?"

Claire thought she did—kind of.

"Because the wraiths are allergic to the sun, right?" she ventured.

"Right!" Sounding pleased, Nett nodded. He held out his glowing moss ball. "That's how the marimo works, too. It's a plant found in the lakes of the Sunrise Isles and is an *excellent* source of sunlight."

"Lecture later," Sena whispered. "Ragweed is going to reach the end of the bank and turn soon. When he does, we'll run to the narrowboat. Me and Nett first, then Thorn and Claire."

Claire tried to ignore the sticky idea that clung to her once she thought it: What if Sena was trying to lose her? She gripped her pencil. She had to trust Sena; there was no other choice.

When Ragweed finally turned, Sena and Nett took off at a

sprint, following the river to the last narrowboat at the end of the line. For a second Claire thought the man would see them scrambling, but he seemed too bored—or sleepy—to pay much attention to the rustle, other than to lob a spark lazily toward the water. The tiny firework kissed the surface, then went out.

Claire and Sophie had always watched the Fourth of July fireworks together. They'd lay out a blanket in the park, separate from their parents, and split an ice cream bar. Sophie would nibble the hard shell of chocolate until only ice cream remained. Sophie didn't really like ice cream, but she loved cold chocolate, and Claire was more than happy to take the half-eaten dessert off her hands.

But two summers ago—the summer before her illness—Sophie had gone to a late-night showing of a new movie instead of the fireworks. That year, Claire had sat on the same picnic blanket as her parents and ate the full Dove bar by herself. When she went to sleep that night, she had a stomachache.

"Ready?" Thorn whispered, jolting her from the memory. "Go!"

Before she could even blink, Thorn took off, leaving her behind. Panicked, Claire burst out of the thicket after him. She ran without thought, trying to keep Thorn in her vision.

A dark shadow loomed suddenly out of nowhere.

Claire's breath scraped across her throat. There by the river's edge, was a wraith . . . and Thorn was running straight toward it.

"*Thorn! Wraith!*" she whisper-yelled, as her vision zeroed in on that pinpoint of darkness. "*Wraith!*"

Thorn pivoted and ran straight back toward her. Should she turn and run in the opposite direction, too? She couldn't think; she didn't know what to do. And then Thorn slammed her to the ground—the second time Claire had been thrown to the ground in less than ten minutes.

"Shh," he urged.

"Somebody there?" Ragweed called out.

Thorn held his finger to his lips in silent warning. Claire could feel her heart thumping against the ground. There was another sprinkle of light, but its glow only reached the water's edge, missing Thorn and Claire on the ground.

"Trouble, Tiller?" A second voice joined the night, this one coming from one of the boats.

"None," Ragweed responded stiffly. "Just a field mouse. You can go back to sleep."

Then Ragweed resumed his pacing, his footsteps leading again to the front of the boat line. Thorn pushed himself to his hands and knees.

"You all right?"

Without answering, Claire jerked her head in the direction of the wraith on the bank.

Thorn furrowed his brow. "What's wrong?"

"Wraith," Claire whispered, wondering if there were glasses in Arden. Thorn looked to where she'd nodded.

Understanding spread across his face. "That's not a wraith; that's a chimera."

"A what?"

"I'll show you." Thorn began to crawl along the bank,

toward the spot of dark against dark. Seeing no other choice, Claire followed.

As they drew closer, the shadow began to have a more definite shape. In fact . . . it looked like a cow. One of those big ones with curved horns on its head that she'd seen pulling covered wagons in history-book sketches. "Cow" wasn't the right word . . . it was an ox.

The ox stood still, one leg raised, about to plunge into the river. But as the seconds ticked by, it stayed still, hoof never touching water.

Claire blinked. It was a metal statue! But the metal caster had made mistakes—the proportions were all off. The ox had too many knees and she was pretty sure it wasn't supposed to have fangs. She felt herself turning red. She'd almost given them away because of a *statue*.

"The chimera can't hurt you. Well," Thorn amended, "it can't hurt you *now*. It's left over from the Guild War. You'll see more as you get closer to Fyrton—they used to be alive, infused with a combination of Tiller and Forger magic, but we've forgotten how to animate them."

He let out a sigh that was more ache than sound. "Just as well. The chimera were vicious. Now, they just stay there, frozen and rusting, a testament to a bloody time."

The crickets' nightly dirge filled the silence as they waited for Ragweed to make his way back up the bank.

Finally, Thorn nudged her. "Ready? Ragweed has his back turned."

Claire nodded, and they crawled to the last narrowboat.

Thorn stood and hopped down onto the deck. He held out his hand, and even though she didn't want to take it, the thought of making another mistake was too humiliating to contemplate.

She swung her leg over the side and let go of his hand as quickly as possible.

"Thank you," she said stiffly, and walked through the hatch.

Claire felt like she'd entered a honeycomb. Everything—from the dinner plates next to the traveling stove to the worn carpet on the floor—was a shade of yellow. The walls were made entirely of small, circular cubbies, in which she could see the polished handles of scrolls. There were hundreds of them, each with their own fluttering tags hanging from different-colored threads.

"What took you so long?" Nett asked. He was already going through the scrolls, eagerly skimming each tag by the marimo's soft light.

Again, embarrassment simmered. "I fell—"

"Just wanted to be careful." Thorn hurried in, shooting a small smile at Claire. She scowled and looked at the floor. She didn't need his help.

"We can hide in the closet," Sena said, pointing to some small doors, "just in case anyone comes in for a scroll or something, but first we should make sure that all the curtains are closed—"

A strangled squeal interrupted Sena, and they all turned to see Nett staring at a rollaway desk covered in sheets of parchment and quills. Nett swiped a stamp from the top and flung it under Sena's nose.

"It's Fray's seal! We're in *Mira Fray's* floating library!" By this point, Nett was practically dancing on his toes. "I've always wanted to meet her, even if she's a Spinner. She's the most famous historian ever!"

"Ever?" Sena cocked an eyebrow. "What about Timsnore and that Dull-pants you're always going on about?"

"Most famous *living* historian," he corrected. "And it's Du*pont*! Anyway. Fray's floating library is one of the largest amassed by a single person. She has books on everything and answers for anything!"

But not for where Sophie went, Claire thought. Eyeing the scrolls, she wondered if one of them could contain information on magical chimneys or adventurous great-aunts. Thinking back to the ladder in the fireplace, she turned over a question that had been bothering her: Had Great-Aunt Diana put the ladder there, and if she had . . . *why*?

"You're bleeding."

Thorn's voice interrupted Claire's thoughts. She looked down to see a small tear at her knee where the fabric had ripped. A tiny blossom of blood stained the ragged edges of her pants.

Thorn quickly reached into his pocket and pulled out a handkerchief. "It's clean," he said as Claire eyed it. Reluctantly, she let him apply pressure to the wound.

While Sena and Nett set about closing the curtains, Thorn leaned in and whispered to Claire. "Can I ask you a favor?" He pulled something out of his pocket. "I was wondering," he said somewhat shyly, "if—*when*—you find Sophie, would you mind giving her this?"

Claire was about to say no—she didn't like the way he pretended to understand Sophie better than she did—but then he placed a small golden bird into her hand. Fine pieces of straw looped and twisted together in an intricate pattern to form wings, plumage, and impossibly tiny feet.

Running her fingers along the bird's back, Claire felt the careful lines that flowed into each other to form feathers and beak.

"I made it for her," Thorn said. "Do you think she'll like it?"

Surprise made Claire forget to be frosty. "You made this? It looks like it's about to come to life!" A thought suddenly struck her. "*Is* it going to come to life?"

"*I lent my magic to the queen*," Thorn replied.

She looked at him blankly. "What? What does that mean?"

"It's a saying in Arden," he replied, looking down at his hands. "It's what we say when a piece of craftsmanship isn't magi—as good as we wanted."

She remembered what Thorn had said Ragweed called him: *Lackie.*

"It's beautiful," Claire said.

He ducked his head shyly. "Thanks. Sophie told me how good you are at drawing. When you and Sophie return maybe you can show me one of your sketches."

The glow of Thorn's praise warmed the smile that was finally on Claire's lips. After all, it wasn't *his* fault that Sophie had kept their crush a secret.

She tucked the golden bird into her rucksack. "I'd like that."

And when Thorn smiled too big, she saw why her sister might *like*-like him.

When Sena was sure the curtains were tight, she, Nett, and Claire all crammed into a closet. Thorn threw a spare horse blanket over them, just in case. Even though Mira Fray wasn't going to be using her narrowboat, they didn't want to take any chances someone else might investigate.

Thorn wished them luck, and with a last quick smile for Claire, he closed the closet doors. She heard him pad to the exit, and a soft thump as the hatch closed. They were alone.

Under the warmth of the horse blanket, Claire must have dozed, because it seemed to be only a few minutes later when she heard people outside the boat calling to one another over the neighs of horses.

But she didn't think it was either of those sounds that had woken her. In her dreams, there'd been a soft *click*. Was someone else on the narrowboat with them?

"Did you hear that?" Claire whispered softly.

"They're just harnessing the horses," Nett said sleepily next to her. "They'll pull us upriver. It's the quickest way to carry a lot of food to the other Spinners, so that it stays fresh."

"How far away is Fyrton?" Claire asked.

"About thirty miles, give or take a few."

A horn sounded, and then whips cracked. The cabin rattled slightly as the boat swayed, and then they began to crawl forward like a caterpillar along a stem.

"The Rhona stretches for hundreds of miles," Nett

whispered, "flowing through the capital before traveling by the Red Mountains, passing the Dale, then Glen Village, then Treeton, then the Gro—"

"Shh," Sena mumbled from the darkness.

Twisting to the right, Claire scrunched up as tight as possible. Hiding in the closet reminded her of the time she'd played hide-and-seek with Sophie and climbed into the wooden chest where the Martinsons stored their spare linens. It had been both the best and worst hiding spot.

The best, because she'd won the game, but the worst because as she lay in the tight darkness, she thought she'd been forgotten.

A snore soon tripped out of Nett, and from the steady breathing to her left, it was clear that Sena had fallen back asleep, too. Claire tried to move her leg without waking either of them and leaned her head against the back panel of the closet. It was strange to be in hiding when she was also the one seeking . . .

A drop of light splashed onto Claire's face. She squinted through half-closed eyes. The doors to the closet were cracked open.

"Well, well, well, what do we have here?"

They had been found.

CHAPTER 12

"Run!" Sena yelled as she surged from the closet, butter knife at the ready.

Adrenaline coursed through Claire's body. Scrambling to her feet, she stumbled out after Sena, the blanket tangling around her ankles. She kicked it off and sprinted to the hatch.

Or at least, she tried to sprint to the hatch.

One second, the world was still, but then it slipped out from under her. Hitting the floor with a muffled *thud*, she had only a split second to catch her breath before the yellow carpet beneath her came alive.

With a *snap*, the corners of the rug lifted into the air, collecting Sena, Nett, and Claire like a net, then squishing them together as it rolled them all up in a big, tasseled burrito, with only their heads peeking out the end.

"And that's why you *always* check to see if there's a Guard-pet around," a silky voice said. A chin appeared above Claire, and then the woman bent over. Eyes shiny as wet ink stared at them behind gold-wire-rimmed spectacles. But it was her hair that caught Claire's attention. Her many braids cascaded down her shoulders, interwoven with colored ribbons and threads.

Their captor crouched, and her hair fell forward like a beaded curtain. She patted the rug. "Good Guardpet."

"Let . . . us . . . go!" Sena wheezed.

"Don't like Spinners, do you Forger?" The voice was a little less silky now, but it still undulated like a mermaid's song. "Not too smart to insult a Spinner when you've been caught. Who—"

"It's an honor to meet you, Historian Fray!" Nett burst out with such force that Claire knew he'd been holding it back. "I'm a *big* admirer of your work, especially your history on the glacial movement across Arden and the Southern territories. Do you really believe that the original cause of glacial deposits was Till—"

"And people often know better than to interrupt me," Fray said. Though her words were harsh, the melody in her tone remained.

"Y-yes, Historian," Nett stuttered.

"As a historian and storyteller, I trade in tales," Fray said, sinking onto the floor next to Claire's head. "If you succeed in telling me a story that is worth the risk of me being caught with Tiller stowaways in a Spinner fleet, I'll let you go. If not . . ."—she shrugged, braids bouncing—"then I'll trade you to Anvil Malchain for one of *his* stories. I hear he's been asking around about you, Sophie."

The rug had been squeezing Claire a moment before, but now it was crushing her.

"How do you know Sophie?" she rasped out.

The Spinner shook her head. "Come now, Sophie. I know it's you."

"She's not," Nett said quietly.

"Not what?" Fray frowned. "Speak up, Tiller. You're too loud when you need to be quiet, and too quiet when you need to be loud."

"That's not Sophie," Nett said in an only slightly stronger voice.

Historian Fray suddenly loomed over Claire. Her arms were covered in thread-woven bangles, making it look like a rainbow slinky had latched on to her. Gently, Fray brushed the tassels off Claire's face.

"You're right," Fray announced. In her surprise, she sounded younger. A white grin flashed across her face. "Well, things just got interesting."

"You know my sister?" Claire asked. "Where is she?"

"I didn't realize Sophie had been misplaced," Fray said, quickly removing a feathered quill from a pocket. "The plot thickens!"

"What does Anvil Malchain want with her?" Nett added.

"And get us out of this rusted rug!" Sena demanded.

"Language, Forger." Fray sat back on her heels. "As I said, I'm a storyteller. A weaver of tales. A keeper of secrets." Her voice flowed around them, dipping into sharp consonants and curving around melodious vowels. "Before I let you go, I need a story from you."

"No," Claire blurted out. Frustration rushed through her veins and into her clenched fists, which were pinned tightly to her sides by the carpet. She was too angry to be afraid.

She hated when people knew things she didn't.

She hated being trapped.

And most of all, she hated getting in trouble for something she hadn't done. This was the third time that she was being held captive, and it *was not fair.*

"We won't tell you anything," Claire continued, "until you get us out of here!"

Fray chuckled. "Sophie was right about you, Claire," she said as she pulled a grubby string with three knots from another pocket.

Curiosity momentarily dammed Claire's fury. "What did Sophie say?" she asked.

"That you're tougher than you look."

Pleasure wafted over Claire like sheets fresh from the dryer. Sophie didn't think she was useless after all.

Claire watched as the historian's fingers deftly untangled the three knots on the little string in her hand. Suddenly, the Guardpet relaxed its grip on her, and Claire found she could move her arms and legs again.

Magic, she realized once again. She wondered when it would stop surprising her. Maybe never. Quickly, the three kids wriggled out of the rug.

Standing up, Claire saw that Fray was shorter than she had thought. And younger, too. Much younger. Why, she couldn't be more than sixteen!

Nett was staring at the Spinner, too—specifically, at her arm, where there was only one white band around her sleeve.

"Get your butter knife, Sena," he said grimly. "This isn't Historian Mira Fray. She's an impostor!"

Before Claire could register his words and what they might mean, Sena threw herself on the Spinner and yanked her arms back.

"Our turn to ask the questions," the Forger growled. "Who are you?"

"Ow!" Fray-who-was-not-Fray yelped. "I may not be Mira Fray, but I *do* have permission to be on this boat. Which is more than you can say!"

"Let her go!" Claire cried, coming to the Spinner's side. "She knows Sophie. She said so."

"She also only has one ring around her arm," Nett said, pointing at her sleeve.

"So?" Claire asked.

"So one ring means she's only a journeyman," he explained. "Two means you're a full member of your guild, three means you're master ranked, and four is reserved for grandmasters."

"Why should we believe anything you say?" Sena asked the

Spinner. Even though the Spinner looked older than Sena, Sena was taller.

"You can believe me or not," the girl huffed. "But if you look in the desk, you'll find traveling papers with my name on them: Kleo Weft. I was Historian Fray's apprentice, but I graduated to journeyman last month. She's letting me use her boat this summer, so I can get a head start on my master ring."

Nett hurried over to the desk and rummaged around.

"Found it!" He skimmed quickly. "I think she's telling the truth this time."

Claire peered over his shoulder to read handwriting that looked like spider legs.

KLEO WEFT
Guild: Spinner
Rank: Journeyman
Occupation: Storyteller-in-Training
Transportation: Water Bobbin Fleet

This document provides access to all settlements along the Rhona River. Visits not to extend more than one night's stay.

Executed by: James Stich, Grandmaster of Ribbonshire

Painted along the edge was a border of unraveling spools, the threads looping up into the shape of a bird with tall legs and a long beak.

"See?" Fray—Kleo—said, her voice once again mellifluous. "I never said I was Mira Fray. You just assumed it."

Nett opened his mouth, then suddenly shut it. "She's right," he said to Sena, eyes wide. "She didn't say she was Mira Fray."

Claire nodded anxiously. She didn't care if this was Mira Fray or Kleo Weft or a snowman. All that mattered was that the Spinner knew something about Sophie.

"Slug soot." Sena seemed to deflate. "I'll let you go. But only if you promise your hands stay away from your hair."

"What do you mean?" Kleo asked, her eyes widening.

"Don't think I don't know the old saying *Spinner's hair, beware*," Sena said. "You're just as dangerous with your hair ribbons as Forgers are with swords."

Claire looked at Kleo's intricately woven hair with new appreciation—and apprehension.

"Fine." Kleo sighed. "I swear by all the unicorn artifacts not to touch my hair. Good?"

Sena grunted in a way that let everyone know it was far from good, but she released Kleo anyway.

Claire could no longer contain the question that felt like it was eating away at her insides. "How do you know my sister?" she asked Kleo. "When was the last time you saw her?"

Kleo eyed Claire warily. "She came to Master Fray with questions every trade day for the past few months. Kept wanting to hear different passages from the poem *The Queen and The Unicorn*." Kleo paused, as if for dramatic effect. "Would you like to hear it?"

"Yes," Claire said automatically, but her mind was more focused on something else Kleo had said. *Months?* The idea that in the four days that had passed since they'd first climbed the ladder, *months* of Arden's time had gone by was similar to trying to balance a spoon on her nose—one moment Claire thought she had it, then it fell away.

"Then I'll need a story from *you* first," Kleo said, her answer dropping so smoothly that Claire knew she'd been set up. "It's only fair."

"What do you want to know?" Claire asked cautiously as Sena let out a low hiss of breath. Claire didn't have any interesting stories—and she remembered Francis's warning. He had said not to let anyone know where she and Sophie had really come from.

"Why was Anvil Malchain asking for Sophie up and down the river?" Kleo asked, gray quill poised above a page.

"We don't know," Nett chimed in. "We thought *you* might. Maybe he mentioned the Uni—perhaps he asked you about a certain item . . . an important object that was stolen from Greenwood Village?"

Kleo's eyes widened. "You mean, an object like a *unicorn* artifact?"

Sena groaned while Nett burst out, "Anvil mentioned the harp?"

"A Unicorn *harp*?" Kleo's eyebrows shot up, and she whistled. "I didn't realize Greenwood had one of those."

"Now you've done it," Sena murmured to Nett.

But Nett continued to look at Kleo in surprise. "But you *just* said—"

Kleo smiled smugly. "Spinners are taught to follow the smallest thread and pull until it becomes something more."

Nett continued to sputter while Sena growled, but Kleo swished over to a yellow pouf and sat down, her skirt flowing around her like a melted sun. Sunlight trickled through the closed curtains along with soft Spinner chatter and occasional whinnies from the horses that pulled them up the river.

"Malchain didn't mention any harp," Kleo conceded as she propped her head on her fist. In her bright yellow clothes and trilling voice, she reminded Claire of a canary. "But it does make you wonder, doesn't it?"

"Wonder *what*?" Sena asked irritably. "Don't think we're going to fall for any of your word traps again."

Kleo adjusted a bracelet. "It's just that I haven't heard of a unicorn artifact stolen from a guild since . . . well, since the Royalists' heists."

Nett's nose wrinkled as though he'd smelled something bad. "You don't think *they* could have something to do with all of this, do you? That Malchain—or Sophie—might be one of them?"

"Please," Sena said disdainfully. "Blaming the Royalists sounds like some knotted Spinner conspiracy."

Kleo's brown eyes flashed, and Claire hurried forward before the Spinner decided to stop talking out of spite. "Sophie might be one what, exactly? What's a Royalist?"

Kleo continued to glare at Sena while she addressed Claire. "They're a society that collects—*steals*—unicorn artifacts for themselves."

"But why?" she asked.

"Because," Kleo said, finally turning to look at her, "the Royalists think that if they can find a unicorn artifact that is powerful enough, they will be able to bring back the last queen and the last unicorn from the stone."

Claire stared at her. "Wait—what?"

"It's an old legend," Nett skipped in. "First started in—"

"It's nonsense is what it is," Sena said. "Anyone who's a Royalist has bolts for brains."

"I've actually met some," Kleo interjected, and peered through her glasses at Sena. "Historian Fray interviewed them, and they seemed perfectly normal. We couldn't see their faces, though, because they all wore hooded cloaks, but they strongly believe in the legend from *The Queen and the Unicorn*."

"The same poem Sophie was interested in?" Claire asked.

"The very one." Kleo cocked her head and studied Claire. "What do you know about Sophie? I sensed she had a great secret, but I couldn't tug it out of her."

Claire shook her head, frowning. "I don't know what—"

"Hold it," Sena said, putting out her hand. She narrowed her eyes at Kleo. "You already got your story. Anvil Malchain is after Sophie Martinson. Greenwood Village is missing a Unicorn Harp. And *we're* looking for both. Now it's time to pay up. Tell Claire *your* story."

CHAPTER
13

*T*he Queen and The Unicorn, the poem Sophie was obsessed with, is Arden's most famed epic," Kleo said as she plucked from the wall a scroll with blue-and-white threads dangling from its end. "It tells the story of how Estelle d'Astora, the last queen of Arden, went to the Sorrowful Plains to save the last unicorn."

Carefully, Kleo unrolled the scroll onto the desk. Claire expected to see words on paper, but instead, she was staring at a beautiful tapestry.

One half of it showed brightly colored gardens, butterflies, and a castle on a hill. The other showed what looked to be a graveyard at night, in obsidian and dark indigos, with skeletal creatures fleeing from the sun. Wraiths.

And in the center, facing the night, was a unicorn.

This creature wasn't docile, like the ones Claire would some-times see on paper plates or gift cards. It was a being wrought of the moon and woven with starlight.

A woman in a midnight-blue dress clung to his back, her fingers lost in the froth of his mane. A circlet of silver and sap-phires glittered at her forehead. Claire longed to brush her fingers against the richness and feel the colorful threads' slip-pery smoothness, but she forced her hands behind her back.

"Wow," Nett breathed as he stood up to take a closer look. "Is this the same tapestry that Jack Tangle wrote about in *Threads of Time*?"

"The one and only," Kleo said, adjusting a few bangles. "I'm surprised you know that, being a Tiller and all."

Nett ducked his head, but looked pleased. "I like to read. Grandpa Francis has the entire epic of *Velvetina Vainglorious and Her Whispering Needle*—"

"I thought you were going to read us a poem," Sena inter-rupted, scowling. "Where are the words?"

"You don't always need *words* to tell a story," Kleo said with exaggerated patience. "Each shift in color tells me what to say and what kind of emotion to convey. Tapestries are by far the most superior way to capture history."

Sena looked slightly confused, but as Claire looked at the rainbow of threads laid in front of her, she thought she understood. In art class, she'd learned that different colors could represent different emotions, depending on the time period or culture. Yellow, for instance, could be joy for some and mourning for others. It didn't surprise her that in this world where art was magic, color was also its own alphabet.

Kleo adjusted her spectacles and lightly pressed her fingertips to the cloth. "We all know the horrors of the Guild War. How the unicorns were hunted down until only one remained."

"Wait," Claire interrupted. "Why were they hunted down? Why would anyone want to kill a unicorn?"

"Because," Nett said, "legend said that if you killed a unicorn, you'd live forever. It wasn't true, of course, but it didn't stop some from trying . . . or from using the unicorns' remains to craft new artifacts."

"Correct." Kleo nodded, hair ribbons quivering. "This is the tale of Estelle d'Astora, a Gemmer, queen of Arden and ruler of the Guilds, who lost everything to save the last unicorn."

Claire leaned forward, feeling the same shivery anticipation she felt as the lights dimmed in a movie theater.

"I begin now," Kleo said, "upon the queen's arrival to the Sorrowful Plains in the light of a lavender moon. When she discovered she was not the only one who sought the unicorn." As she spoke, Kleo sank into her storyteller's voice, her words wrapping around Claire, as bright and vivid as any screen.

And so the queen strode into the night,
   Seeking,
   Waiting,
   Watching,

Arrow drawn tight.
Then—
> *Sharp brilliance of moon,*
> *Scorching glory of sun,*
> *Furious splendor of stars,*
The unicorn stepped onto the plains.

As she spoke, Kleo transformed. She seemed less like a canary, and more like a hawk, her eyes flashing with a predatory gleam as she spoke of wraiths, her voice galloping along with the unicorn's hooves. Claire leaned in to catch the story.

> *Then—*
> *Behind the rocks,*
> *A foreign movement.*

The queen saw a flash—
> *Of Gemmer greed,*
> *Of Spinner jealousy,*
> *Of Forger rage,*
> *And Tiller apathy—*
The queen saw a flash of moonlight on steel.

A hunter stalked the unicorn.

The poem marched on, pulling Claire into Queen Estelle's terror as the hunter and the unicorn battled on the Sorrowful

Plains. Just as the hunter raised his ax above the creature's neck to strike, the last queen of Arden flung herself over the unicorn.

> *Her arms armor would be:*
> *Her hair, steel;*
> *Her bones, a shield.*
> *Her heart in exchange,*
> *For Arden's last hope.*

Claire sucked in a breath, and Nett turned his cheek. Sena stayed still, but her knuckles were white as she clenched her hands into fists. Kleo continued.

> *Queen and unicorn lay on the ground—*
> *Stayed still on the ground,*
> *Bled on the ground—*
> *Queen and unicorn dying on the ground.*

"She dies?" Claire cried out. "What kind of story is this?!"

"Shh," Nett said as Kleo glanced over her spectacles. "It's not over. Continue, Kleo."

> *The last queen whispered:*
> *"The end can be found*
> *Where fire meets water,*
> *At the edge of day and night.*
> *My grief, your gift.*

My rock, to protect.
All yours to neglect,
Until time
Is right."

A wind filled the plains—
   Lashed the plains,
   Cleaned the plains,
   A rushing light burned the plains—
Driving back the dark.

And in the light of a lavender moon,
   Two stones gleamed—
   Queen and unicorn: gone.

Silence filled the room. The words seemed to linger in the air, the way sweetness lingers after a spoonful of honey, present but faded.

"So . . . queen and unicorn turned themselves into rock statues to protect themselves?" Claire asked hesitantly, in case she hadn't understood.

"Boulders, actually," Nett said.

Kleo nodded. "The Royalists believe they can free the queen and the unicorn from the stones—they just need to find a unicorn artifact powerful enough to help them reverse the spell. A single unicorn treasure—*the* Unicorn Treasure—that can be found where fire meets water."

"And when they do," Sena cut in, "our guild magic will

thrive again, the wraiths shall be defeated, and all will be happy and wonderful within Arden." She rolled her eyes and made a face. "Rusted hinges, if you ask me. We all know that Estelle was killed in the final battle of the Guild War."

"What matters at the moment is not whether the story is true," Kleo said, taking her spectacles off and cleaning them with her skirt, "but whether the Royalists still believe it. And whether they are, in fact, the ones who stole the Unicorn Harp."

"And how we're going to get it back," Nett added. "If Malchain is a Royalist and Sophie saw him steal the harp, well, it would make sense that she would run."

"Where can we find the Royalists?" Claire asked. "Maybe Sophie is already there, trying to steal the harp back from them!"

Suddenly, Kleo put out her hand, gesturing her to stop. "Do you hear anything?" she asked.

Claire listened. Silence. The *jangle* of the horses pulling the boats up the river had stopped.

"That's strange," Kleo said, glancing at an hourglass balanced precariously on a tower of books. We're not supposed to break until Fyrton—and we're still at least a mile away." She stood and pushed aside a yellow curtain. Peering out the window, she gasped.

"What is it?" Nett asked as Claire leaped to her feet.

Kleo turned, her pupils large. "Forgers—they're inspecting the boats!"

From the round window, Claire could see the glint of swords and axes as Forgers in chain mail boarded the boats. She could hear *thumps* as doors were taken off their hinges, and cries of protest as the crates on the rafts between boats were overturned.

Kleo ran into the closet and pulled out two bundles.

"Forger clothes," she said, shoving the first bundle at Sena. "For when you've escaped."

"But how are we going to escape?" Sena asked, her eyes darting around the narrowboat.

"With this," Kleo said, handing something to each of them from the second bundle. Claire stared at it. It was a piece of cloth that looked similar to a dentist's mask.

"What are these?" Nett asked as the fabric dangled from his finger.

"Aqua Masks," Kleo said. "We wove air pockets into them."

Suddenly, Claire understood. "You want us to swim off the boat?"

"Yes," Kleo said, braids and ribbons whipping as she turned to her. "The masks won't last long, probably only fifteen minutes, but it should be enough to swim underwater to the far banks. The current is gentle here."

"How do they work?" Nett asked, holding his mask up to the light. "I mean, I think I understand enough air theory—"

Kleo shoved him to the back window. As the last boat in the fleet, they were hidden from the Forgers' sight—for now.

"Out!" Kleo ordered breathlessly. "They'll start working as soon as they touch water."

Nett eyed the round window skeptically. "I don't know if I can fit."

From down the line came sudden screams.

"I can fit," Nett yelped. He grabbed his rucksack and pulled the mask around his head. Using a pouf, he heaved himself up to the window and wriggled through.

A moment later, there was a *splash*.

Claire quickly strapped her own mask over her mouth and nose. Though it looked like normal cloth, next to her skin it felt more like a heavy gel.

Then she climbed onto the pouf and poked her head out. The muddy water lapped gently below.

THUMP THUMP THUMP!

"Fyrton inspectors! Open up!"

"Go on," Sena said bravely to Claire, as she slung her rucksack over her shoulder. "I'll follow."

As much as Claire wanted to put distance between herself and the sharp swords coming nearer and nearer, she hesitated at the darkness and dread in Sena's eyes. She remembered what Francis had said: that Sena was banned from her guild forever. What would happen to Sena if she was caught by the Forger inspectors?

"No," Claire said, stepping back down. "You go first."

Sena gave her a determined nod, then hurled herself out the window.

"In the name of the Guilds, open this door!" the inspector demanded again.

"One moment!" Kleo called out in her sweetest voice, while she waved at Claire to go. The Spinner had pulled a ribbon from her hair and wrapped it tight around the doorknob. Claire could only imagine what the ribbon was supposed to do—there wasn't time to see what would happen next.

As she scrambled on top of the pouf, the Forgers announced, "By the order of the Grand Council of Arden, Fyrton has the right to inspect all boats traveling within three miles of Fyrton's gates. If you resist inspection, you shall be taken to Fyrton to stand trial. This is your last chance. Open up!"

Claire heaved herself through the window, expecting to hit water any second . . . but the impact never came.

She was stuck. Thrashing, she tried to wiggle herself free.

"Just trying to find my keys," Claire heard Kleo call out. "You wouldn't understand, since I'm sure you've never lost metal."

Claire strained toward the river. The water's muddy freedom dipped tantalizingly close!

"No need for keys," the inspector said through the door. "Stay back." There was a soft *ching* from behind her.

"They're removing the hinges!" Kleo hissed.

Claire heard the Spinner's footsteps patter across the cabin, and then she felt a strong shove. An instant later she was tumbling through the air. Claire only had a glimpse of brown water and bubbles before she splashed under.

CHAPTER 14

It was dark in the river, mud turning everything murky. Claire didn't know which way to go, but she kicked out. Any direction would put distance between her and those terrifying Forgers.

Something brushed against her. She caught a glimpse of red river weed. No, it was hair! Sena! And next to her, his dark hair a wild cloud above his head, was Nett.

Sena motioned with her hand, and they kicked upstream.

By the time Claire's feet touched the shallows, she was chilled to the core despite the bright sun above. As she collapsed onto the bank, she wished she had remembered to grab her cloak. But if she had, it probably would have wrapped around her body, sinking her to the bottom.

Claire unhooked her Aqua Mask. Before she had plunged

into the water, it had been made of a tight, thick fabric, but now it was no more than a wet net. The threads of air that Kleo said had been woven into it were now depleted.

"W-we n-need t-to move," Nett chattered. The water had slicked back his hair, making him look like a seal. "The inspectors might come back this way."

Tired, but terror still fresh, Claire pulled herself to her feet and followed Nett and Sena, who were clambering up the bank.

They had flowed toward fields of tall, swaying grass about a mile away from the base of a hazy mountain where a town had tucked itself next to its foot. Drifting above the town's many chimneys were multicolored clouds that looked more like puffs of sidewalk chalk than the smoke Claire knew they must be.

Fyrton.

"This way!" Sena called, hurrying toward a cluster of large metal objects in the grass. Claire had to run to keep up. As they got closer, she saw an iron lion with six legs, eternally growling, while a stag with a scorpion's tail pawed the ground.

"Chimera Fields," Sena said, a little breathlessly. "We can hide here while we warm up."

The sun was high, and Claire had to put a hand on her forehead to shield her eyes from the glare, for the field between the river and the Forger town was littered with metal bodies. The sight was almost enough to make her forget how close they'd come to getting caught. Almost enough to make her forget she was drenched and freezing.

Sena waved Claire and Nett over to a large copper bear, whose bulk was enough to hide them from the view of the river.

Nett flopped onto the ground, Claire not too far behind. She wrapped her arms around herself, shivering in her soaked clothes.

"I n-never thought I'd see this," Nett said, his awe clear even though his teeth chattered. "After the G-Guild War, the knowledge of how to care for and maintain chimera was forgotten. These stopped moving more than two hundred years ago."

"Hold out your hands," Sena instructed, ignoring Nett's reverie. She pressed a coin into each of Claire's palms and did the same for Nett.

As her fingers curled around the coins, Claire felt a delicious warmth seep into her bones. Looking over, she saw Sena rubbing her hands together quickly. Every so often, she'd stop and blow gently before rubbing again. Finally, she placed a new coin on Claire's feet. The warmth spread there, too.

"What?" Sena said as she took in the surprise on Claire's face. "Just because I was exiled doesn't mean I didn't pick up anything. Even toddlers can heat metal."

Claire opened her mouth to say it wasn't that she was surprised Sena knew how, only that it was possible at all. But Sena was already working her magic on the next batch.

"Thanks," Nett said, holding some coins to his cheeks.

Sena nodded. Her eyes were bloodshot, though whether

that was from the use of magic or their near escape, it was impossible to tell.

Sena's braid had come loose, and Claire watched as she deftly divided her dripping hair into sections to redo it. "You're next," she said, catching Claire's eye. "Everyone in Fyrton wears their hair up so it doesn't accidentally catch on fire."

When Sena had secured her braid around her head with iron pins, she motioned to Claire to sit in front of her. The Forger's fingers worked through Claire's tangles. She was surprisingly gentle, and a long-ago memory came rushing back to Claire.

A ten-year-old Sophie had declared they needed the Experience of going to a ball. Sophie had pretended to curl her own wavy hair with the round brush. Claire's hair naturally curled, but she wanted the big, smooth curls of magazines. Sophie had been happy to oblige, wrapping a section of Claire's hair around the round brush. Then she'd pulled.

But as hard as Sophie tried, the brush did not budge. It was thoroughly snarled and completely stuck to Claire's head. Afraid of getting in trouble, Sophie had made Claire wait two hours before telling Mom.

Claire smiled at the memory. Sophie had felt so bad about Claire's ragged haircut that she'd let her use her favorite nail polish afterward.

Sena's fingers rhythmically separated snarls, while Nett hung the Forger clothes on the bear chimera to dry. Claire realized she'd stopped shivering.

"All done," Sena finally said. She eyed Claire critically.

"With the right clothes, it shouldn't be *too* hard to pass as a Forger. We can maybe pick up a hammer on the way, just in case."

Claire reached back and felt the even bumps of a short braid. She had the sudden image of a younger Sena surrounded by other quick-tempered girls braiding their hair at recess. That is, if they had recess in Arden. Either way, Sena was definitely an experienced hair braider.

"Why are you the only Forger in Greenwood?" Claire blurted out. "Why were you exiled?"

Nett froze, a Forger's black tunic dripping over his arm. "*Claire,*" he whispered, widening his eyes at her.

An array of emotions washed across Sena's face, though Claire didn't know how to name them. If she were using Kleo's color alphabet, though, Sena would have been a swath of twilight shades, shifting, caught in transition.

Sena sighed and lay back in the grass, snow-angel style, as though Claire's question—and her un-nameable reaction to it—had made her exhausted. But then, staring at the sky, she began to speak, voice flat.

"I was born in Fyrton, under the shadow of Arden's tallest bell tower. My parents, Sylvia and Mathieu Steele, were two of the most respected alchemists in Fyrton."

"Alky-what?" Claire asked, pulling her knees in to her chest.

"Alchemists," Sena corrected. "They are the craftsmen who take all the best parts of metals, like silver's willingness to reflect, gold's flexibility, and iron's strength, to try to create new metals—at least, that's what it is *now.*"

Sena turned her head, her cheek resting in the grass as she looked at Claire. "But before—like *before*-before—alchemy wasn't just the merging of metals; it was the merging of guild magics. The metal plant cage in Greenwood? That was the work of ancient alchemists. So are the chimera. Both the cage and the chimera represent different combinations of Tiller and Forger abilities."

To Claire's astonishment, she saw a single tear roll down Sena's cheek.

"You don't have to talk about this if you don't want to," Nett broke in.

"I'm fine," Sena said. Taking a deep breath, she began again. "My parents experimented with ancient alchemy, researching the knowledge that was lost when the guilds separated from each other. They were good at what they did. Too good. When I was eight years old, they crafted the first walking chimera in three hundred years. A little copper kitten with mouse ears."

"But . . . ," Claire said slowly, a question forming at the tip of her tongue, "didn't you say chimera are made by a combination of Forger *and* Tiller magic? How did your parents craft a chimera without a Tiller?"

Sena pushed herself into a sitting position. "Because Mama was a Forger, but Papa . . . he was a Tiller."

"What?" Claire sat up straight. She glanced at Nett, to see if he was also in on the joke, but his face was completely serious.

"I never knew that Papa was a Tiller until the day we were arrested," Sena continued. "He was born Mathieu Frond, but became Mathieu Steele to hide his true guild so he could marry Mama."

"But are *you* a Tiller?" Claire asked.

"Guild magic is kind of like eye color," Nett jumped in. "Just because your mother has blue eyes doesn't necessarily mean you will."

Sena nodded. "My parents were lucky I was born a Forger and not a Tiller, but that's where their luck ended. Their secret shattered when the chimera kitten escaped. I had left the door open by mistake. The Fyrton inspectors arrived that night."

Sena gazed into the distance, seeming to see something Claire couldn't—and didn't want to—see.

"Mama was imprisoned someplace secret, and Papa . . ." Sena swallowed. "Papa was executed."

Claire didn't know what to say to something so awful. Not sure how Sena would react to a hug, Claire settled on scooting closer to her.

"The Grand Council of Arden didn't know what to do with me," Sena said. "I was too young to be punished by Forger law. Francis had been Papa's teacher in Greenwood, and when he learned what had happened, he volunteered to take me in. I've lived with him and Nett ever"—she took a deep shuddering breath—"ever since," she finished gruffly.

Wiping a hand across her cheek, Sena lurched to her feet and marched away from them, disappearing into the yellow grass. Nett moved to follow.

"Wait," Claire said. "Give her a minute."

"But," Nett said, looking anxiously toward where Sena had disappeared, "we need to keep going."

"Sometimes people need a little time by themselves," Claire said. "To . . . to process."

When Sophie had her first surgery, there had been an ongoing line of people visiting the house, bringing flowers and gifts. Claire knew they wanted to make everyone feel better, but Claire had just wanted to be with Mom and Dad. No one could have understood the numbness that had dropped into Claire's stomach, and that had only recently begun to thaw.

"Give her a minute," she repeated.

Nett exhaled loudly. "I'm going to go keep an eye on the river. If she doesn't return in ten minutes, we go after her."

Nodding, Claire reached for her rucksack. Everything in it had stayed miraculously dry. Or maybe it wasn't so much miraculously as *magically* dry.

She pulled out her pencil, glad that it had been spared the Rhona's waters. With it in her hand, she felt more like herself. She might not know how to make plants spark or rugs roll or coins heat, but she *did* know how to draw.

Pulling one of Francis's parchment-wrapped bundles from her bag, she carefully set the clump of dried blossoms she found inside next to her. Then she smoothed out the thick paper and sat down again, making sure she was still well hidden behind the bear chimera.

Not thinking about anything in particular, Claire let her hands take over. Her pencil skated over the page, sweeping curves trailing behind it. After a moment, she realized what her hands were drawing.

A unicorn.

Queen Estelle's story glided into her thoughts. The queen went searching in the midst of terrible danger, and had been brave even when the hunter went after her and the last unicorn. She had done what was right, even though she must have been scared. The queen was brave. A hero.

Claire wondered what it had been like when unicorns roamed Arden. Did they travel in herds, like wild horses, or alone? Did they have sisters?

A flowing tail and inquisitive ears blossomed beneath her pencil. Claire drew a smaller set of ears. A unicorn mother and its foal grazed in a sun-dappled grove, a sunbeam entwining with the mother's horn.

A sweet sorrow nudged Claire.

Mom. Dad.

Sophie.

If Mom were in Arden, she would have wanted to stay on the Spinner boats, looking at the different threads, while Dad probably would have chatted with Francis about which flower bloomed best in the shade. After they'd both gotten over the shock of a magical land above the chimney, of course.

But Sophie . . . Claire couldn't even begin to guess. Sophie liked everything spectacular. Every Experience. She was the kind of girl who could make even the dreariest day feel like an adventure.

"Hey, that's pretty good!"

Claire started as Nett suddenly appeared before her. Hastily, she covered the sketch with her arm. "Oh, no, it's not done yet—"

"Seemed great to me," Nett said, looking impressed. "I once tried to draw Francis, but everyone thought I'd done a portrait of a hairy cabbage."

"I'm sure you're not that bad," Claire said. She stuck her pencil behind her ear and shook out her fingers. They were tingling a little. Maybe they were still cold from the river. "Is Sena back?"

"Yes, and the clothes are dry," Nett said. "Sena tried to steam them with some coins. They smell a bit, er, *strange*, but with all the smoke in Fyrton, no one should notice." He handed her a short-sleeved black tunic and leather vest.

Claire quickly changed behind the bear chimera. The vest laced up the front and was heavier than the clothes she was used to.

"Ready?" Sena asked. Dressed in Forger black, her red braid stood out like a fiery nest. Determination shone in her eyes and she stood straighter as she gripped her butter knife. She looked like a girl about to do battle.

And in a way, maybe they were.

"Should we disguise you more?" Nett asked, peering at her. "Rub some walnut juice in your hair, or something?"

Sena waved her hand impatiently. "We've lost enough time. Besides, a lot of Forgers have red hair."

"But aren't you worried someone's going to recognize you?" Claire asked.

Shrugging, Sena adjusted her tunic. "A little, maybe, but it's been five years. Fyrton is one of the largest towns in Arden. And I had a growth sprout this summer. Now, get moving—I've met *slugs* faster than you!"

Nett caught Claire's eyes and made a face before breaking into a grin. Claire returned the smile. Sena's edge was back.

"Are you ready?" Nett asked. The Forger vest was too big for him, the thick strap slipping a little off his shoulder, but it was the best they could do.

The memory of loud voices and sharp swords came back to Claire. The inspectors. Forgers.

Certain death, Francis had said.

She shook it off. They *had* to go to Fyrton. Everything Sena needed for a Looking Glass was there, and Claire couldn't back out now.

Rolling up the parchment, Claire noticed something off about her sketch. She thought she'd drawn both mother and foal grazing, horns pointed down. But now the unicorn foal was staring straight at her with big mournful eyes.

She blinked. Perhaps she was more tired than she thought.

But then she realized Nett and Sena were looking at her, waiting.

"Yes," she said. "I'm ready."

CHAPTER
15

Though Mount Rouge protected one side of Fyrton from invaders, the Forgers clearly did not take any chances. High gates edged the city like a pointed crown, each of the golden curlicues tapering into a sharp spear that made it impossible to scale. Luckily, Claire, Nett, and Sena didn't have to climb over.

In their black leather clothes, they were well enough disguised that the inspector only glanced before waving them through. Sena mumbled something about the woman being lazy, but, as Nett pointed out, most people probably weren't foolish enough to even try to sneak in.

The first thing Claire noticed about the Forger town was the *noise*. Great bells called out from the tops of buildings, drowning out and interrupting one another like squabbling children. Even then, the tolling couldn't stifle the sounds of daily Forger life: the scrape of knife against whetstone, the clatter of pots, the rhythmic *ching* of hammer on metal.

Sena led them through the smoke-scented streets. Sparks flew from forge windows and, underneath the clamor, the hiss of hot metal drowned in cold water whispered: *rush, rush, rush.*

Occasionally, Nett pulled on Claire's arm and shared tidbits of Fyrton's history.

"The Steel Mouth! It used to be a Spinner theater, back when all the guilds lived in the same cities, but now it's an arena where weapon masters show off their skills . . .

"Ooh! I think that's the bell tower where Threadrick Tenacious tested out the very first flying carpet. It was a good thing he had a parachute . . ."

"How do you know so much about Fyrton?" Claire asked during a lull in Nett's wonder-filled chatter.

He shrugged. "I read. I've lived practically my entire life in Greenwood, but . . . I don't really *fit.*" They stopped for a moment to let a cart full of rattling copper pans pass by. "What do you mean?" Claire asked.

"Other kids live with their parents, but since my parents are both gone, I had to live with Grandpa Francis," he said as they hurried to catch up to Sena, who'd gotten ahead of them. "Even though my father's side has been in Greenwood since the guild founding, my mother was from the Sunrise Isles. I wanted to prove to everyone that I belonged in Arden, so I learned everything I could about our country's history."

He grinned and ducked his head. "Besides, it's fun to be able to tell Sena she's wrong—oh! Look!" he interrupted himself, and pointed to an empty street display. "Invisible shields! I can't believe I get to see one of these! Or, *not* see them. You know what I mean."

Left, right, straight, right again. They stopped once to buy some small hammers which they added to their belts, then kept going. The roads ran in a haphazard dash, leading them past rows of soot-singed town houses.

"Why do all the doors have scissors hanging on them?" Claire asked. In fact, as they'd rushed by the markets, she'd spotted displays of golden scissors for sale—not just practical ones for cutting, but little ones meant to be worn as necklaces.

"They're charms against Spinners." This time, it was Sena who spoke. "Spinners are deceitful and traitorous," she continued. "They spin lies upon lies until you are so tangled you will never know yourself again."

"But Kleo helped us," Claire pointed out.

"She only helped us to save her own skin," Sena said with her usual vigor, but then she dropped the subject and doubled her pace. "Come on, we're going to be late!"

"For what?" Claire asked.

"School!"

Claire almost stumbled. "*What?*"

Sena whipped onto an avenue and gestured in front of them.

A cluster of turrets sprang up from behind a stone wall like paintbrushes in a jar. White clouds of smoke and steam wove between chimneys, making it impossible to tell how high the towers truly were, or what lay beyond the thick wall. Through a set of wide-open double doors, a stream of kids flooded into the building. Above them, a sign read

PHLOGISTON ACADEMY

Knowledge Withstands the Flame

"The School of a Hundred Bells," Nett said in an awed voice. "Each of the academy's headmasters has crafted a bell for it." He craned his head. "This is bigger than anything we have in Greenwood."

"It has to be," Sena said. "All Forgers come to the academy when they turn twelve, then train as apprentices until they are sixteen, when they graduate to journeymen, and gain a ring."

Claire saw Sena's expression darken slightly, and she thought that Sena, as loud and confident as she was, was sad that she'd been sent away before she had had a chance to come here herself.

But Sena pressed on. "Forger magic is a little more unpredictable than the others and we need more tools than most. It's not like you can burn down a village by planting a rosebush or quilting a patch, but when you're pouring red-hot metal . . . well, let's just say things can get dangerous. It's important that Forgers know what to do before they begin to travel as journeymen."

Sena waved her hand in the direction of the other kids. "Hurry up. Now that midday break is over, we'll stick out like unhammered nails. But in there, we'll just be three more students in a sea of hundreds. Then tonight, we can break into a Forger's workshop and I can craft the Looking Glass."

Nett looked at her doubtfully. "Wouldn't it be easier if we just found an alley to hide in until nightfall?"

"I thought you of all people would *like* to sneak into school," Sena said.

"I *like* to keep myself in one piece," Nett replied, crossing his arms. "Come on, why do you want to go in there?"

Sena looked like she was about to argue, and then suddenly, her shoulders sagged. "I don't exactly know how to craft a Looking Glass," she admitted. "There's a book in the academy's library that will tell me how."

Claire gaped at her. "You said you knew how to make one!" Pressure built behind her eyes. "You said you *knew* how to find Sophie!"

"Cool your coals," Sena said, though she had the decency to blush. "I just need a refresher, that's all."

Nett cocked his head, and Claire could tell he didn't quite believe Sena, but the tug of a forbidden Forger library must have been too strong, because he caved. "How are we going to get in? They just closed the front doors."

Claire turned to realize he was right. The double doors had just slammed shut and bells were chiming. They were too late!

Sena was silent as she studied the enormous wall in front of them. Slowly, a wicked smile spread across her face, and when she faced Nett, Claire saw her golden eyes dancing dangerously. "That's where you come in."

Nett didn't say anything, but Claire could practically hear him gulp.

Fifteen minutes later, Claire's heart skipped a jagged side step as she watched Nett grind an acorn in a small bowl with something that smelled like a cow farm. They were in a dirt alleyway squeezed between the most remote wall of the school and another wall that Sena said belonged to a covered market. The alley was so narrow that when Claire spread out her arms, she could easily rest one palm against each wall. Claire doubted that most passersby even noticed the tiny street.

Taking a seed from his rucksack, Nett placed it in the dirt, then glopped the smelly mixture on top. Finally, he took out a vial. Sitting back on his heels, Nett addressed the girls.

"This is Water Extract," he said, holding out the vial. "It's water in its purest form. Once I combine it with the Insta-Grow, we'll only have sixty seconds before the wisteria becomes fully mature."

"What happens after sixty seconds?" Claire asked.

"It will begin to wilt, and I can't promise the bines will be able to hold your weight."

Claire tilted her head. "Don't you mean 'vines'?"

"No, I mean *bines*—they're like vines, but feel more like wood. Now"—he looked up, making sure to meet both Sena's and Claire's eyes—"you *must* be over that wall in sixty seconds unless you want to break a leg. And be caught by the Forgers. And then be imprisoned in a dark, damp—"

"We get it," Sena snapped. Though her tone of voice was scornful, Claire noticed the skin around her lips was white. Claire didn't feel so great herself. She tried to breathe deeply.

Nett looked at them, the eyedropper of Water Extract held over the small mound. "Ready?"

Sena and Claire nodded.

"Then here goes nothing!" Nett squeezed a single drop onto the newly planted seed. Immediately, he lurched back, covering his head with his arms. A second later, Claire knew why.

A great column of dirt shot up like a fountain, covering them in soft soil. Twisting green arms wriggled from the earth like snakes that had had four cups of coffee.

"Grab on!" Nett cried, and he wrapped his hand around one of the flexible branches. The plant jerked him into the sky as the wisteria raced up the wall.

"Don't just stand there, grab on!" Sena called as she took a running start and leaped for a climbing bine with the ease of a flying squirrel.

Claire stumbled forward, trying to catch one. Newly sprung, they were rubbery and slick, sliding between her fingers as soon as she brushed them. Finally, she managed to catch hold of one.

Her stomach left the ground as the bines yanked her upward in a burst of purple petals and spring-green leaves. A plant growing fifty years' worth in fifty seconds was louder than she had expected, and she hoped no one would come to investigate what must have sounded like a mini-tornado. But in a town of swinging hammers and heavy bells, Claire thought the inhabitants of Fyrton were probably used to strange, loud noises.

Wrapping her legs tight, she kept her eyes up—she was close to the top of the wall now, but would she make it? The flowers around her were beginning to brown and their sweet smell had been replaced by the scent of dead rot. She had taken too long on the ground; the wisteria would wilt before she could get to the other side!

And then she was above the wall, the bine flopping over as it spooled down toward the courtyard where Nett and Sena had already landed. Claire could see they were staring up at her, their mouths open. Were they saying something to her? She couldn't hear—the rush of air and rattle of leaves were as loud as waves pounding on sand.

She was almost eye level with Nett and Sena when—
CRACK!

The withered bine beneath her snapped, tumbling Claire the last few feet to the ground.

She lay there, winded. It hurt, but only a little, like jumping off a swing at the wrong time.

"Are you all right?" Nett asked.

"I'm fine," she said, slightly out of breath. He offered a hand, and she let him pull her to her feet. They'd landed in the northwest corner of the campus, and in front of them was the sprawling complex of Phlogiston Academy.

Claire had an impression of towers, arched doors, pillars, and silver edges before Sena hurried them toward one of the side doors. Glancing behind her, Claire saw that the wall they had popped over was bare now, the gray rock devoid of any flowering bine. The only evidence that there may once have been an enormous plant was a scattering of dried leaves at its base.

She tore her eyes away and jogged after Sena and Nett. As she approached the door, Claire couldn't help but feel as though someone were watching. Scanning Phlogiston's windows, she didn't see any curious faces peering out. She tilted her head farther back and finally realized where the icky sensation was coming from.

Gargoyles, at least a hundred of them, glared down from the sloped roofs.

"I feel like they're looking at us," she murmured to Nett.

He followed her gaze. "They are. Those are the Gemmer gargoyles. They can be whistled awake if you know the right tune."

Claire took in their long fangs and pointed horns, imagining what it would be like to see one charge, the strength of stone behind each step. If they were awakened, they would form an army of rock teeth. Except . . .

"What happened to their ears?"

"When the Forgers took over the Gemmer Hearing Hall,

they hammered their ears off so they wouldn't be able to hear the tune," Nett said as he adjusted the straps of his pack. "The gargoyles will never be able to move again."

"Don't feel too bad," Sena said, seeing the look on Claire's face. "Those rock beasts took out an entire regiment of Forgers during the Guild War. They and their Gemmer masters were ruthless." And with that, Sena opened a door and waved them into the Forger academy.

Classes were in session, and the hallways were wide and empty.

"The library is in the main courtyard," Sena whispered. "If we can make it there without being seen, we'll be golden. Just . . . *try* to act like you belong here. Forgers are known for being strong and passionate and—"

"And full of themselves," Nett muttered.

"We're proud of what we do." Sena rocked on the balls of her feet. "Claire, for soot's sakes, stop slouching, and Nett"— her eyes lingered on the soil under his fingernails—"keep your hands hidden."

They quietly rushed past open doors, hearing snippets of the classes within. Each time she dashed by a doorway, Claire felt her heart rise into her throat. If someone spotted them . . . if Sena were recognized . . . the Forger inspectors had been terrifying enough!

Soon, they settled into a kind of pattern. Stride, stride, stride—quick dart by an open door! Stride, stride, stride— quick dart!

Claire began to sweat under the black leather vest. She had

expected the stone building to be cool and drafty, but instead it was as warm as a sweater in summer. But of course a school for Forgers was hot; they needed fire and heat to be able to bend metal's magic to their will.

She caught glimpses of students hunched over metal sheets, older kids teaching younger ones how to grip swords, and an entire class whose hair had turned blue when a student played the wrong note on his golden flute.

Claire wondered how much farther the library was, and how much more they could push their luck.

"Almost there," Sena hissed. "Mama was a scholar and taught alchemy at Phlogiston. She used to bring me here when I was little, even though I wasn't apprentice age yet." They whipped by the last corner—

—and smacked into a thin man carrying a pile of books.

The man was able to right himself quickly, but Sena, Nett, and the books toppled to the ground in front of Claire.

"No running in the halls!" the man ordered as he retrieved his books. He was wearing what Claire thought was Arden's equivalent of safety goggles, but while they must have protected his eyes, they had the added effect of making them look big and round, as though he were constantly surprised.

"Sorry," Sena said as she began to inch away.

"One moment," replied the teacher. He pursed his lips and pointed at Nett. "Second-form boys are getting fitted for hammers in the lower forges," he said. "You better hurry before Scholar Burns puts out the coals!"

Nett's eyes shifted to Sena, and Claire could see he was

begging her to tell him what to do. But it seemed even Sena had run out of ideas.

The man's eyes grew even wider. "You don't need your friend's permission to get to class. Go, or I will report you!"

Claire held her breath. They were being split up! There was no way she or Nett could survive the Forger academy without Sena's help. But from the set of the teacher's wire-thin lips, she realized they might not have a choice.

"Yes, Scholar," Nett croaked out. With one last glance, he scurried off in the direction the man had pointed.

"As for you"—the man pointed at the girls—"first- and second-form girls are reviewing for summer examinations. Just because Scholar Ember has a cold today *does not* mean you can skip class."

Sena suddenly clutched her stomach. "I'm sorry," she gasped, stepping away from the man. "It's my stomach—must have been something I ate . . ." Then Sena was sprinting away, leaving Claire to deal with a very annoyed Forger all by herself.

The man shook his head in exasperation. "*This* is why I don't teach lower years! What room are you in? First-year, right?"

Claire nodded, relieved at least that the teacher didn't seem to realize they didn't belong here.

"Come along with me, then," the man said. Putting a hand on Claire's shoulder, he began to briskly walk her down the corridor. Though Claire's mind whirled, she couldn't think of any way to get out of the man's grip—not without calling more attention to herself.

"Ah, yes," the man finally said. "Room 501—here we are!"

He pushed Claire into the classroom. A warm, wet heat engulfed her like a summer's day that begged for a storm. Stone benches were arranged along three of the walls, but an enormous clay dome with a glowing red eye took up the fourth wall. It looked a little bit like the rounded ovens found in fancy pizza restaurants.

Fifty or so girls—all Sena-sized or taller, with hair carefully braided away from their faces and hammers hanging from their belts—stared back at Claire.

Claire's palms began to sweat.

A teacher from a different class might not be able to identify a new face, but she knew from experience that kids always recognized an outsider.

CHAPTER
16

A stern voice rang through the thick steam in the classroom. "Have a seat, Abigail," the teacher said. She was squinting, her glasses fogged. With her tight topknot and gray gown, she looked exactly like a pin Mom used when she sewed.

After a second, Claire realized the teacher was talking to *her*. She had mistaken her for someone else. Before the teacher could realize her error, Claire dropped her rucksack down and plopped into the closest chair, which happened to be directly under a wall display of wicked-looking spearheads. The weight of the other girls' eyes and whispers pushed her farther down in her seat.

Looking around, she saw each girl was equipped with a notebook, hammer, and what looked like a large pair of tweezers. Claire reached her hand into her pocket and clung to her pencil, trying to calm her nerves. At least she had a hammer.

"Who are you?" a girl whispered nearby. "You're not Abigail."

"Quiet," the teacher said. "Please turn your attention back to our practical review. I will ask each of you a question, and you must demonstrate the answer in the central forge. Everyone, form a line."

There was a flurry of scraping and jangle of hammers as the girls hurried toward the far wall, Claire a beat behind. Nerves turned to a strangling panic as she fought to keep her breath steady. She was going to have to do Forger magic in front of everyone.

Or rather, *not* do Forger magic since she had no magic to begin with.

Claire's grip on the pencil tightened as the first student took her place at the forge.

"I am thinking of a number between one and five hundred," the teacher said. She threw something small and shiny at the student, and the student caught it one-handed.

"Tell me exactly which number I am thinking of."

Next to Claire, a girl in braided pigtails murmured to her friend, "Hazel lucked out."

"I *know*," her friend whispered back. "We've been able to do Penny for Your Thoughts for ages."

Standing in front of the forge, the student, Hazel, sorted through a pile of objects on the stone table. She selected a tapered candle, and lit it with a spark from the forge. With thumb and forefinger, the girl held the penny over the flame.

One minute passed, then two.

Claire clenched her fingers into a fist, wondering how the Forger was able to keep her bare hands next to the fire for so long. When Dad took Claire and Sophie camping, Claire always had to have an extra-long roasting stick for her marshmallows.

The coin began to glisten, then drip, melting like ice cream. Suddenly, the penny flared red. Hazel let out a yelp and dropped it into a bucket of water. A second later, she plunged her hand in. Opening her fist, she displayed a copper *22* to the classroom. The others clapped politely.

"Not bad," the teacher said. 'But you forgot to keep your body temperature at the same heat as the metal, didn't you?"

The girl nodded, looking sheepish.

"Had you remembered," the teacher continued, "you would have been able to keep melting the penny until it formed the actual number I had in mind, which was two hundred twenty-*three*." The teacher turned and addressed the class. "Does anyone have suggestions for how Hazel can work at building heat resistance?"

A discussion began, using a lot of words Claire didn't understand, like "flame retardant" and "thermal shielding." As the teacher scanned the room for students to participate, Claire lowered her eyes to the flagstone floor. If she was called upon, she'd have no idea what to say. She curled her fingers around the pencil in her pocket again. Where were Sena and Nett?

Some of the students around Claire wrote in their notebooks, but most whispered among themselves, clearly bored.

"I don't know why we even have to review," Pigtails whispered to her friend. "I have an essay on smelting due tomorrow."

"I thought you were going to have your papa help you with that," the friend said as she twisted the end of her French braid.

"He was supposed to, but he came home late." Pigtails pouted. "Didn't you hear about the inspectors' raid on the Tiller narrowboats last night?"

French Braid's eyes widened in surprise. "I knew there was one this morning, but I didn't know there were raids yesterday, too!"

"Silence!" The teacher's voice rang out from the front.

The two girls immediately quieted. As the next student went up to the forge, Claire scrambled to think of an escape plan. If she wanted to reach the door, she'd have to walk in front of the entire class. And the windows were too high up to climb out.

The chatting Forgers soon resumed their conversation, their voices a low scratch now.

"Apparently," Pigtails whispered, "Anvil Malchain requested the extra raids!"

French Braid gasped, which was lucky, because it covered the sound of Claire's squeak of surprise.

"What's Malchain looking for this time? Do you think he finally found D.J. Scorch's magic spear?"

"Papa said he's after a girl."

Claire's breath caught. Sophie. It had to be.

"A *girl*?" French Braid paused. "Why?"

Pigtails adjusted the hammer hanging at her waist. "Apparently, she stole something from him."

Questions slipped and skidded across Claire's thoughts before she could properly grab them.

French Braid gaped at Pigtails. "Who would be reckless enough to steal from Anvil Malchain? Everyone knows that his double-headed ax can slice through stone."

"I know," Pigtails agreed. "Mama says he's always had a temper, and—"

"Girls!" the teacher said again. She pointed at Claire. "Abigail, to the front!"

"But I'm not—" Claire squeaked. Then she stopped herself, because the other girls were staring at her.

What would Sophie do? Claire didn't know. She could hardly think. Hurriedly, Claire picked up her rucksack and moved toward the forge, her legs shaking. Laid out on the table were several sharp instruments that looked like dentists' tools—if the dentists were seeing to giants' teeth.

"Demonstrate for the class how to craft a skeleton key," the teacher ordered, the tool belt at her waist rattling ominously. "Begin."

Claire stared at the teacher blankly. A skeleton key . . . Was that a key *for* skeletons or made *from* skeletons?

"Is there a problem, apprentice?"

"I don't see any bone," Claire mumbled, trying to keep her voice steady.

The class snickered, and the teacher's eyebrows shot up so fast Claire thought they would fly off her forehead.

"Are you trying to be funny, apprentice?" The woman seemed to grow in fury with each word. "One more misstep, and we'll see how funny the headmaster thinks you are."

The headmaster! If he were anything like her principal at home—a woman who seemed to know everyone's detention count—the headmaster would definitely know that Claire wasn't enrolled in Phlogiston Academy.

It would only take a few more minutes after that for people to realize Claire wasn't a Forger at all. And if she was caught, who knew what would happen to her.

Who knew what would happen to *Sophie*.

The memory of swords and chain mail on the river flashed through her mind. Dread pooled in her chest. Arms heavy, Claire reached for a hammer.

But before she could do anything with it, a loud bell rang out.

The teacher furrowed her brow and shook her head. "Class doesn't end until a quarter past and it's only—" But the rest of whatever she was about to say was extinguished by a bellowing ruckus that sent little vibrations shooting through Claire's bones.

The bells of Phlogiston—all one hundred of them, from each and every tower—were clanging at the same time.

Claire clapped her hands to her ears while the apprentices around her grinned gleefully, grabbing their tools and notebooks before rushing toward the door. The teacher shouted something above the din, but it was impossible to make out.

Snatching up her own rucksack, Claire hurried out the

door. The previously empty halls were now packed. Students milled about, shouting and laughing, knowing that they really shouldn't have been dismissed.

And throughout it all, the bells kept clanging.

A hand suddenly gripped Claire's arm. She whirled around.

"Nett!" she yelled joyfully. She would have hugged him, but he grabbed her hand and began pushing his way through the crowd.

A few times Nett tried to say something, but each time Claire just shook her head, unable to hear. It was only when they turned the corner to a small spiral staircase that the clanging finally stopped.

"Ow," Claire said, rubbing her ears. "What's going on?"

A second later, the answer descended the stairs.

"You got her!" Sena said delightedly. Her coronet braids had fallen out, and her hair radiated around her face like spokes on a wheel. It almost looked as though she had stuck her finger in an electrical socket.

"What worked?" Claire asked in a still-too-loud volume. Even though the bells had stopped bellowing, a tiny *ring* seemed to outline everything she heard.

"Our plan to get you out of there," Nett said with a grin. "Sena, you look like you were caught in a lightning storm!"

"Well, at least it's a new look for *me*," Sena drawled. "You always look like you've combed your hair with lightning."

Claire looked at the Forger incredulously. "Did you set off all those bells?"

Sena held out her wrist. A silver bracelet Claire had never seen before dangled there. It took her a moment to recognize it for what it was—or what it had been.

"My butter knife," Sena said. "I convinced it that it actually wanted to be a magnet. A magnet that would be powerful enough to give all those bells"—she waved her hand airily above her head—"one really good *tug*, which would set them off for a while. Or at least, long enough to distract everyone as we rescued you."

"What Sena didn't mention," Nett said as he checked to make sure the coast was clear, "is that she may have overdone it. Just a bit."

He glanced behind at Sena. "One bell would have been enough. We didn't need all of them."

Sena grimaced slightly. "*You* try something you haven't trained for. Besides, any guild magic can be a little . . . *big* if you're scared."

"Ha! So you admit that you get scared!" Nett said.

"If you're scared *or* feeling any strong emotion, like excitement," Sena added with dignity.

The threesome walked quickly, making their way into a large courtyard. A marble building stood in its center, round and tiered like a wedding cake. The silver terraces that edged the tower's levels only added to the confectionary effect.

"*Tower Library*," Nett breathed. His brown eyes filled with wonder. "Sena, you never said your home was so beautiful!"

Claire expected Sena to be smug, but the Forger girl just

shrugged and marched between two snarling bronze bears at the entrance of the library.

If Tower Library had seemed like a cake on the outside, inside it was all swooping arches, rambling staircases, and books. Hundreds and thousands of books. So many books that Claire thought her school library, Dad's library, and her own public library could have fit in there and had room to spare. It was the kind of library princesses had, or the kind Sophie dreamed of building once she was a famous actress.

For the first time since arriving in Fyrton, Claire heard blissful silence. It was as though the thick leather volumes that coated the walls soaked up any insolent *chimes* and discourteous *clangs* that dared to enter the library.

Sena put her finger to her lips and pointed toward a corner staircase. Carefully, she, Nett, and Claire made their way past students hunched over tables, scrawling hasty notes, and quietly giggling in groups while their books lay open, forgotten.

As they climbed the staircase, titles popped out at Claire: *History of the Forger's Forge, Rust and Its Prophecies, Platinum: Myth or Fact?* There was an entire floor dedicated to *Coins of Our Time.*

When they reached the eleventh floor, Claire was out of breath.

"I think the book I need is somewhere up here," Sena whispered. They wove their way through narrow aisles. While most of the shelves were heavy with books, some didn't have a single volume on them at all. Instead, they held items that looked like they belonged in a museum: carved masks, silk fans, and even a goblet of solid gold. The collection made Claire think of Great-Aunt Diana's gallery and its pedestals of beautiful and curious objects. Again, she wondered if Great-Aunt Diana had ever climbed the chimney. She had never met her great-aunt, and now she intensely wished she had.

"What is all this?" Claire asked, as she stopped to examine a coronet that appeared to be made of crystal or glass. It was inside a clear display case, sandwiched between a silver key and an empty spot. She peered closer at the empty space and saw a label that read *Unicorn Tooth*. "Why are there other things in a library besides books?"

"A statue or piece of jewelry can hold as much information as a thousand pages," Nett whispered. "You just have to know how to look at it."

He pointed at the coronet. Its tapering points glowed in the chandelier's light, creating an illusion of icicles on fire.

"Take this, for example," he said. "It was carved in the year 987 CE. If you know Arden's history, then you know that same year a rock slide on Starscrape Mountain destroyed an entire Tiller village. They might not seem to be connected—until you realize that this diamond was mined *from* Starscrape Mountain, and that the Gemmers severely weakened the mountainside in their search for a single diamond large enough to carve a crown."

Diamond. Claire knew from science class that diamonds were one of the strongest gemstones in the world, impossible to be scratched unless by another diamond. The Gemmers had to be very powerful indeed to craft this treasure.

Nett was leaning so close to the coronet, Claire worried he might leave nose smudges on the case.

"So," he went on, "this crown tells me that the Gemmers are selfish, for ignoring the safety of the Tillers; stubborn, for refusing to change their plans; and heartless, for continuing to carve the diamond even after the tragedy. Looking at this crown, I can see exactly *why* the other guilds rebelled."

Sena blinked at him. "You got all that from a crown?"

Nett shrugged, seeming slightly embarrassed.

"But wasn't Queen Estelle a Gemmer?" Claire asked.

"She was," Nett admitted, "but she's the only Gemmer in the history of Arden who can be called a hero—and that's only if the legend is true, which I doubt. Gemmers are ambitious, stubborn, and as unmovable as the stone they carve."

Claire felt a shiver pass through her. She remembered what Francis had told her in his cottage, that the Gemmers had enslaved Forgers before the war.

"I hope I never meet a Gemmer," she said with feeling. "They sound evil."

"Don't worry," Sena assured her. "The Gemmer Guild is the smallest of the four. Most were killed in the Guild War, especially with the death—or transformation, if that's what you believe—of Queen Estelle. Now they live in a few scattered settlements in the mountains."

Claire nodded, drawing a map in her mind of what she'd learned so far: Tillers were spread out everywhere, in woods and villages. Forgers lived in proper towns and cities like this one.

Spinners roamed, like Kleo and the historian Mira Fray. And Gemmers lived in the mountains. With every new piece of information, her understanding of Arden deepened, like a painting that begins as a light sketch, then gets shaded in, and then, slowly, is filled with color.

She leaned in to read the little silver plaque next to the crown.

GEMMER CORONET
Carved from Starscrape Mountain diamond by
Grandmaster Mica Mantle, circa 987 Craft Era.
A present to Queen Estelle d'Astora
on her thirteenth birthday.
Recovered by Aquila Malchain in the year
1179 Craft Era.

"Aquila Malchain," Claire said. "Is she related to Anvil Malchain?"

Sena nodded. "The Malchains are one of the oldest families in Arden, and the best treasure hunters. They're the only ones who know how to make Kompasses."

Claire frowned. "It's not hard to make a compass. We made one once in fourth grade with magnets."

"No, Kompass-with-a-*k*," Sena explained. "Compasses-with-a-*c* always point north, but a Kompass-with-a-*k* will only point toward the specific thing it was forged to find. If Anvil Malchain has forged a Kompass specifically to find Sophie, then he *will* find her. It's only a matter of time. Let's keep going—we're looking for *Junior Year Metallurgy*. Come on, Nett, I thought you were good at these things."

"I *am*," Nett protested, giving Sena's back a hurt look, but he hurried after her.

Claire stood for a moment longer, staring at the shimmering crown and thinking of what the students in class had been whispering about: Anvil was looking for a girl who had taken something of his. It *had* to be Sophie, but why would she have taken something from *him*? Unless . . . maybe Anvil had stolen the harp, and then Sophie had swiped it from him and was already on her way back to Greenwood to return it.

But Claire had a sense there was something she was missing—like when she stepped back and realized the perspective in a drawing was off.

She dragged her finger along the glass display case, captivated by the glimmering crown, wishing her mind felt as clear as the carved diamond. And then . . . she felt something.

A low rumble moved through her, starting from her fingers, almost as if the display was electrified. She yanked her hand away and stared. Her fingertips were red, like she'd touched something hot.

Suddenly, the small golden horns that hung on each shelf crackled to life, and a man's voice floated onto the air. "Attention, apprentices."

"Slug soot!" Sena whispered. "Oh slug soot, slug soot, slug soot!"

"What's wrong?" Claire asked, swiveling around. And then she found out.

"There has been an intrusion," the voice said. "All apprentices must report to the central courtyard."

"They know!" Sena said, and in the distance, Claire heard quiet thumps as students shut their books and hurried to the stairwells. "We have to get out of here, now!"

"But the Looking Glass!" Claire cried. "We need to get that book!"

Nett looked at Claire as though she'd sprouted wings and antennae. "Don't you remember the inspectors?" he asked. "Big muscles with big swords?"

Claire shuddered.

"I found it!" Sena said triumphantly, before Claire could respond to Nett. Sena slipped a blue volume from an upper shelf. "Let's get out of here, now!" Sena practically flew down the aisle, with Nett at her heels.

Breathless, Claire pounded after them, so terrified of the inspectors that she hardly noticed that the burning in her fingertips had disappeared.

CHAPTER
17

The windows of Fyrton began to glow orange with candle-light. Smoke and steam still puffed through the darkening streets, as though a dragon lay sleeping beneath the cobble-stones. Claire hugged her rucksack tighter to her and hurried behind Sena and Nett.

To her relief, no fast-growing bines had been needed for them to sneak out of Phlogiston Academy. After the alarm, the apprentices had been corralled into the courtyard. Despite inspectors swarming the school, the students were giddy—delighted, even—by the second interruption of the afternoon. They had dashed from friend to friend, each swapping different rumors and theories on the question of who had broken in . . . and why.

"I heard something was *stolen*," Claire had overheard an apprentice whisper to his classmate.

"Please," the classmate had said disparagingly. "It's only a mistake—the bells probably set something off. Or it could be a practice trial."

Practice trial or not, Claire had been grateful for the pandemonium. Though she had seen some teachers trying to take a headcount, they appeared to be too distracted to question why their numbers included three more than usual.

When Phlogiston's students had finally been allowed to leave, Claire, Nett, and Sena had managed to exit without notice, tagging along on the fringes of a group of older apprentices. After tidying up, they had celebrated their success by purchasing meat pies, and Claire, with a full stomach, had begun to feel truly hopeful for the first time.

Now, they rounded a corner and, through the haze, Claire glimpsed drifts of snow against the buildings. Snow—in this heat? Squinting, she took a second look and realized that the drifts were actually piles of gleaming silver bits, the leftover scraps from a full day in the forge.

"Silver Way," Sena said with obvious pride, the book they'd stolen from the school tucked under her arm. "Fyrton's silversmiths are the best in the world."

Her eyes rested on a window display of spears fanned like a peacock's tail. Claire recognized the longing on her face—it was the same feeling she had when she saw one of those beautiful cases of pastels that were only affordable on birthdays.

They passed by a row of silversmithies. Each one was dark, though many still steamed as though the fires had only recently been put out.

"How about that one?" Nett asked, pointing to the smallest silver shop. It was tucked slightly behind two larger ones. "I think we could probably hide any firelight we make from the street."

Sena shook her head. "That one doesn't have what I need."

"How do you know?" Nett adjusted his rucksack, grunting a little as its contents shifted. "Do Forgers have a secret ability to see through walls that the rest of Arden doesn't know about?"

"It just won't work, all right?" Sena snapped.

Claire saw Nett jerk back, recoiling from the anger in her voice.

"Relax," he said, his smile still in place. "I was only joking."

"Well, stop joking! This is serious."

His smile tumbled off. "I'm just trying to help."

"Well, you're not."

Looking at Nett, Claire felt sorry for the Tiller. Claire knew how it felt to be unfairly yelled at by an older sister, and even though these two weren't related by blood, it was clear they were each other's family.

Sena must have realized she'd gone too far, because she suddenly said to the air, "I'm just jumpy. There's so much at stake . . ." She trailed off. It wasn't really an apology, only an explanation, but Nett nodded.

The sun was now completely gone, and the only light that came their way was from candle lanterns strung above the cobblestones. The lamps' shadows flickered on the ground, a mirror of Claire's own darting thoughts.

Where was Sophie spending the night tonight?

Why was Malchain so interested in her?

And most traitorous of all . . . Had Sophie been part of a plan to steal the harp all along?

At last, Sena stopped in front of a forge. Above the door in a curling script were the words:

Master Scythe's Silverorium

"This one," she said quietly. "This is where I can make the Looking Glass."

From the outside, it didn't seem much different from the other forge she'd so quickly rejected. It was slightly larger, but it wasn't as well hidden from the road.

Nett opened his mouth to protest, but Claire quickly spoke up.

"It's fine," she said, her eyes sliding to Nett. It didn't matter to Claire *where* Sena would forge the Looking Glass, only that she *did*—and soon. "How are we going to get in?"

"Not through the front doors," Sena said thoughtfully. "Forgers are proud of their locks. The more puzzley, the better."

Looking resigned, Nett raised his hand.

Sena sighed. "What?"

With a slight tilt of his round chin, he nodded upward. The girls followed his gaze to a side window, hidden from the main street, that was cracked open slightly.

"That could work, I guess," Sena mumbled.

Nett climbed onto Sena's shoulders while Claire kept

watch. The streets were almost entirely empty now, except for an occasional cluster of older apprentices who drifted by, talking loudly as if to prove they weren't scared of being out in the night. But Claire, who had learned that details in faces mattered when drawing a portrait, noticed that it was often the loudest students whose eyes searched the shadows the longest.

A hooded figure on horseback clipped by as a nearby tavern door swung open. A new group of journeymen burst into the night. They laughed and yelled, playing pranks on one another. One cheerfully stole his friend's pliers while another tugged on her friend's cloak and accidentally undid the clasp. The cloak slithered to the ground.

The movement startled the horse, and it bucked, dislodging the rider's hood. Claire got a glimpse of blond hair and large ears . . .

Claire blinked. Was that *Thorn*?

Her feet took an involuntary step away from the wall as she tried to see better, but the rider had already pulled his hood back up and urged the horse into a trot, putting distance between himself and the boisterous journeymen.

Claire shook her head and scolded herself. She was letting her nerves get the better of her.

"Nett's in!" Sena whisper-called. "Come on!"

Entering the silver forge was like stepping into a mirror— or a mirror *within* a mirror. Wherever Claire looked, a girl with a messy braid and wide, lost-looking eyes stared back at her in the endless rows of polished bells, armor, and buckles.

"The workshop is in the back," Sena whispered, and they wound their way through precariously balanced silver trays and mounds of silver vases. The oddly shaped stacks reminded Claire of coral reefs found under the sea.

Clang!

Claire jumped. Looking back, she saw Sena closing the door of a display cabinet. "What are you doing?" Claire asked.

Sena went to the next cabinet and opened it. "Looking for a tool I need."

"The tools are all here," Nett said, gesturing to the back of the shop. A large forge similar to the one Claire had seen in the classroom looked back at them, cold and black. Forging instruments—ham-sized hammers, tongs with stork-leg handles, and nails that were as long as Claire's forearm—all hung on the wall next to it.

"Not the tool I need," Sena said. Her head disappeared into another cabinet.

"What does it look like?" Claire asked, eager to start the magic. "Maybe we can help you look for it."

Sena pulled her head out. "Stop pressuring me!"

Claire stepped back, startled at the anger in Sena's voice.

"Sena," Nett said soothingly. "Claire was only trying to help."

"I don't need help." Sena slammed the cabinet shut. "I can do it myself!" She disappeared among the piles of silver.

Claire looked at Nett, who ran his hand through his hair. "I know it's hard for her," he muttered. "But this is ridiculous."

"What's hard for her?"

Nett pulled his marimo out of his pocket and gave it a pat. The moss began to glow. "Seeing all those Forger students . . . seeing other kids learning her craft while she's not allowed to . . . That had to be hard for her."

Claire briefly touched the pencil in her pocket. She didn't have magic, but she knew that if someone told her she wasn't allowed to draw or paint she would be miserable. Gloom settled over her, and she looked around for a way to cast it off.

"I can build a fire," she offered. "Dad used to take me and Sophie camping a lot before."

"Before what?" Nett asked.

"Before Sophie was sick."

"I didn't know that Sophie is sick."

"Well." Claire quickly backtracked. "She's not sick *now*. But she used to be."

Nett tilted his head. "You know, unicorns strengthened guild magic, but they were also able to cure any illness with just a touch of their horn. And one or two people say that unicorns could even turn back death—Historian Eric the Loquacious said that's how the rumor that killing a unicorn makes you immortal came to be. Some say unicorn artifacts, like the harp, have the same power."

"Sophie's not sick anymore," Claire hurried to explain. "The doctors didn't know what was wrong with her, but she's better now."

"That's good," Nett said. "I'm glad the healers were able to help. Sometimes, they can't." Loss tinged his words the way yellow creeps into autumn.

"Who are you thinking of?" Claire asked quietly.

Nett gave her a crooked smile. "Wraiths attacked my parents seven years ago. Though the Wraith Watch found them before the monsters could finish them, they were injured beyond magic. Mama died the next day, but Papa lingered for weeks before he finally gave up."

"You must miss them," Claire said.

Nett shrugged, not as though he were dismissing his pain, but in the same way he'd adjust the rucksack on his shoulder, settling it so it would be comfortable. "When I think about Papa, I can kind of remember his scratchy beard, like bark. Mama is just the scent of jasmine. Grandpa Francis tells me stories about Papa growing up, but I don't know much about my mother or her relatives at all. All I have from her is the marimo."

Nett stroked the fuzzy moss with his pinkie, and the light became brighter. "They're common in the Sunrise Isles, but rare in Arden. I like that her light guides me, even though she's not here."

Claire patted him on the shoulder. He smiled at her, though the melancholy lingered as they began to stack logs in the hearth. Nett rubbed two bits of kindling together. Sparks instantly flew into the hearth. The flame caught and held. In the new light, Claire could see Nett whispering something over the fire.

"What are you saying?"

Nett stood up, stretching. "Words of thanks. It's Tiller custom to acknowledge wood that burns for our comfort. Our magic is a bit different from the other ones. If you ask a Forger, she'd say metal is alive, and a Gemmer would say that stone is, too. But they don't *live* the same way plants do."

He frowned. "Speaking of Forgers, we should probably check on Sena."

They searched for her through the aisles of silver. Only when they passed the same ugly bust of a bulbous-nosed woman for the third time, did they realize Sena was not in the Silverorium at all. But before Claire's alarm could give way to panic, Nett held up his hand.

"Do you hear that?" he asked.

Claire strained her ears. A sniffling was coming from somewhere inside the shop.

They followed the sound to a large wardrobe that stood against the wall. Nett slowly opened the doors.

"Sena!" Nett gasped as he pushed aside hanging leather aprons. "What happened? And—oh. What . . . what is this place?" His voice had taken on a note of wonder.

Claire peeked around Nett to see that the back of the wardrobe was open . . . and that instead of pressing up against the wall, it framed the entrance to a secret room.

Though the light of a solitary torch barely illuminated the objects within, Claire could see that the contents of this room weren't just silver. Dried herbs, coils of rope, spindles, rings, shields, and lumpy packages that seemed to be leaking lined the shelves that were built into the wall.

And in the center, sitting on the ground, was Sena, her face streaked in tears.

"Sena, what's wrong?" Claire exclaimed. "Are you hurt?"

"It's gone," she said. Her braided crown had flopped.

"*What's* gone?" Nett asked. "Sena, what's going on?"

A shudder coursed through Sena, and Claire knew that whatever Sena was about to say, she wouldn't like it.

"The Unicorn Harp," Sena whispered. Her eyes dropped to the floor. "It's not here."

Claire's heart began to drum in her chest. "Why did you think the harp would be here?" she demanded. The whole point of coming here was supposed to be to make a Looking Glass so that they could *find out* where the harp—and Sophie—were.

Slowly, Sena raised her head to look at Claire. "Because," she hiccupped, "it was me. *I* stole the Unicorn Harp."

CHAPTER
18

"What?" At first, Claire didn't think she'd heard correctly.

Sena put her face in her hands and repeated, "I stole the Unicorn Harp."

Nett started to yell at Sena, but in her shock, Claire couldn't make out exactly what he was saying. She felt both heavy and hollow.

The last time she had felt like this was when she'd been called to the principal's office last September. Dad was there, and in a voice that didn't belong to him, he told her that Sophie had collapsed during her class field trip and that she was at the hospital in a very deep sleep. Mom was with her, and he was taking Claire to see her now, too. She couldn't remember walking out of the office, or much about the days immediately after. Her memories from that time were like blurred streaks of paint, hazy moments of smudges, confusion, and cold.

Looking at Sena, Claire's world once again felt like an art-ist's messy palette. "I don't understand," she said slowly. "*You* took the harp? Then—" She thought about what Thorn had told them, and Kleo. How the girls at the academy, too, had said Anvil was looking for Sophie. "*Then why is Malchain after my sister?*"

"I don't know," Sena said. She pushed her braid up off her forehead. "I don't know."

"I don't get you, Sena," Claire said. Her voice sounded diamond-hard; she barely recognized it. "You're always saying how Spinners are the liars. That they're the ones I have to watch out for. But you—you've been lying all along!"

Sena flinched.

"You've put us all in danger!" Nett burst out. "You put Fran-cis in danger! He's the reason you're not in an orphanage." Nett looked like someone had punched him. "Sena, what were you thinking?!"

"I wasn't," she said miserably into her hands. "I thought no one in Greenwood would miss it. The harp just stays in the Hearing Hall, out of sight. I thought by the time anyone real-ized it was gone, I would already be out of Greenwood and with my—" She broke off, shrugging.

"Your mother?" Claire guessed quietly.

Sena nodded and closed her eyes. "When my parents stud-ied ancient alchemy, they sometimes had to buy things off the black market. Nothing *bad*, of course, just unregistered pieces of jumbled magic. Master Scythe knows lots of people in his line of business. If anyone could track down where Mama is, it would be him. So I snuck a letter to Fyrton using a merchant, and told Scythe about the Unicorn Harp. I told him I'd give it to him in exchange for more information about Mama." She hiccupped. "When the Forger boats came to Greenwood to pick up their harvest, I brought the harp to Master Scythe."

Wiping her nose on her sleeve, she looked at them defensively. "No one noticed the harp had been gone for a whole week. And I promise—I didn't know the harp was unregistered with the Grand Council *until* the hearing. I didn't know the Unicorn Harp was a secret that could bring war to the guilds again."

"But you know stealing is wrong!" Nett exclaimed.

"So," Claire said, her fury building, "my search for Sophie was just an excuse for you to travel to Fyrton so you could get the harp back? Were you even going to try to make a Looking Glass?"

"*Yes*, of course." Sena raised her head, her mouth a quivering line. "Sophie is my friend. I didn't mean for her to get blamed, but when Ragweed accused her, it was just easier for me to let her take the fall since Arden isn't even her home. It wasn't until we found you near the well and you said that Sophie was missing, that I realized Sophie could *actually* be in trouble."

Sena's voice wobbled. "I thought if we returned the harp to Greenwood, everyone would leave her alone. I haven't had much training, but Claire, I will try to find her. I *promise*." She hid her face with trembling hands again. "Please forgive me."

Claire didn't want to say it was all right, because it wasn't. Each hour gone was another hour Sophie was getting farther away from her, or getting deeper into trouble. Or possibly both.

Claire reached into her pocket once again and gripped her pencil. It made her feel slightly—*slightly*—calmer. She knew that if she'd been in Sena's position—if it were Dad and Mom she was trying to get back to—she would have done the same.

She couldn't completely forgive Sena, but Claire gave her the tiniest nod. Nett's nostrils flared. However betrayed Claire felt, it must have been a hundred times worse for Nett to learn his best friend had lied to him and endangered Francis.

"Nett?" Sena asked, voice tiny.

Nett glared at her, eyes narrowing into thin lines that paralleled his mouth.

"*Please*," Sena begged. "I'm sorry I lied. I'm sorry I put Francis in danger." She buried her hands in her palms. "I'm just—I'm *scared*."

As Claire watched, Nett's mouth twisted. He peered down at the marimo as though it would tell him what to do. Slowly, his scowl loosened. Stroking the shaggy moss with his thumb, he let out a sigh.

"Did you learn anything about where your ma is?" he asked.

Sena looked up with red-rimmed eyes. "When I traded the harp, Master Scythe said there were rumors she might be in the Constellation Mountain Range, but he'd find out more."

"Are you *sure* the harp isn't here?" Nett asked. "Maybe we should all look one more time. For Greenwood."

"I'm pretty sure," Sena said. "But the shelves . . . they're *awful*."

Claire didn't understand what Sophie meant, but when Nett inspected the wares, he looked repulsed.

"Aphids," he cursed softly. "Is that, do you think—the shield?"

Sena and Claire looked at a tarnished shield against the wall. Sena nodded grimly. "It's *definitely* a Revealor."

Nett walked over to the shelves. "And right underneath that is *Somno libertas*, and that black ribbon next to it is a Choker. What is Master Scythe doing with all this stuff?"

As Nett listed the items, Claire's skin began to crawl. "What *are* all these things?"

"A Revealor is silver that has been directed to only reflect a person's greatest flaw," Sena said in a hushed voice. "Long ago, nobles forced their enemies to look into them, so they could learn how to destroy them. It's a horrible thing to have the nastiest, most secret thoughts within you revealed to all."

"And *Somno libertas*"—Nett pointed to the twisted herbs— "when eaten, will take away the eater's ability to make decisions for an hour, or for years, depending on the amount consumed. The Choker, well, the name says it all."

They began to hastily scan the shelves, being careful not to touch the items directly. Claire lifted the corner of a dusty sheet and saw a viney rope with hooked thorns, a gemstone, and a metal helmet that made Nett extremely nervous. ("A confusion cap. It scrambles your thoughts.")

Suddenly, the light in the room dimmed.

"Nett, can you make the marimo any brighter?" Claire called. She didn't want to rummage through a bunch of dangerous magical objects without seeing what she was getting into.

When no one answered, she glanced up. Sena's mouth was a round O of surprise.

"By all that's rusted," a voice growled from the doorway, "what are you doing in my shop, Sena Steele?"

Dread locked her muscles as Claire saw the form of a man outlined by the light of the main forge. As the man stepped into the hidden room, Claire could see he was built roughly along the lines of a boulder. His chest strained with muscles formed from years of forging, but his head was round, and as bald as a baby's.

"Master Scythe!" Sena scrambled to her feet. "Let me explain!"

"And let *me* explain that you are breaking and entering," As Scythe stepped toward them, Claire heard the heavy *clank* of metal. Chains and knives hung from the man's belt.

"Please, Master Scythe," Sena begged. "The Unicorn Harp—I need it back."

Scythe's thin eyebrows lifted incredulously. "You do, do you? And did you ever consider that if you gave away my operation, nothing in the world—and that includes the Unicorn Harp—would stop me from handing you over to the inspectors? You're exiled. And if someone saw you come into my shop, you and I will be locked in an inspector's cell before you can blow out a candle. Reckless, Steele. Very reckless."

Sena shook her head. "Please, I just need the harp back."

Master Scythe clicked his tongue in mock sympathy. "Even if I wanted to give the harp back to you, I couldn't. An item like that doesn't sit long in my trade."

Though her throat felt like it was swollen to twice its normal size, Claire stepped forward.

Master Scythe's eyes flickered over to her, then went back to Sena, as though Claire were too unimportant to notice. And Claire was sick and tired of being overlooked.

"Excuse me, but the person who bought it?" Claire said, trying to put all Sophie's confidence into her own voice. "Was she a girl who looked like me, just a little older?"

Scythe looked at Claire again, and she had the distinct impression he was amused by her. "The man who bought it hid his face, and had the sense to not ask questions."

"Do you have any idea who he was?" Nett asked, stepping forward.

Scythe glared at Sena. "Who are these fools you've brought with you, Sena?"

But Claire wasn't finished. "Who is the man?"

Scythe put his hand to his forehead and rubbed his temples. "The man didn't wear a guild's colors, but he had the calluses of someone who swings a hammer."

Or a double-headed ax with blades that look like a bat's wings, Claire thought. The man could be Anvil Malchain. But Sena had stolen the harp, not Sophie or Malchain. And if Malchain had the Unicorn Harp now, maybe he was no longer tracking her sister.

Claire waited to feel comforted by her reasoning, but the relief never came. Instead, another thought drifted in: *What if Sophie had found out Malchain was after the harp, and was going after* him?

"Did he say anything? Anything at all?" Nett asked. Claire was grateful that he was able to ask the question she couldn't.

"Nothing," Scythe said. "Except that I should let him know if another unicorn artifact appeared in my shop. Which should be soon. The Unicorn Tooth was stolen just this afternoon."

The children looked at one another in surprise. Claire remembered the missing item next to the diamond coronet. Had the inspectors not been searching for them, after all? Had they actually been called to Tower Library because someone— maybe even Anvil—had stolen the Unicorn Tooth?

The chains on Master Scythe's belt rattled ominously as he took a step toward them. "Do you children happen to know anything about the missing tooth?"

"*No*," Sena said sharply. All traces of the tearstained girl from minutes before had disappeared. She stood straight as an iron rod.

A wry smile appeared on Scythe's face, then it disappeared. "You knew the price of coming back," he said to Sena. "And now you must pay it from behind inspector bars. By the time you're out, I'll have set up a new secret store, and you'll never be able to compromise my business again."

He snapped his fingers. A hard *jangle* clanged above them.

Claire looked up just in time to see a large gleaming net descend from the ceiling and drop over their heads, the force knocking them to their knees. Before they could throw it off, the edges of the chain net latched with metal locks along the floor. Sena yanked at a link, but the net stayed put. They were pinned in place.

The three of them sat back-to-back, the weight of the chain net pressing down on them. But even though Claire was tired and sore, she did not want morning to come.

Scythe had left a few minutes ago to fetch the inspectors. And when they arrived, it would all be over. She would have lost her only chance to find Sophie.

The chains jingled as Nett squirmed. He seemed unable to keep still for more than a minute.

"Stop moving," Claire said as a chain link dug into her arm. "You're making it worse."

"I'm just trying to see if there's a way out."

Claire pushed against the chains, wishing she knew how to snap them. She bet any of the kids in Phlogiston Academy could have done it in a minute. Sena's sharp elbow pushed into her back, and even though Claire thought she already knew the answer, she had to know for sure.

"Sena, isn't there something you can do?" she asked desperately. "Melt the net or something?"

The chain links rattled as Sena shook her head. "I could try, but I'm not trained. I might melt *us* instead."

But Claire didn't think anything could melt her—her insides felt frozen solid. And trapped in the ice was one question that she couldn't let go: "Why is Malchain asking about Sophie?"

There was a hiss as Nett slowly let out his breath. "Now that two unicorn artifacts have gone missing, I think it's clear that Royalists are involved. Anvil Malchain must be a member. It kind of makes sense, though, doesn't it? That one of the most famous treasure hunters of Arden would join a society obsessed with finding powerful unicorn artifacts."

Claire nodded in agreement, but she was far from comforted.

"But why now?" Sena asked. "They must be organizing, collecting artifacts for some reason."

"No idea," Nett said seriously. "But I think we must assume that Sophie *does* know. And that she's either joined them, or is trying to stop them. Claire, which do you think it is?"

But she was spared having to answer as suddenly there was a muffled *thud* from beyond the wardrobe. All three of them started, the net rattling with their surprise.

"The inspectors!" Nett hissed. "They're here!"

They could hear footsteps now, pacing around the silver columns beyond the false wardrobe.

"I can't go back to the inspector cells—I can't!" Sena moaned. "The *cold* . . ."

The footsteps stopped just outside the wardrobe door. Pressed against Sena's back, Claire could feel the girl shaking in terror. The secret room was suddenly lit from the light of the main forge.

"You!" Nett gasped.

Claire heard a familiar voice. "Looks like you're in a bind."

Thorn Barley was in Fyrton.

CHAPTER 19

"What are you doing here?" all four asked at once. And all four replied:

"Searching for the harp—"

"The smith—"

"We need a Looking—"

"To help you."

The last was Thorn, who had knelt down to examine the silver links. His cheeks were red, as though he'd been running, and his scarlet tunic was askew. So Claire *had* spotted him in the street.

"That's a Forger journeyman's tunic!" Sena said. "How did you get that?"

"I don't think that's really the most important question right now," Nett said, frowning. "Why are you here?"

Thorn pulled halfheartedly at the net. "Like I said, I came to help."

"But how—"

"Look," Thorn interrupted. "I'm happy to answer your questions, but we need to get you out of here first. That bald Forger will come back with the inspectors soon."

"I think I saw some skeleton keys in that box over there," Sena said.

Claire felt her stomach turn. The academy teacher had asked about a skeleton key, too. "What . . . kind of bones do you use for them?" she asked tentatively, not sure she really wanted to know the answer.

"It's not what you're thinking," Sena said, and even though Claire couldn't see her face, she could practically hear her eyes roll. "A skeleton key is a key that has been forged to open any lock. Most Forgers build locks that can withstand a skeleton key, but if there are any skeleton keys in this room, then the chances are they're particularly strong."

Thorn hurried to the corner to retrieve the box.

"Do we trust him?" Nett murmured under his breath.

"No," Sena whispered back. "Not until we find out *why* he's here. Or *how* he got here."

Claire remembered the look on Thorn's face when he had asked to see her pictures, and the little golden bird in her ruck-sack. "I think we should trust him," she announced. "He helped us before, didn't he?"

Sena nodded. "We can trust him until he gets us out of here. Then . . . we'll see."

Thorn returned and held up keys for Sena to inspect. Each time she shook her head, Thorn would pluck out another one.

"Why are you here?" Nett asked again.

Thorn held up another key, this one brass. "If I want Greenwood Village to stop treating me like a weed—to take me *seriously*—then I need to do something to change their mind."

Sena shook her head, and Thorn held out a new key, an iron one with pointed teeth.

Claire felt a twist of sympathy as Thorn continued to explain. "I thought that if I help find the harp and prove that Sophie is innocent, then maybe they'll respect me more."

He set the pointed-teeth key down when Sena shook her head, and presented the next. "I went back to the narrowboats, but the Spinners were already awake. So then I thought I could ride a horse fast enough to catch up in Fyrton. I've been looking for you all day."

There was a silence as Claire debated whether she should tell Thorn the truth about the harp. What if, in his mission to impress Greenwood, Thorn reported Sena as the thief? As difficult as the Forger was, Claire didn't want to see her go into the inspector cells.

She kept quiet, as did the other two.

"That one," Sena said suddenly as Thorn held up an unremarkable-looking key. "That's a skeleton key!"

Thorn slipped it into one of the locks, and after a moment of silence there was a soft *click*. As he went to the different locks, the chain's pressure lessened. Soon, they were able to cast off the net like a winter coat on the first day of spring.

They hurried out of the secret storeroom, and Claire was glad when Nett shut the door on the creepy objects behind them.

In his haste to fetch the inspectors, Scythe hadn't completely smothered the fire Claire and Nett had built. Smoldering embers remained. Nett hurried over to stir up the fire, while Sena beckoned Claire over to her.

"Stand here," Sena ordered as she placed the library book on the Forger's table. "I'm going to need your help."

"What can I do?" Thorn asked, standing awkwardly at Claire's elbow.

"Keep watch," Sena said. "This is our one chance to find out where Sophie is, but Scythe will be back with the inspectors any moment."

"We have a little time," Thorn said. "When I saw you slip inside here, I went to tie up my horse. I returned just in time to see the Forger enter his shop. So I *might* have untied his horse and then tied him up a few streets down. He'll need to either find his horse or walk."

Nett looked impressed. "Good thinking!"

"Thanks." Thorn grinned, then hurried to the window.

Claire watched as Sena read from the book, then, looking up from the pages, dropped a few of her silver coins into a small clay pot. Next, she put on a pair of leather gloves. Once Nett had the fire going strong again, Sena used a pair of tongs to place the clay pot in the flames.

As the coins melted, Sena placed a small metal box on top of the worktable. She opened it to show Claire a mirror-shaped indention inside.

"This," Sena told Claire, "is called a sand cast."

She closed the box and pointed to a hole at the top. "We're going to pour the metal through here, and it will fill up the impression you just saw."

"*We're?*" asked Claire.

"Yes, you're going to help me. Now, for this to work, though, I need you to start thinking of Sophie. Concentrate on what she looks like, how she stands and moves, the faces she makes, how tall she is, how heavy or light, the way she wears her hair. And think of *who* she is. Got it?"

"I thought you were making the Looking Glass?" Claire asked, confused.

"Each mirror is crafted to a single person," Nett called over as he pumped the bellows to push more air into the forge. "If, say, Sena used your Looking Glass, she'd only see what she normally sees in a mirror—a frizz ball with a booger hanging out of her nose." Nett dodged Sena's punch to his shoulder. "But *you* should be able to stare into your Looking Glass and see where Sophie is since she's the thing you most want to find."

"Exactly," Sena agreed. "When I say so, you must take the crucible—that clay pot—out of the flames and pour the silver into the sand cast. Understand?"

Astonished, Claire nodded nervously and Sena handed her

a pair of leather gloves. They were heavy, and she hoped she'd be able to grasp the tongs well enough with them on.

"But why do you need me for this part?" Claire asked. "What if I accidentally drop it?"

"You won't drop it because you can't afford to," Sena said, wiping sweat from her face. "You're the only one in all of Arden who *has* lost Sophie. She wasn't anyone else's to lose."

Claire nodded, and picked up the tongs Nett offered to her. Dutifully, she closed her eyes. What had Sena said? Think of Sophie. Was she big or small? She was taller than Claire, that was for sure. But Claire didn't know exactly how tall she was, or how much Sophie weighed. How precise were the details in her head supposed to be? Claire knew Sophie was heavy enough that when her sister would flop onto the couch pretending not to see Claire already there, Claire struggled to breathe. And as for her height—Sophie was tall enough to hide her piggy bank on the highest closet shelf where Claire couldn't reach.

It was hard to think of Sophie as a list of facts, because she was so much more than that. Sophie had always been there, adding excitement to Claire's memories, coloring in her days. Sometimes, during long car trips or a boring class at school, Claire would assign colors to her friends and family. Mom was the blue of a shallow sea while Dad was a humming-bird green. She knew that Sophie was some kind of purple, but it wasn't until she'd seen a rare Vanda orchid on a field trip to the botanical garden that she'd known exactly which shade her sister was. The flower was the perfect blend of a vivacious, temperamental red and the strong, loyal blue of the ocean. Together, it was dramatic. It was fun. It was Sophie.

"It's time!" Sena yelled.

Claire opened her eyes, and the furnace's heat scraped across her face. Gasping from the shock, she accidentally inhaled the smoke. She began to cough.

"Keep your eyes open!" Sena shouted above the roar of the flames. "Timing is everything!"

Tears streamed down her face as Claire nabbed the pot from the fire. Arms trembling with effort to hold the tongs steady, she tipped it into the cast. Molten silver flowed quickly from the pot.

"Ah!" Claire yelled, dropping the tongs as the heat chewed through her leather gloves. The clay pot clattered to the floor, but luckily it was empty. Peeling off the gloves, Claire stuck her burned fingers into her mouth.

Suddenly, Nett was there with a tin cup of water. She wrapped her fingers around its coolness and sipped gratefully. She felt dry and cracked, as though she'd been in a forge and not simply next to one.

"Is everything all right?" Thorn reappeared from his post at the front window. When Claire nodded, Thorn whispered, "Try to be quieter—people might hear you! I'll go out to the front and see if anyone has come to investigate."

Sena swiftly undid the latches of the cast, the trunk splitting down the middle into two halves. Each side had been packed with sand, and the molten silver had pooled into a hollow dent to form a small hand mirror.

Claire looked at it incredulously. It was as dull as an old pan. She couldn't imagine how this thing would help her find Sophie.

Sena ran her fingertip over the cooling metal, then handed it to Claire. The handle fit in her fist as comfortably as smooth stone.

"I don't see anything."

"That's because I haven't polished it yet," Sena said as she picked up a file. She read a line from the library book. "I hope."

Claire passed the Looking Glass back to Sena, her hand feeling strangely empty without it. Looking for something to do, she pulled out her pencil while Sena methodically swept the file across the rough silver. Around, down, repeat.

"Metal, especially silver, wants to reflect," Nett said, settling on a nearby stool. "But a Forger helps direct *what* it reflects."

"'Ow 'ong 'ill it 'ake?"

"Sorry?"

Claire hastily removed the pencil from her mouth. "How long will it take?"

"It depends on the Forger. Sena is . . . inexperienced."

After a few minutes, Sena stood up and walked over to Claire. Up close, Claire could see sweat beading her forehead. Sena grasped her right hand as though it pained her.

"See if it works," she rasped.

Wrapping her fingers around the handle, Claire looked into

the glass. Even though Sena had been polishing, the surface remained dull, a mix of white and gray, like the bathroom mirror after a hot shower.

There wasn't anything to see. Or was there?

Claire squinted, holding the mirror an inch from her nose. A delicate shape drifted like mist against cloud, coalescing into a spiral and the slenderest of tips . . .

A dazzling hope almost broke the surface of her thoughts, but then she blinked. The image was gone.

With a feeling of helplessness, Claire shook her head. "I thought . . . for a second, but no."

Sena gritted her teeth. "Give it back."

With a new ferocity, Sena attacked the metal. She pushed into the surface with her entire being, her shoulders moving like pistons. Claire wrapped her arms tight around herself to keep from pacing.

"Look now," Sena panted. As Claire took the mirror from her, she saw Sena's hands were trembling. Magic, it seemed, came at a price.

Once more, Claire looked into the mirror. Its face was still dull, but this time, there was color. A black smear streaked across a background of trees. The trees seemed odd, though. Trunks, leaves, even the roots tangled on the forest floor were all the same color: a dark, rusty red. The color was only broken by the glimpse of a dusty plain beyond the strangely still branches.

Claire squinted, and the black smear became a galloping

horse ridden by a cloaked man, with a double-headed ax slung across his back.

Anvil Malchain.

He galloped toward another, smaller shape, in a tunic Claire had never seen before. A shape wearing a moonstone necklace and a purple ribbon that was about to slip out of her hair.

CHAPTER
20

In the Looking Glass, Anvil Malchain reached down and pulled Sophie up onto his horse without breaking stride, the man's bat-winged blades gleaming even in the night. For a moment, it seemed the man felt Claire's eyes on him, and he turned to look right at her. Malchain had the oddest gray eyes she had ever seen—as dark and lusterless as charcoal.

Claire screamed and dropped the mirror. It clattered to the ground face-first and skidded along the stone floor.

"What's wrong?" Nett leaped off the chair.

There was a patter of feet as Thorn raced from the front window to join them. "We need to get out of here!" he whispered. "Someone must have heard that."

But all Claire could manage to do was wrap her arms around herself and try to keep from shaking as she looked at her circle of friends. "He's found her! Malchain's found Sophie!"

Her throat felt raw, as though she'd scraped it. Over and over again she replayed the scene. She felt a hard shake to her shoulders.

"What else, Claire?" Sena's yellow eyes glared at her and each word was punctuated with a shake. "What else did you see? Come on, stay with us!"

"She should look into the glass again," she heard Thorn murmur.

"It's too badly scratched," Nett replied quietly. "It won't work again."

Claire closed her eyes, trying to remember details—and, almost at once, trying to forget them.

"A forest," she croaked. "But the forest looked weird. The trees were too still and everything was the same color—a rusty-brown red."

Sena and Nett looked at each other and Thorn let out a soft whistle. "The Petrified Forest."

Claire's eyes snapped open. "You know where they are? How do we get there?"

"Claire." Nett looked at her solemnly. "*No one* goes to the Petrified Forest. It's a forest that was turned to stone during the Guild War. It makes Tillers sick to be there, and Spinners and Forgers avoid the cursed place at all costs. Gemmers might go, I don't know, but they almost never leave their mountaintop."

"But they were at the edge of the forest. I could see an open plain just beyond the trees," Claire protested.

"The Sorrowful Plains?" Thorn's voice cut in. "You saw the Sorrowful Plains?"

Claire shook her head. "I don't know. Wait, isn't that where Queen Estelle went to save the last unicorn?"

Nett and Sena exchanged a look.

"It is," Nett said. "And it has to be the Sorrowful Plains. If you could see it from the Petrified Forest, there's no other place it could be. But remember, Sena isn't a trained Forger, so the mirror may not be *that* accurate."

"What do you mean?" Claire asked.

"I mean," Nett said, "whatever you saw in the mirror could have happened yesterday, or it might happen tomorrow. It's always hard to get it exactly right, even if the Forger has training."

"But if Malchain already caught up to her, there's no way we'll get there in time," Sena said, her voice hard and low. "The Sorrowful Plains are days away."

"Not necessarily," Thorn said. He ran his fingers through his blond hair. "My grandmother was a Tiller Trader in her younger years, and she told me that Fyrton's Mount Rouge contains many secret passages, including one that leads straight through the mountain and directly into the Petrified Forest."

"A secret passage?" Sena asked, distrust written all over her face.

Thorn nodded. "The silver mines," he said. "They're

abandoned now, but I've heard other people say, too, that the longest passage will still take you all the way to the Petrified Forest."

Underground mines. That meant more dark. More uncertainty. Claire nervously tapped her finger against her pencil. But if that was the quickest way to get to Sophie, she'd do it.

"Can you take me there?" Claire asked, taking a step forward.

Thorn smiled at her. "Yes. We need to leave right away."

Sena opened her mouth, closed it, then opened it again. "I don't think it's a good—"

"But it's an idea," Claire pointed out. "You don't have to come with me, but now that I have a clue of where Sophie is, I'm not going to just give up."

"I'm ready," Nett said, picking up his pack. "Sena?"

But Sena was already walking away from him and over to a barrel of swords. She wrapped her hand around different hilts.

"What are you doing?" Nett asked.

"Hang on." Sena pulled out a small sword. The hilt was plain, except for gold wires melted into a Forger's hammer on the pommel. Sena swished the blade through the air in a figure eight. "She fits perfectly. If we're going into the mines, we better be prepared."

And for the first time since Claire had met her, Sena truly grinned. The difference was so startling that Claire didn't think she'd recognize her if she saw her in a crowd.

Sena quickly buckled the sword around her waist and threw a few coins on Scythe's table.

"You're paying that horrible man?" Nett asked incredulously.

"Yes," Sena said. "I'm done being a thief. And Fireblood deserves a clean start."

"Fireblood?" Claire asked.

"My sword," she said, patting the hilt. "Let's go."

They were a little way up the mountain when the sun rose in its full glory, dripping scarlet and orange onto the earth below. Sena and Nett marched in front, while Claire lagged behind with Thorn, who was carefully leading his horse along the rocky path.

Thorn murmured something.

"Sorry?" Claire asked. She was only half-awake, which meant she was actually mostly asleep.

"I was just thinking how the sunrise makes the sky look like it's on fire," Thorn said. "It reminds me of a poem Grand used to like:

The end can be found
Where fire meets water
At the edge of day and night.

"That's from *The Queen and The Unicorn*, right?" Claire asked, surprised. "Was your grand a Royalist?"

"You know about the Royalists?" Thorn asked, equally

surprised. "Yeah, she was one. She didn't talk about them that much, but whenever there was a blue moon—the second full moon in one month—she'd disappear for a few days, saying she had Royalist business to attend to. They're a pretty quiet group. How did you hear about them?"

"I learned about them on the narrowboat," Claire said. "I think that maybe they—" She was going to say that Anvil Malchain might be a Royalist, and that maybe the Royalists were organizing, up to something secret and bad, something that her sister was trying to stop. But what if he didn't believe her? Or was offended? Or worse, what if he told Greenwood Village before she knew how to clear Sophie's name . . .

"Maybe, what?" Thorn prompted.

Claire squinted at the bluing sky. "Do you think the poem means anything or is it just a bunch of pretty words?"

"Grand thought it meant something," Thorn said. He clucked, and the horse's head jerked up from the scrubby grass he'd been sniffing. "She said she became a Tiller Trader so that she could travel and maybe one day find a place where fire meets water. She believed a secret, all-powerful unicorn artifact—the Unicorn Treasure—that could wake the queen would be hidden there."

"What kind of artifact?"

Thorn shrugged. "I don't know. I don't even know if Grand knew what it was."

"Do you believe in the story?" Claire asked, curious.

The boy shrugged. "I don't know what I think. I will say

one thing—I like the idea of a queen coming back to restore Arden to the old ways, to the way it was before the war. To make magic *thrive* again."

Once more, Claire thought about how the Tillers of Greenwood treated Thorn, how they called him lackie. It made sense that he would want to believe in the poem's promise.

Looking over at Claire, Thorn smiled. "That's what's so nice about Sophie. She doesn't let her lack of magic get in the way of having adventures."

No, Claire thought. *She certainly doesn't.* And finally, a puzzle piece fell into place.

"So that's why you really came after us," Claire said. "Because you realized you could actually help, even if you didn't have magic?"

Thorn looked at her in surprise. "You're pretty smart for your age, you know that?"

"I'm eleven," Claire said automatically, but she was pleased.

Falling into a friendly quiet, they continued to walk for what felt like hours until Nett called back to them, "Thorn, is this the entrance?"

In front of them in the earth was the dark mouth of a mine shaft. The opening was about six feet wide, but it was much too dark to be able to tell how far down it went. A boulder stood next to it. Drilled into the stone was a metal loop, through which a chain was threaded and connected to a wide wooden platform. The other end of the chain was wrapped around a large spool with a handle.

Claire hoped she was wrong, but the whole contraption did look an awful lot like a very old, very dangerous elevator.

Sena went over to examine the pulley. "It's not magic," she said. "Someone will need to stay behind and pull it back up. If no one does, it'll be obvious to the inspectors where we disappeared to."

Claire looked at her toes. There was no way she would be the one staying behind, but she hated the thought of going on without Sena, Nett, or Thorn. The more people there were to rescue Sophie, the better she felt.

"I'll do it," Thorn volunteered. "I'll pull it back up after you. It makes the most sense," he added when Claire opened her mouth. "It's dangerous for Sena to stay—what if someone recognizes her? And Nett is trained with magic. I'm not adding anything."

Claire felt a little guilty. Poor Thorn, always wanting to be a hero, but always being left behind. She knew how that felt.

"Thanks," she said.

He smiled at her. "Follow the trail of moonmilk. Where the rock shimmers white, you'll definitely be able to breathe. Where there's no moonmilk . . . it could be a sign that the air is becoming too thin."

Claire didn't understand, but Nett and Sena nodded.

"Go," Thorn said, walking over to the handle.

Reluctantly, Claire stepped onto the platform, and Sena and Nett followed. Maybe if she closed her eyes, she could pretend that the platform was solid ground. But that was going to take a lot of imagination.

"Are there wraiths in the mines?" Claire asked timidly.

"Maybe," Nett said softly. "But we have the marimo. And Sena's sword. Besides there are worse things dow—"

"All set?" Thorn interrupted.

"We should hold hands, I think," Sena said, reaching for Nett's and Claire's. "It'll keep us from slipping off the edge."

Thorn began to turn the handle. The chains creaked, and the platform lowered a few inches.

"Remember—follow where the moonmilk flows! Don't stray," Thorn warned as the top of Claire's head became level with the ground. "Good luck!"

"Thank you!" Claire called up.

Though Thorn's face had turned red with the effort, he still managed a grin for her. "Anytime, Clairina. We'll see each other in Greenwood soon!"

And Claire, who should have been annoyed at this boy for using Sophie's nickname for her, was surprised to discover she didn't feel bothered at all.

They dropped farther into the dark. Claire thought she heard Thorn add something else, but now they were too far away to make out his words.

Trying to push out the growing darkness, she focused on the shiny spot of Thorn's blond hair hovering over the opening above. But sooner than she thought possible, Thorn became a dot, blurring into the sky. Still, Claire told herself, as long as she could make out the bright blue of sky, all would be well.

Farther and farther they dropped, until the shrinking circle of light looked like a tiny sun in a ring of blackness.

As long as she could just see *light*, it would be okay, she told herself.

And then that, too, disappeared.

CHAPTER
21

The mines. Claire pulled out her pencil and held it in a death grip. But the platform tapped the ground more gently than she expected. In fact, she wasn't even sure they had reached the bottom until Nett took out the marimo. A quiet light appeared around it, its brightness only a glimmer of what it had been the night they snuck into Thorn's stables.

Nett looked at his little plant in dismay. "I'm not sure it'll be able to get us all the way through. It needs time to soak in more sun."

With a loud *creak*, the platform began to lift off the ground. Thorn was pulling it back.

"Hurry!" Sena said, and they hopped off the platform onto the floor of the mine. With less weight, the platform rose much more quickly than it had descended.

"If we don't find the tunnel how are we going to get back up?" Claire asked.

There was an uncomfortable silence.

"Well, I guess we'll just have to find the way," Nett said forcefully.

"What did Thorn mean when he said to follow moonmilk?" Claire asked.

"Moonmilk is a kind of living stone," Nett said. "It's found in caves, and the little creatures that live within it produce enough breathable air so that it's safe to walk underground as long as you're next to it."

"Here's some," Sena said, pointing. Claire followed Sena's finger to see a wash of white against the red of mountain rock. The substance was lumpy, like snowballs strung together and hung in a garland.

Nett pushed his palm against it. "Ugh." He made a face. "It feels like eyeballs."

"Nett!" Sena admonished.

"What? It *does*!"

"Never mind," she said quickly. "There's the tunnel we need to take."

The mines weren't as bad as Claire had feared. Their path seemed obvious. There were other tunnels, many in fact, but only one glowed with moonmilk. Most of the other passageways had been boarded up or had caved in, but here and there, Claire spotted caverns that had been carved into amphitheaters, or a brush of dye on stone that seemed to indicate gowned figures, snarling dogs, and bloody spears—brief glimpses into Arden's past, she guessed.

Down and down they went, passing pockmarked walls and abandoned pickaxes. Claire's ears popped. And then they popped again. As the three continued through the dark, Claire noticed that metal beams no longer supported the tunnels. They had passed through the mines and were now walking through natural corridors of the earth. And though she knew that she was deeper underground than she had ever been before . . . Claire wasn't afraid.

Maybe it was because she was sandwiched comfortably between Nett and Sena, who had her sword, Fireblood, at the ready. Or maybe it was the cool air that seemed to hum a quiet lullaby around her.

Claire let her fingers drift over the rock, skimming the time-smoothed curves as though she were trailing her hand into the lake as Dad rowed their boat. Her fingertips tingled.

Adjusting her rucksack, she gave her hand a hard shake. The tingling didn't stop. If anything, it intensified. Now it seemed as though the soft hum she'd heard in the air had actually been inside her bones.

"Do you guys feel funny?" Claire asked.

"Funny how?" Sena asked from behind.

"Like your hands are about to fall asleep?"

"Nope," Sena said.

Claire kept walking. She remembered feeling a slight tingling in her fingers when she'd climbed the chimney, too. In fact, she'd felt more than that—a reverberation that she thought would shake her apart. But this feeling was more gentle, soothing even.

Nett stopped. "Oh no."

Claire's heart leaped in her throat. "What's wrong?"

"This." He held up the marimo, and Claire peered around him. They had come to a fork. One path was made of the sandy-red rock that had been common in the higher chambers, and the second was gray. In the gray, she spotted the spiraling imprint of a long-ago sea creature.

But there was no moonmilk to be seen in either one.

"Slug soot," Sena said. "Slug soot, slug soot, slug soot!"

"We could go back—" Nett suggested.

Sena whirled on him. "And do what? Thorn's probably left by now—there's no way to get back up!"

Nett jutted his round chin forward. "But if we keep going, there's no way to know *where* we'll end up! We might end up in a tunnel with no air! Claire, what are you doing?"

Claire had brushed by Nett and was standing in the sand-colored tunnel. She wasn't sure what was happening but a sudden warmth—happiness, maybe, or excitement—zipped through her veins, feeding the hum. It was similar to the triumphant rush of letting go of her bike's handlebars for the first time. Or when she'd won the school-wide drawing contest.

And that's when Claire knew what the hum was. Not happiness or excitement, but *exhilaration*. She felt a surge of rightness.

"We need to go this way," she said.

"Why?" Sena asked. "What makes you so sure?"

Claire didn't know herself, but she wasn't going to admit that.

"My mom always says to trust your gut," Claire said, hoping they wouldn't question her too much. "And I think my gut is telling us we need to go left."

Sena let out an exasperated sigh. "So that's what it's come to? Guts?"

Claire snuck a glance at Nett. He was staring down at his toes, scuffing a triangle into the dirt. The dust of travel dulled his clothes, and his bundled energy seemed to have dissipated. Was he feeling all right?

As though he had read her thoughts, he looked up and gave her, if not a full smile, at least a shadow of one. "Guts are guts," he said. "And Claire's are as good as any. Let's go left."

After a moment, Sena nodded. "All right. Give Claire the marimo."

They resumed walking, Claire in the lead. If only Sophie could see her now. She'd know that her little sister was up for any Experience—and had even had some without her.

The passageway twisted and turned. Sometimes, it grew so narrow that Sena took Fireblood off her hip to stop the scabbard from scratching against rock. Other times, it was wide enough that the marimo's light only served as a reminder of how little they could actually see. The hum in Claire's bones lessened, and she no longer felt the gentle tug that had drawn her left instead of right.

She had been so *sure* that this was the way out, but with

each passing step, Claire felt her newfound confidence fade. She wished Mom and Dad were here to tell her what to do.

"Nett!" Sena's voice cut through the air. "If you don't keep moving *right now*, I'm going to—"

"I found something." Nett was studying the cave wall, nose almost brushing the rock.

Claire backtracked to them. "What did you find?"

Nett held his hand out for the marimo, and Claire placed the feathery plant in his palm. Its captured sunlight spilled over the rock.

"See there?" With the tip of his finger, Nett touched a fuzzy red dot on the wall. "It's . . . well, it *feels* like a plant, but it's . . . strange." He looked up, and Claire saw that there was a gray tinge to his usually brown skin. Claire suddenly wondered if people, like flowers, would wilt without sunlight.

"Let's keep going," Claire said. "The sooner we get out of here, the better."

Nett stood up, swaying slightly.

"Hey, Sena?" Claire said. "We're going to need a little help."

"I'm fine," Nett protested. "I just—it's too quiet down here. I can't even feel *tap*roots anymore."

Sena took in the dark circles under Nett's eyes. "You're fine, and I'm a rooster," she said, as she grabbed Nett's arm and put it around her shoulder. "Take his other side," she ordered, and Claire hurried to slip Nett's other arm around her.

"Get moving, lily pad," Sena said to Nett. "You plant people are as delicate as your garden flowers." But beneath the sting of Sena's words, Claire heard a deep concern. She tried to push back her own worry as the three of them lurched into the darkness.

Nett must have been heavier than his slight frame appeared, because Claire found herself struggling to breathe a few minutes later. Claire hoped it was because Nett was heavy, and *not* because they were running out of breathable air. Without the moonmilk, it was impossible to know what was truly safe.

Trying not to panic, Claire focused on drawing the damp air in through her nose and pushing it out through her mouth. It left an earthy taste in the back of her throat.

Nett suddenly stopped. "Look up," he wheezed.

Claire did as he said, and saw another splotch of red fuzz, this time tipped with a fine white powder. Nett's head fell back down, his breathing shallow.

"Why isn't he getting any better?" Claire asked Sena. "There are plants everywhere! Don't plants produce oxygen?" She thought she remembered a teacher mentioning that.

"Not . . . plants . . . ," Nett wheezed. "Mold . . . white dust is spores . . . poison. Can't breathe."

"I *knew* we should have gone right," Sena muttered. "*Useless* . . ."

The Forger's words felt like punches. "Then why did you follow me?" Claire retorted. "Why did you listen to me if I'm so useless?"

Nett let out a low moan, and both girls looked at the Tiller. His chin was resting on his chest. Claire adjusted her grip on his arm.

"I'm sorry," she whispered to him.

"Sorry isn't going to help," Sena said, her red braid whipping as she turned. She began to walk again, practically dragging Nett and Claire behind her. "We need to get out, now!"

"Sena, slow down," Claire said. "I'm going to—" Her foot caught on something. She stumbled, but managed to steady herself before she brought all of them down.

"Nett. The light?" Claire asked, and Nett handed the marimo to her.

She shone the light on the ground, and for the very first time in her life, Claire wished it were still dark.

Because the marimo's pearly light shone directly onto a rib cage. A large, very human rib cage. And a skull.

Claire screamed. And screamed. And screamed.

Flinging herself away from the splayed skeleton, she took a heavy step toward the cave wall, twisting onto loose soil. No, not onto—*through*.

Claire was falling!

She thought she heard Nett and Sena falling beside her, but it was hard to tell in the sudden thunderstorm of rock and grit. Long moments later, Claire's breath rushed out of her as she landed on something spongy.

"Nett! Sena! Are you okay?"

"Fine." Claire heard Nett's voice a little to her left, faint and barely audible above the last *plinks* of pebbles falling down the hole.

"Sena?"

"Slug soot, slug soot, slug soot!"

They were all okay! If Claire's ribs didn't hurt so much from the fall, she might have laughed with the sheer relief of it. She saw the marimo shining a few feet from her and scrambled to pick it up.

Her eyes adjusted slowly. They had fallen into a vast cavern with dagger-sharp stalactites reaching down toward them like teeth. Some were so long that they had fused with a few stalagmites shooting up from the ground, forming large columns of rock.

And everywhere—above Claire, below her, and around—there was more red mold.

It pulsated slightly, making it seem as though the cavern had a heartbeat.

Claire gasped—and immediately wished she hadn't. The mold's powder trickled into her lungs, and she began to cough. Hard coughs, the kind that made her think her ribs would break. No, she couldn't think about bones! She almost retched.

Claire felt something soft being tied over her mouth and behind her head. She started.

"Relax," Sena murmured, as she pulled the knot tight. "It's just some muslin we . . . use to collect . . . seeds." She spoke slowly and with great effort, sucking in breath. "It's not perfect, but it . . . should help filter."

Sena took the marimo from Claire and handed it to Nett, who appeared somewhat recovered. He, too, had a cloth over his mouth and nose. Then Sena drew her sword.

"I don't see any way out," she announced. "The walls are too steep, and it's too dark. And the sunlight in the marimo is going to run out soon." The pearly light wavered, as if agreeing with the Forger's words.

"Well," Nett wheezed. "At least it can't get . . . any worse."

Grrrrrrrrrrrr.

A low growl echoed around them.

Sena immediately raised Fireblood.

"What was that?" Claire asked.

"Shh." Sena planted her feet, staring into the shadows with Fireblood raised.

Wraiths? Claire gulped, and followed Sena's gaze but didn't see anything. She felt Nett shift slightly next to her.

A moment later, Claire thought she heard a slight *rasp* coming from the other side of the cave. She turned.

Suspended high in the darkness were two glowing eyes.

Claire screamed.

Nett swerved, twisting the marimo hard. The plant burst into a hard light that lit the entire side of the cavern—as well as the creature that half-slithered, half-flew down toward them.

"Wyvern!" Sena yelled. "Nett, don't let the light die! Claire, hide!"

At first glance, Claire would have said it was a dragon, except she'd never heard of a dragon with only two legs, both at the front. Its hindquarters resembled a snake's body—long and whiplike. Delicate, narrow wings jutted from its shoulders, too fragile, it appeared, to lift the giant creature from the ground.

It propelled itself forward with its body, swaying its wings from side to side to keep its balance as it charged straight down the cavern wall, long front claws gripping the rock like it was soft cheese.

Claire watched in horror, too frozen to move, as the dragon—*wyvern*—hissed, tucked its sleek wings into its body, and dropped to the bottom of the cavern.

"Go!" Sena yelled, holding Fireblood up. Finally, Claire shook loose from her terror, and ran.

In the dark, she almost darted straight into one of the cave's natural columns. She quickly dove behind it. From the other side of the pillar, Claire heard a high-pitched scream followed by a loud *crash* that shook the entire cavern.

Her stomach curled. Was that Nett? Sena?

Claire placed her hand against the rough column to brace herself—and the hum that had left her flooded her again. But whatever she had felt before was a kitten's purr compared to the lion's roar that now rushed through her.

With hands splayed against the column, Claire was suddenly aware of a deep resonance that ran beneath her feet, rose into the pillar, and into her. She realized that the hum had never come from her bones—it had come from the *rocks* around her. She lifted her hands, and the hum lessened. She placed them back against the rock column, and the vibration surged again.

She had the sudden sense, wild as it seemed, that she could actually *feel* the constant, perfect push and pull of millions of crystal structures that formed the geological base of Arden.

Crystals that she knew from science class linked together to form rock. To form a cave. To form a column.

With her fingertips, Claire found a weakness in the column, a hairline fissure that broke the crystalline pattern and created the tiniest of cracks.

There was another *crash* and a deafening *clatter* as a few stalactites plummeted to the cave floor.

She thought, strangely enough, of Kleo Weft, the Spinner girl on the boat, and how she'd managed to control her magical rug just by knotting a thin thread in her hand. Claire didn't know why that image came to her, but it reminded her that something small can set off something bigger.

Time moved like honey. Without fully understanding *why*, but knowing she *must*, Claire pulled her pencil from her trousers' deep pockets and lodged its point firmly into the split in the stone. With her left hand, she held the pencil steady, and with her right, she quickly felt around her feet for a palm-sized rock.

With the power of the cave humming through her, Claire swung the rock like a hammer, and drove her pencil deep into the stone.

The column buckled, sending tremors high up into the cave's ceiling. The next moment, the world trembled as dozens of stalactites broke loose from the ceiling and crashed down onto the rock floor with the fury of an earthquake.

Claire screamed and fell to the ground, her arms over her head. The hum began to fade and the noise quieted. Still, she remained motionless, exhausted and too scared to look. But she had to look.

Scooting to her hands and knees, Claire peeked around the column.

The tree-sized stalactites had fallen in a perfect circle around the wyvern, forming a sort of rock-cage. The creature growled and thrashed angrily, but the prison held.

Across the cavern, two pairs of eyes—one amber, the other brown—stared at Claire from above dirty muslin masks, blinking in surprise.

CHAPTER
22

A thousand questions exploded like fireworks inside Claire, each one sparking off another that left her dizzy. So she asked the simplest one first. "What just happened?"

There was a *crash* as the wyvern threw itself against its rock bars. It howled in anger, but the cage held.

"Well," Nett said with a nervous glance toward the beast, "you just captured a wyvern."

Claire turned to look at the wyvern, which was pushing its large, scaly head through the bars. Now that she wasn't running away, she could see it a little better. It was massive, and Claire could clearly make out a ropy black scar cutting across its chest and the milky white of its rolling eyes. The creature was blind.

"I don't understand," Claire said. Shock made her voice surprisingly steady. "What *is* it?"

"They are the Gemmers' war pets," Sena said. Still holding

Fireblood tightly in her hand, she walked over to Claire. Nett stumbled after her. "They can only be killed by drowning," Sena continued. "Their stone hearts make them sink. The oceans, rivers, and lakes are littered with their bodies."

The wyvern strained, its shoulders pounding against the rock-cage. To Claire's dismay, the wyvern's scales seemed to be chipping away at the bars, widening the space little by little with each forward thrust.

Claire looked back at Sena and Nett. They were staring at her like she was a stranger.

"What?" she asked.

"Nothing," Sena said. "It's just . . . *lucky* the stalactites fell when they did. And how they did." Something strange lurked beneath her words.

"Did you help?" Claire asked, surprised. An uncomfortable thought began to prowl the corners of her mind. "Was it magic?"

But Sena's face stayed carefully blank. "I'm a Forger. I don't do rock stuff."

"Sena," Nett rasped, his voice muffled by the muslin cloth. Exhaustion had carved shadows beneath his eyes. "You know that there . . . is sometimes . . . metal in rock. You must have been . . . too scared to realize . . . you crafted something."

Sena stared hard at Nett. "That must be it," she finally said.

At her words, Claire should have felt relief. And maybe she would have, if she believed Sena. She glanced at the fissure. The only thing that remained of her best pencil was a small wooden circle around a gray dot.

For a second, the cave was quiet. The wyvern was mountain-still. Then the creature erupted, its shoulders slamming the rock bars one final time.

They cracked.

The wyvern whipped out with a scream, wings tight against its body as it streamed toward them like an avalanche.

"*STOP!*" Claire screamed as she threw her hands into the air above her head. She squinched her eyes tight, waiting for the beast to make contact with her soft body, grinding tissue and muscle into the ground.

But impact never came.

Slowly, she opened her eyes. Two white orbs like clouded marbles peered into hers. The wyvern's legs were twice as long as Claire was tall, but its neck curved down like a question mark so that it could stare directly into her eyes.

Her hands shook as she slowly lowered them to her sides. Out of the corner of her eye she saw Nett and Sena standing absolutely still.

The wyvern snapped its teeth and emitted a sound like crunching gravel. Suddenly, an image of a small tree balancing on the edge of a rock popped in Claire's mind. Its roots squeezed around a boulder, its fibrous hairs stretching, feeling out the rock's weakness, breaking it into crumbs, and then finally—dust.

"I—I think she's scared," Claire said slowly.

"*She?*" Nett asked.

"Yes," Claire said. The wyvern opened her jaw, and again

spoke in her crunching language. This time, Claire saw pick-axes streaking through the air as they hollowed out the mountain. Fear and anger from an unknown source whipped through her. She took a quick step back from the creature.

"I don't think she likes Tillers or Forgers very much," Claire said slowly. "I think—I'm not sure—but I think she can smell the plantness and metalness that runs in your blood."

Nett and Sena stared at her.

"Plants and metal can both destroy rock," Claire said with an apologetic shrug. Then, turning to the wyvern, she added, "They won't hurt you. I promise."

The wyvern dipped her head.

"You *are* talking to it—her—aren't you?" Sena said, adjusting the muslin cloth around her nose and mouth. "Nett, have you ever heard of something like this? Why can Claire talk to it?"

"I don't know . . . much about wyverns," Nett said, his voice still weak. "There aren't many left."

Nett's eyes tracked the wyvern's flicking tail. "Maybe it's . . . because you're not from here," he continued. "Maybe all people from where you're from can speak to wyverns, they just have never . . . had the chance to meet one . . ."

"Maybe," Claire agreed.

"This isn't a time to speculate," Sena said, not taking her hand off her hilt. "We need to get out of here."

"But how do we do that?" Nett looked up into the cavern. "The only entrances are above the hole we fell through . . . in the ceiling . . . and the wyvern's exit. The rock face is too steep for us."

Claire's eyes darted to the wyvern, a plan forming. "There is the obvious way—"

Nett stared at her blankly, and then his eyes widened. "You can't be serious."

Standing up, Claire walked over to the wyvern. The creature's nostrils flared as she neared, and she took a deep breath to steady herself. How did one address a wyvern?

"Excuse me." She bobbed her head in a kind of half bow. The creature tilted her head, and Claire knew she had her attention. "Would you be so kind as to lead us to the exit?"

The wyvern's growl rolled and crunched again. Claire closed her eyes, trying to make sense of the cadence, to latch on to an image. And when she finally did, her eyes opened with wonder.

The wyvern had stretched her neck along the cavern's floor.

Cautiously, Claire laid her hand on the wyvern's bumpy neck. Its scales weren't smooth like those of a fish, but knobby, as if river-worn rocks had been glued onto it.

Swinging a leg up and over, she settled just in front of the two wing joints and gripped two scales in front of her. The wyvern's wings rustled like paper bags as she adjusted for Claire's weight.

Giddiness swept through Claire and she had to hold back nervous laughter, scared that if she started, she'd never stop.

After counting to three—once for Mom, once for Dad, and once for Sophie—she looked at Sena and Nett. "Coming?"

For once, Nett had no answer.

Sena sheathed Fireblood. Gingerly, she pulled herself up onto the wyvern, too. On the ground, Nett seemed to be having an inner battle with himself. His tousled hair was a storm cloud above his head. He muttered something that Claire couldn't quite make out, but after checking the straps on his pack, he placed his hands on the wyvern's scales and scooted on, behind Sena.

As soon as he stopped wriggling, the wyvern rose to her feet and began to run. Unlike horses, which move in a straight line, the wyvern's serpentine body whipped from side to side as she picked up speed. The cavern's wall loomed suddenly out of the darkness—they were headed straight for the rock face!

Claire screamed. They were going to crash!

But at the last moment, the wyvern jumped, launching itself up and toward the wall, clawed feet outstretched.

THUMP. It grabbed on to the cavern's side.

The wyvern's body swung like a pendulum, and Claire shut her eyes tight against the image of sliding back, all the way down the wyvern's tail and into the dark, red world below.

But the wyvern's claws hung tight, and as it unfurled its wings, the world stopped swinging. Claire had only a second to catch her breath before the wyvern leaped again. Wind stung her eyes as they bounded up the cave's wall. The sensation was like sledding, but if you sledded *up*. It was the same wild, out-of-control exhilaration that could end in a split second of catastrophe.

The wyvern crested over the last outcrop and surged into a wide tunnel that gleamed white. Moonmilk!

Claire tore off the bit of muslin cloth and gulped in the cool, clean air, free of mold dust. It was too much, too fast, and her head throbbed as though she'd slurped a milk shake too quickly.

From behind her, she heard a feeble moan. "I think I'm going to be sick," Sena said.

Again, the wyvern picked up speed, and they hurtled through twisting passages. Keeping her wings tucked tight against her sides, the wyvern bounded with the flexibility of a slinky, narrowly missing jagged crystals and dripping stalactites. The world within the mountain was just as varied as the one outside. At one point, Claire even thought she saw an entire side passage of deep blue light that must have been sapphires, but the wyvern twisted down another path before she could take a better look.

Only once did the wyvern lessen her pace, when they neared the smooth black surface of a lake. Carved into the rock wall behind it were two giant figures sitting on stone thrones. The first was the image of a girl in a long flowing dress. She wore a serene expression on her face, and her hand held a small bow, the kind for shooting arrows.

Next to her, smaller, was the figure of a boy with a crown on his head.

"The last queen, Queen Estelle, and her brother, Prince Martin," Nett said, his voice full of awe. "This must have been done a long time ago—after the war, the Gemmer Guild retreated up to their mountain top and have hardly ever traveled back down."

"I didn't realize the queen was so young," Claire said. She felt a renewed sense of belonging when she looked at Estelle's likeness. If Estelle could find her unicorn, Claire could find her sister.

Claire's eyes flickered over to the other statue. The little brother. "What happened to Prince Martin?" she asked.

"He died late in the war," Nett said. "It was his death that led Queen Estelle to reconsider the Guild War.

"At that time, the Gemmers were losing badly and many of them went on a unicorn hunt to gain immortality for the final battle. But from her loss, Estelle was able to gain the courage to stand up to the rest of her guild and try to save the last unicorn from them."

With new eyes, Claire studied the queen's face. Now that she knew the story, she thought that Estelle's expression wasn't serene, but sad. How could she not be?

The wyvern had carefully edged around the lake. As soon as they were on the other side, the stone beast resumed her gallop.

Soon, they were moving upward through a narrow passage, and the children had to lean forward, flattening themselves against the wyvern's serpentine neck as her wings folded and brushed against them.

Finally, the wyvern slowed, then stopped. She rumbled, a sound like ocean waves retreating from rocks.

"This is as far as she goes," Claire said, slipping off the wyvern's neck. "This tunnel will take us to the surface."

Sena wobbled off, and immediately braced herself against the wall. The green tinge of her skin contrasted vividly with her red hair.

Nett seemed to have fared better. He was staring down the tunnel, and it was clear he was ready to run all the way back to the sun. Claire hoped he wouldn't, though. Her knees were shaky from holding on to the wyvern and there was no way she could manage more than a slow hobble.

"Thank you," she said to the wyvern. She placed her palm flat against the creature's neck. The wyvern cocked her head at Claire, her rumble growing louder.

This time, as the vibrations moved through Claire, she not only felt what the wyvern felt—she remembered the beast's memories: warm sun and blue sky. She realized with a start that the wyvern hadn't always been blind. She knew color. Dry pine needles pleasantly scratched her tail and tiny bird feet ran along her spine, as birds picked itchy bugs out from between her scales.

And curled next to the wyvern's tail, in the hazy memory made of hums and pulses, was a smaller rock pile. Another stone heart that beat as one with the wyvern. A tiny creature that was taken away too soon.

A tear slipped down Claire's cheek. She'd been in the

wyvern's heart, and for just a moment, she'd seen what was inside it: the wyvern's baby, who had died long ago. The mother's sadness lingered, and her loneliness tucked into Claire.

"Maybe she could come with us?" Claire asked.

Nett shook his head, though his eyes looked glum. "In an earlier time, wyverns used to live aboveground, but if she went out of the mines now, she'd only be hunted."

Already the wyvern was turning around, her scales whispering against rock. She wouldn't be able to see the world anyway. She'd lost her eyesight over centuries of darkness. Gifts not used withered and died.

And besides, the wyvern purred in her grumbly language, caves weren't bad—they were warm, filled with salt licks and sapphires and diamonds that tasted of stars. There could be joy and warmth and coziness tucked into shadowed places.

Soon, the wyvern's long tail slipped into the safety of darkness.

"Good-bye," Claire called. "Thank you for showing us your home."

And as she followed Sena and Nett up the passageway, Claire knew that if she ever again had to travel without light, she'd be okay.

After all, now she had learned there were things worse— much, much worse—than the dark.

CHAPTER
23

Light!" Nett let out an excited whoop. He ran down the tunnel, hair and pack flapping behind him.

The girls looked at each other and Sena grinned. "Race you?" the Forger asked.

Claire was off before Sena reached the end of her question.

They had made it through the mines! She'd ridden a wyvern! She was getting close to Sophie!

Soon, she'd be able to tell Sophie all about her Experiences—though she didn't know if she'd start with the narrowboats or the Forger school or that she'd saved them from a dragon-like beast or—

A terrified wail echoed down the tunnel.

"Nett!" Sena yelled. She overtook Claire within two strides, and disappeared out of the tunnel's mouth. Claire pumped her legs harder, and soon burst out into a green world.

Trees the width of school buses towered above her and white butterflies fluttered in golden slants of sunlight.

And in front of her, near her knees, was the very angry head of Nettle Green.

Sena was bent over with laughter, startling a flock of swamp wrens into the air.

"It's not funny!" Nett shouted, clearly enraged. From the shoulders up, Nett looked normal, but the rest of him had sunk into brown, soupy muck.

"Sena, stop laughing and help!" Claire yelled frantically. "He's going to sink!"

"No, he's not," Sena said, catching her breath. "Nett's a Tiller. He can get out of this, no problem. In fact, he should have been able to avoid the bog to begin with if he'd been paying attention."

"There wasn't supposed to *be* a bog," Nett grumbled. "Thorn said the mines would take us to the Petrified Forest."

"The wyvern must've taken us another way," Sena said.

So they were lost. Trying to ignore the kernels of worry that had suddenly appeared in her stomach, Claire asked Nett, "Do you need help?"

"No." Nett sighed and closed his eyes. "I got this." He dropped a pellet on the bog, and it floated a moment, before sinking beneath the muck.

Looking around expectantly, Claire wondered if a nearby vine would suddenly start to grow. Instead, the bog began to bubble.

Claire blinked. "Are you getting taller?" she asked. The

muck that had been up to Nett's chest was now at his waist. And as she watched, it slipped to his hips.

"Nope," Nett said as he pushed down on the earth. His hands, instead of sinking through muck, stayed on top. "I just convinced the roots beneath me that they're thirsty. They're sucking up all the water, so the ground will be firm enough to step on. It'll go back to normal in an hour or so." With a loud *slurp*, he pulled himself onto firm ground.

Sena wrinkled her nose. "You smell like rotten eggs."

Nett flicked mud in Sena's direction, and she burst into laughter again. Ignoring her snorts, Nett began to hit the mud caked onto his clothes. It broke off in great clumps, as though the mud had been on him for days rather than minutes.

"Nett got Mud Repellent last Namesday," Sena explained as Nett tackled the dirt on his boots. "If you brush it onto your clothes, it makes the mud flake right off. Useful, when you're a Tiller."

Suddenly, Nett let out a sharp cry and crumpled to the ground. His body twitched and jerked, and to Claire's horror, she saw a rash march over his body like a colony of red ants. He began to scream.

"Grab him!" Sena cried as she dumped the contents of Nett's carefully organized travel pack. Leaves and packets and twigs and barks fell onto the soft ground. Claire ran to Nett, trying to stop him from rolling back into the mud as he writhed in obvious agony. What was happening?

Sena elbowed Claire to the side, and plunged a sharp

needle into Nett's arm. "Keep him still," she said grimly. "I've injected him with luna syrup. It cures almost everything, including razor mud."

"Razor mud?"

"Looks like regular mud, but it's toxic—and potentially lethal. If he's clear for a day, then he'll be all right, but if he relapses before then . . ."

Nett suddenly shuddered, then stilled. The tightness around his lips loosened, and he let out a long sigh. Claire thought she saw his eyes open for a moment, but then his eyelashes fluttered and they closed again.

"Do you think it's working?" Claire asked.

Sena rubbed angrily at her eyes. "What?"

"Is it working?"

Giving her red-rimmed eyes a last swipe, Sena leaned down and put her ear to Nett's chest.

One Mississippi passed, then two. Claire closed her eyes, as though a thin layer of skin could protect her from a stark reality.

"Getting all moss-soft on me, Forger?"

Claire's eyes snapped open.

The warm undertone of Nett's skin was back, and his hair, though not at its fluffiest, looked less trampled.

"You're alive!" Claire yelled, so happy that she flung herself over Nett and Sena, arms wrapping around them tightly.

"Yes—and in pain." He prodded Claire with his index finger. "You're suffocating me!"

"Geroff!" Sena mumbled.

Claire sprang back. Sena sat up, but not before she pinched Nett's ear. "That's for scaring me."

"Ow." Nett shook his head, then winced. "I've definitely felt better, but nothing some willow bark can't fix."

"Don't complain," Sena said, and handed him a piece. "People don't always survive razor mud."

It was only after Nett had sat up, eaten some seedcakes, and made fun of Sena two more times, that Claire finally felt herself relax enough to focus on what would be next.

"Where are we?" she asked. "How far are we from the Petrified Forest?"

How far from Sophie?

Sena pulled a crumpled map from her rucksack and smoothed it on top of a rock.

"Here's Fyrton, at the base of Mount Rouge," she said. She traced her finger east across the mountain and stopped at a small label: *Petrified Forest*. Then her finger drifted north. "I'm guessing we're somewhere here, in the Foggy Bottom."

Claire glanced around at the turtles that lounged on moss-covered boulders. The swamp was more soggy than foggy, but the name seemed to fit.

Sena sighed. "I'm just not sure exactly where 'somewhere' is."

"We're near New Road." The girls looked up to see Nett licking the last crumb of seedcake from his fingers.

"How do you know?" Sena demanded.

"The wisdom of my Tiller-sense," Nett said solemnly. "Also, there's the sign."

Claire followed Nett's finger to a sign and, next, to a path. She hadn't seen them behind feathered ferns.

"The Tillers of Dampwood laid the road a few years ago," Nett said. "It was a huge undertaking. They had to pick the perfect plants that would firm up the land. Before that, there had been no way to cross the swamps at all. We would have been completely stranded here. The Tillers built lighthouses all along the way to keep travelers from straying off the road in a fog and sinking into the swamp."

Nett studied the map. "The first lighthouse should be on our right," he announced. They packed up, and Nett tied the marimo to his shoulder so that it could soak up sun as they walked.

They began to follow the road, Claire hurrying, determined to get to the forest. They'd already lost another day and by now, Anvil Malchain surely must have caught her sister. Besides, hurrying helped her forget the strange humming she'd experienced in the mines, and the even more curious looks that Nett and Sena had given her. And, of course, the enormous, unthinkable question of how she'd been able to understand the wyvern when the other two could not.

She knew Sena and Nett must still be wondering about it, too, but they said nothing. Their silence made her nervous. It had a weight to it, a deliberate quality that Claire had used herself when classmates whispered behind her back.

Finally, Claire spotted something high in the branches. It looked like a great gust of wind had blown a garden shed into the tops of a tree. A turret with an observation deck tilted from the roof, and a rope ladder hung down from the platform, as though it were anchoring sky to earth.

"The first lighthouse! We're going in the right direction!" Nett said happily. He eyed the sun. "I think we can make it past six lighthouses before it gets dark, and, well, you know. Wraiths. But we'll be able to spend the night safely inside a lighthouse."

They followed the path, rambling over small streams, mossy rocks, and tangled roots. Lily pads the size of hula hoops dotted the swamp and stick-legged birds waded through grass and water with ease. But as they trudged on, Claire's calves began to ache. They stripped off their leather Forger vests, damp with sweat, and left them dangling on a bush. By the time they reached the third lighthouse, the day had begun to feel endless, and despair squirmed through her.

How far were they from Sophie? How much time had passed back at home? Would there ever be answers or just more questions?

"Tell a story, Nett," Sena said suddenly. Mud speckled her trousers and sweat plastered tendrils of red hair to her neck. "Distract us."

Nett was quiet, then began to speak. "Time before memory and time before blood, the people of Arden were cold. They had offended the Sun, and he punished them by withdrawing his face. The world became a white and barren place.

"From Arden, there came a great and terrible wail. But the Moon heard their cries and wept for them. As the Moon's tears fell to earth, they did not disappear. They continued to shine, becoming bright, and brighter, and brightest. Unicorns."

Claire thought for a moment of meteor showers she'd seen at home. Sophie preferred to call them waterfalls of wishes, and maybe she wasn't so far off.

"When humans looked upon the beauty of the Moon's children," Nett continued, "they could not help but laugh. The Sun, drawn by the unexpected sound, turned his face again toward Arden. Upon seeing his sister's children galloping the earth, the Sun was filled was such joy that the world immediately warmed under his own laughter, and became warm and softly green again."

"Beautiful," Sena murmured, and Claire agreed.

By the time they reached the fifth lighthouse, Claire's feet felt as heavy as bricks, and her hands grasped at her empty pockets, missing the pencil that had given her comfort since she left Windemere Manor, however long ago that really was.

To her great relief, they reached the sixth lighthouse quickly. If it had been any farther, she wasn't sure they could have made it.

Climbing up a swinging rope ladder, they reached the treehouse. It was surprisingly spacious, and even had a turret complete with observation deck. Sena spread her cloak out like a picnic blanket and Nett handed them each two seedcakes.

"My mama is an amazing cook," Sena sighed, looking at

the dry cake in her hand. "She used to cook wild boar in sweet carrot sauce."

"Sena," Claire said after swallowing her first nibble. It didn't taste bad, it was just hard to chew. "If you're looking for your mom, why don't you just make a Looking Glass to find her?"

"Because all Forger prisons plan for that," Sena said, leaning against the rough treehouse walls. "Mama's kept someplace that can't be traced. She could be anywhere."

Sena poured water from her canteen over her seedcake, and the water hit the floor with angry *plops*. Claire suddenly wasn't hungry. Even though she knew where her mom was— fast asleep in a world away—she felt her stomach turn with missing.

After dinner, Sena used her pack as a pillow and curled into a corner. In a few seconds, she was fast asleep.

Claire knew she should sleep, too, but she didn't want to— not yet. She studied the moon through the cracks in the roof. The moon's belly was round, and tomorrow night it would be completely full.

"I'm not too tired, are you?" Nett whispered across the lighthouse.

"I don't want to sleep, if that's what you mean."

He made a face. "Me neither. After the razor mud I still feel a bit . . . off. Too hot." Standing up, he gestured for her to follow him.

They climbed up the little turret and out onto a narrow

observation deck. The swamp was velvet black, except for a few white lights that looked like shooting stars that had gotten tangled in branches. It was funny how distance and time could alter appearances, Claire thought. After all, she knew those lights weren't stars at all, but the dim beacons she'd passed beneath only hours before.

"Pretty, aren't they?" Nett said. He was backlit by the lighthouse's beacon, his hair a ragged halo. "I think there is only one more lighthouse until we reach the Petrified Forest. And then, only a few hours' walk until the Sorrowful Plains. We'll be there tomorrow."

Tomorrow.

Sophie always liked tomorrows and their unspoken promises, but Claire preferred yesterday's knowings. That was yet another difference between them. Claire read the last word of a book before starting, while Sophie liked the surprise.

There was another thing Claire needed to know. "Nett?"

"Yeah?"

"In the wyvern's cave . . ." She hesitated. Once she said the words, she couldn't take them back. "I don't think it was Sena who made the rock-cage."

Nett paused. "I don't either."

Claire took a deep breath as the stories she'd heard over their journey came back to her.

"Do you think . . . Am I a Gemmer?" she asked so quietly she barely even heard herself.

Nett was slow to answer the question. "I don't know what

to think," he finally admitted. His eyes crinkled in thought. "It's *possible* that a long time ago a Gemmer found your world and stayed."

Stones replaced Claire's heart and stomach. "I don't want to be a Gemmer!" she said. "They enslaved the Forgers. They hunted unicorns!"

"All the guilds did evil things during the war," Nett said. He sat down, dangling his legs over the deck. When he patted the wooden planks beside him, Claire thumped down next to him.

"The Guild War was a terrible time," Nett continued. "And don't forget, there's Queen Estelle. She was a Gemmer. She's a hero for all of Arden. Even if she didn't save the unicorns, she tried. That's more than anyone else did."

But misery had hooked its teeth into Claire and wouldn't let go. Without thinking, she reached for her pencil for comfort, but, of course, it wasn't there. She slammed her hand down on the wooden planks.

"What's wrong?" Nett asked.

"My pencil," Claire said. "I know it's silly, but without it, I feel—" She broke off as Nett's eyes widened. "Why are you looking at me like that?"

"Your pencil," he said, "it's made from letter stone."

Claire shook her head. "It's graphite."

"Maybe it's called that where you come from," Nett said, a new seriousness in his voice Claire had never heard before. "But I saw your drawing. It's called letter stone here. It's not exactly a rock, but it's a mineral on its way to becoming one. How do you *feel* when you draw?"

Claire pulled her knees to her chest, and stared out at the swamp. "Like all the levels of my brain are working at the same time, but not thinking at all. I lose track of everything except what is right in front of me."

"That's how Tilling is for me," Nett said. "Only, I hear a kind of *song* coming from my plants. And I can hear when the tune is flat or sharp, and I work to make it sweet again." He shrugged. "But it's different for everyone, even people in the same guild."

With a groan, Claire lowered her head onto her knees.

"Even if you are a Gemmer," Nett said softly, "you're still *Claire*. A name doesn't change that."

They were quiet, though Claire's mind was a whirl as she ran through the possibilities. Could Dad know about Arden? Did Mom? But if they did, they definitely would have protected their daughters from passages into other worlds masquerading as chimneys.

Great-Aunt Diana, a voice whispered to her. Great-Aunt Diana with her treasures would know. But she was dead.

"There," Nett said suddenly. "It's starting!"

Claire lifted her head. "What—?" But before she could finish her question the answer came in a spark of orange. A single firefly, an ember in the night, flashed in the bushes below.

Soon another joined its pinprick of light, and then another, and then another, until the air around Nett and Claire was bursting with the dazzling pattern of firefly dances.

It was beautiful. It was *glorious*.

"Do you know if a group of fireflies is called anything?" Claire asked. "You know how lions live in prides and oysters are in a bed?"

"I know that a bunch of crows is called a murder, but I don't think anyone has a name for a gathering of fireflies," he said. "Why, do you have a name for them?"

And for once, she had an answer. "I think they should be called a glory—a glory of fireflies."

Nett didn't say anything, but in the scattered bursts of light, Claire saw him smile thoughtfully.

"A glory of fireflies. I like that. Countess Molly, a poet from the Golden Age, once said that to call a group of unicorns a 'herd' is to liken a diamond to a brick. A gathering of unicorns should not be compared to a herd of cattle. Rather, more than one unicorn at any time is a blessing."

"A blessing of unicorns and a glory of fireflies," Claire said out loud. The words sounded pretty and protective somehow, though she didn't know why.

"Sophie would like that," Nett said.

"Yes," Claire said softly. "I think she would, too."

They watched in silence together as the fireflies swirled up from the ground to eventually rest on branches.

"Are you feeling better?" Claire asked.

"A little. Still hot, and I'm so . . ." A soft snore punctuated the end of his sentence. Claire smiled, and gazed at the moon. It looked so round and ripe, she half-wondered if it might break off from the sky and fall into her hand. With Nett by her side, she slipped into sleep.

But in the morning, Nett was worse.

CHAPTER 24

Gray edged Nett like frost on a leaf. His chest rattled with each breath and his eyes, though open, didn't seem to look at the others.

Sena placed her hand on his forehead. It came away slick with sweat. She pushed his sleeve up gently, and Claire gasped.

His skin had risen in lumps, swollen as though the razor mud rash from before had settled beneath his skin onto muscle and bone. And maybe that's exactly what had happened.

"He needs a Tiller, maybe even a master Tiller," Sena said grimly. "There's no plant or poultice I know of that will stop him from—I mean, that will help him make it through."

The air was suddenly impossible to breathe. It *hurt* to breathe, as though all the oxygen had turned into a fine glass dust. The memory of IV drips and clear tubes surfaced, its snapping jaws threatening to pull Claire down. The doctors had said the tubes that linked under and through her sister were there to help Sophie stop hurting, but the hospital hadn't done anything for Claire's pain.

Yet Sophie had healed; nothing was impossible. Claire forced herself to take deep breaths and focus.

Sena had pulled her hair into a single thick braid over her shoulder, and she tugged on it as she thought. "Dampwood, the Tiller village Nett mentioned, isn't too far from here. It's the best chance we have."

Claire clamped down hard on her disappointment. She knew they must be close to Sophie. She could *feel* it. But she couldn't abandon Nett.

"Let's pack up and get him there," Claire said. She gave Sena's cloak a hard flap and a cloud of dust billowed in the sunlight.

"No." Sena's yellow eyes met Claire's. "You need to find Sophie. I know what it's like to have lost your family. Don't make my mistake and wait too long. There's only one more lighthouse between here and the Petrified Forest. Do you think you can manage?"

Claire's answer came to her swiftly: *No.*

She didn't know Arden, didn't know how to avoid all its dangers. And even if she made it to the Sorrowful Plains, how would she get back home? She didn't know the way to the well. But even though Claire knew the impossibility of what Sena was asking, it didn't mean she wouldn't try.

"Wraiths, wyverns, and Malchain?" Claire smiled nervously. "Shouldn't be a problem."

Sena laughed, but it was a hollow sound, like a door closing on an empty room.

Claire looked down at Nett. His eyes were thin crescents on damp skin. Her small courage fumbled. "Let me help you get him to Dampwood first," she said. "He's too heavy for you to carry all the way."

But Sena was already lifting Nett up by his armpits. "I'll be fine. If I put him on one of those giant lily pads we saw, I can drag him, like a sled. It won't be fun, but it's the quickest way. You need to leave now. You can*not* be on the Sorrowful Plains when the sun sets, got it? The plains are the location of one of the bloodiest tragedies in Arden's history, the Unicorn Massacre. More than a hundred unicorns were killed that day. There are more wraiths on the plains than anywhere else in Arden."

Suddenly, Sena's strong arms shot out and wrapped Claire into a hug. She let go just as quickly and began unbuckling the belt around her waist. "This is just a loan," she told a stunned Claire as she handed over her sword. "But by accepting Fireblood, you're promising to return her to me. Do you understand?"

"Sena, I can't—"

The belt was suddenly around her waist, the strap pulled tight. "Too late. She's in your hands, and now you've made the promise."

Scared that her voice would be as high as a mouse's squeak,

Claire just nodded. The blade was surprisingly heavy, and she felt herself listing to the side. Sena tugged Fireblood, spreading the weight evenly across her hips.

Claire wrapped her hand around the hilt, her thumb and fingers barely meeting. Would she even be able to lift it if—*when*—danger came for her?

Sena nodded her approval and gave Claire a gentle shove. "I'll take care of Nett. Now go."

As Claire squelched away, she turned back, only once, to see Sena straining against a swamp-vine harness, Nett unnaturally still on the lily pad.

The Petrified Forest had once been called the Hollow, a small strip of towering pines, feathered warblers, and furred creatures of all types that had edged the Sorrowful Plains— or so Nett had told Claire yesterday as they'd navigated the swamp.

The Tillers of the Hollow had been the most skilled of all, even, legend said, coaxing four living trees—oak, sycamore, pine, and hawthorn—to bend and grow together into the throne of Arden.

Nett's eyes had gleamed when he spoke of the throne, the thought of such a wonder overshadowing the tragedy of its demise. In the midst of the Guild War, Tillers had persuaded the throne to grow thorns, piercing deep into the flesh of the unsuspecting Gemmer king, Estelle's father, and leaving him badly scarred.

In retaliation, the king had the throne burned to ash, and the Gemmers attacked the Hollow, turning their homes into rock. Like winter's first frost, stone crept over the forest, suffocating life from it.

Claire knew that Arden was full of monsters—wraiths, chimera, even wyverns—but the Gemmers seemed to be their own kind of monster. They had killed an entire forest for revenge, not caring about the innocent lives of those who had made their home in the Hollow. The Gemmers sounded *evil*. She thought briefly of her conversation with Nett last night and then shoved it away. She didn't want to think about Gemmers anymore.

Claire gripped Fireblood's hilt as she moved past the seventh and final lighthouse. Fog was descending and she was worried about the possibility of losing the road or getting turned around. But soon she felt a change in the air. The ground beneath her began to harden, and stagnant puddles gave way to saplings. Pushing aside a last fern, Claire knew she'd finally reached the Petrified Forest.

In front of her was a forest of red—not the cheery red of fire engines, but a red that had been mixed with brown. What was that shade of paint called? Russet? Carmine? Whatever it was, it was the color of dried blood.

You're stalling, she heard Sophie in her head. *Stop looking—do!*

She pulled Fireblood out of its sheath. She didn't know how to use it, but Sena's blade made her feel less alone. With one glance back at the swamp, Claire stepped into the Petrified Forest.

It looked like someone had brushed stone glue onto everything in the woods, cementing branches, twigs, and brush to the forest floor. A single narrow path cut through the trees like a scar, and Claire followed it. She couldn't hack away at the rock-hard undergrowth with Fireblood, and instead had to clamber over bushes and crawl under low-hanging branches.

As she was keeping her eyes on her feet, it was only luck that saved Claire from walking straight into a vine with a flower as round as a fist. Instinctively, she tried to push it aside, and her hand slammed against rough rock.

"Ow!" she yelped. She looked at the stone flower. If she were a Gemmer, wouldn't she be able to sense the magic within the rock?

Cautiously, she reached her finger out and brushed a stone petal. There was no hum against her fingertip, no tingle in her bones. Closing her eyes, Claire strained to feel *something*.

But there was nothing.

She drew her hand back, not knowing whether to be pleased or disappointed. She didn't *want* to be a Gemmer, of course, but it would have been nice to have magic—and even nicer to be able to do something other than run away if anything terrible showed up. Though, so far, nothing seemed too unusual, except for the amount of rock.

Turning away from the stone vine, Claire resumed walking. Had Queen Estelle gone through this path to reach the last unicorn? Had she seen this stone-barren place and wanted to return it to its green glory with the help of unicorn magic?

She wondered how much time it had taken her to get to the Petrified Forest, and how much longer she needed to go until she reached the plains. The light that managed to trickle through the stone branches was dull and unchanging. Any amount of time could have passed. Remembering Sena's warning, Claire broke into a jog.

Her breath became ragged as she pounded down the stone path. Sweat dripped in her eyes. The air was hot and still and quiet, except for the rustle of leaves.

She stopped short.

There was no wind. So how could the leaves be rustling? Could stone leaves even move? It didn't seem possible, and yet she was definitely hearing *something*.

Straining her ears, Claire listened.

Now the rustle sounded more like whispers. Voices. She looked around wildly, but no one was there. The skin on the back of her neck prickled. Holding Fireblood tight, she turned and plunged into the thickest part of the forest. Her feet slammed against the ground as she darted from tree to tree, her entire being screaming at her to put as much distance as possible between her and whoever was out there.

She heard footsteps behind her—someone was following her!

Her breath came in tearing gasps as she willed herself to go faster. But the pounding of her heart was soon replaced by something else: the pounding of hooves.

She would never be able to outrun a horse!

With growing horror, she realized the hooves weren't just coming from behind her—they were also coming *toward* her.

Had Fyrton's inspectors come for her?

Though she was hot, Claire's blood went cold. She pivoted left, but instead of getting softer, the hoofbeats only grew louder, as though a herd of a hundred horses was racing through the forest.

And above the bass of hoofbeats were equine screams of fear, the treble of dogs' whines, and human voices:

"Don't let them escape!"

"Beware their horns . . ."

"Sound the hunting bugle!"

Tucking Fireblood under her arm, Claire covered her ears. With her elbows close to her chest, she tried to outrun whatever horrible thing was happening.

"In the name of the queen . . ."

"They're on the plains!"

"For the Gemmer queen!"

The screams pulled at Claire, wanting to smother her in their terror. Blinded by panic, she didn't realize she'd come upon a stream. Tumbling, she fell into the water—

—and into blissful silence.

Claire stood up in the ankle-deep water, hands on knees as she gasped for breath. The screams, the hoofbeats—the fear—were all gone. The only sound now was the rush of water flowing over rock.

Looking toward the rocky shore, Claire expected to see an

army of men and hounds burst out from the trees at any moment. At the very least, she thought she'd see a flash of mane.

But there was nothing.

Claire wrapped her arms around herself, trying to keep from falling apart.

Scanning the russet forest around her, she held Fireblood out in front of her and cautiously walked out of the stream.

As soon as she took a few steps away from the water, the whispers stirred.

A few more steps, and the whispers turned again into the clear sound of screams and hoofbeats.

Claire fled back into the stream.

Peaceful quiet, again.

Confused and overwhelmed, she sat down on a rock that poked out midstream. Her boots grew heavy with water, but she didn't care. She was sure about one thing now: the hoofbeats and the voices weren't really there.

At least, not there in the same way *she* was there.

There was magic at work here—she just had to figure it out.

Splashing cool water on her face, Claire tried to remember what Nett had said about Arden's magic. Magic was in the raw material; it wasn't housed within him—or any of them—but in all the possibilities of what a seed could eventually be, or a thread, or a scrap of metal, or a . . . a pebble.

A curious thought sparked, then glowed.

In a way, rocks in her world spoke, too—through echoes. Claire vaguely remembered a science teacher once mentioning something about sound waves reflecting off surfaces. She wasn't really sure how it worked, but why couldn't the same principle be applied here?

What if, when the forest had been newly changed to rock, the sounds of the past had somehow gotten stuck here, reflecting and bouncing endlessly, never to fade?

And if that were true, it was no wonder the Tillers and the rest of the guilds avoided this place. It was haunted by horrible deeds of the past.

The hoofbeats hadn't been from horses at all, but—her stomach twisted—from unicorns.

Claire had heard the sounds of a unicorn hunt.

Only that could explain the anguished braying and snarling dogs.

"Okay, Claire, okay," she muttered to herself. "Get a grip." She didn't want to leave the safety of the stream, whose running water must somehow disrupt the echoes, but Sophie needed her.

"It's just sound," Claire told herself firmly. "It's like thunder; it can't hurt you."

But as she waded out of the stream and away from its protective babble, the wailing sounds of the hunt slammed into her again. Her knees trembled. She pushed on, and the voices began again, clearer this time.

"We've herded them into the plains, Your Majesty."

"Then do what you must." A cool, light female voice drifted between stone branches.

Keeping her eyes on her feet, Claire tried to ignore the snippets of sound.

"*Estelle, don't do this!*" a boy's voice urged.

She stopped in her tracks, fear momentarily forgotten. Estelle! Claire's heart pounded. She knew coincidences happened, but the queen had continued to appear along her journey: on the Spinner boat, in Fyrton's library, in the wyvern's cave, and now, here. It was almost as if Queen Estelle were guiding her. Protecting her.

Straining her ears, Claire listened, hoping the echo had caught the queen's voice.

"*Put your ax down,*" the same female voice ordered.

"*I won't,*" the boy replied. "*You can't!*"

"*I must, Martin. There is no other choice. You missed much when you deserted my armies.*"

Claire's heart picked up speed as she stepped in the direction of the conversation. If she had to guess, she thought she was hearing a conversation between Estelle and her younger brother, Prince Martin. This must have been shortly before Martin was killed—a little before the queen had done her grand deed.

"*No, you don't,*" Prince Martin said. "*There are other ways. Alloria Malchain says—*"

"*Alloria Malchain does not understand.*"

There was a pause, and Claire thought she'd lost the conversation. But then Prince Martin's voice spoke again.

"*I'll stop you, then,*" Prince Martin said. "*I swear I will. I cannot let you kill Arden's last unicorn.*"

Confusion crashed into Claire, tugging her down into churning white bewilderment. She tried to hold her breath so she could hear properly, because it was clear she *wasn't* hearing things properly at all. Hadn't Nett said Martin died near the end of the Guild War, and that it was his death that led to Queen Estelle's quest to save the last unicorn from the hunters?

"*The last unicorn is mine,*" Queen Estelle's echo hissed. "*His heart is mine. Stand aside, rebellious brother, or I shall have to kill you as well.*"

"No!" Claire's cry burst from her and flew into the empty trees. The phantom trumpets and shouts began again, concealing the rest of the conversation. She spun wildly in all directions, trying again to catch a snippet of Queen Estelle's cool voice. But all she heard was the hunt.

Gripping Fireblood tight, Claire tried to keep following the path. Kleo, the Royalists, the poems . . . all of Arden had been wrong. The hunter in the poem hadn't been a nameless person at all—he'd been Prince Martin of Arden and it wasn't he who'd wanted to kill the unicorn . . . And Estelle hadn't saved the unicorn by transforming him into rock.

The last queen had killed the last unicorn herself.

The sounds of the hunt grew into a crescendo. Claire broke into a run. The eternal echoing screams of unicorns filled Claire's ears as she imagined them galloping toward the Sorrowful Plains, where Claire knew they would meet their death. The hunts that drove the unicorns to extinction must have been arranged by the queen, too.

Claire fought to escape the echo she was caught in, but no matter where she turned, she couldn't break the sound. For an instant, she wondered if the screams weren't coming from the past at all, but were erupting from her.

She dropped to the ground, covering her head with her arms while Fireblood clattered to the stone ground. She needed a way to break the echoes. She needed to drown them out.

"Once upon a time," Claire whispered, her voice so soft she could barely hear it over the thunder of unicorn hooves, "there were three little pigs . . ."

There was a sharp neigh. *"Got it! Hand a knife . . ."*

Claire scooted to her knees and raised her voice. "Their mother sent them off in the world to seek their fortunes . . ."

Though she could still hear voices, the unbearable screams were muffled now, as if the hunt were moving away. Hurriedly, Claire continued the story. By the time she got to the first "Huff and puff and blow your house down," the Petrified Forest was quiet except for the sound of her own voice.

Relief coursed through her, but she dared not stop.

She finished *The Three Little Pigs* and then went through *Cinderella* and *Sleeping Beauty* in rapid succession. As Claire spoke, she wished she'd thought to fill her canteen with water. In the heat, her throat was drying up quickly. If only Nett were here—he'd have stories to tell.

After two more princess stories and a haphazard rendition of *The Ugly Duckling*, she longed to break, but she couldn't. She pushed on through the thin path in the bloodred forest. Taking a deep breath, she began a new tale.

"Once upon a real time, there were two girls, sisters. The little one followed the elder like night follows day, and they were as different from each other as sun and moon, but like the sun and moon, neither would be the same without the other . . ."

Claire told the trees the stories of her and Sophie's adventures. The time they'd followed the Amazon River (in reality, a drainage ditch) two neighborhoods over and their parents had called the police to search for them. The time Sophie had decided she wanted to be a pastry chef and they'd spent a weekend trying to learn French from flash cards. (Claire still knew how to count to ten.) She told the stone ears about Sophie's papier-mâché diorama and how the paper-paste concoction had plugged all the plumbing in their home.

Were the trees thinning? Claire didn't look too closely; she didn't want to know if they weren't.

And finally, she told one more story. A story of the little sister watching the older one close her eyes in a gray bed, tubes and needles stuck into her as though she were a display in a children's museum. How even then, when Sophie couldn't speak and barely breathed, she'd squeezed Claire's hand. Still comforting her. Still taking care of her.

As she neared the end of this tale, she stepped onto something soft.

Grass! Actual grass that smooshed under her weight.

Looking up, Claire saw a plain. Dust blanketed the yellow grass that spread out before her like a tattered fan, reaching toward a hazy horizon. Nothing broke the monotony except for two obsidian monoliths: Unicorn Rock and Queen Rock. They were encircled by a ring of smaller stones, the shortest of which was at least as tall as Sophie.

Claire sucked in her breath. The formation reminded her a little of Stonehenge, another set of mysterious rocks that had enthralled Sophie and had kicked off a monthlong obsession with Camelot and star charts.

Scanning the plains, she searched for movement. But there was none. It was eerily still—no rustle of hidden mice or squawk of birds in the air. But then again, there was no sign of men with double-headed axes.

Not sure whether to feel relieved or scared, Claire slowly let out her breath. Estimating by the slant of the sun, she guessed that there was still time to search before it would set and wraiths would appear.

Giddily, she addressed the stone branches above her. "And that's why the youngest sister went after the oldest, as annoying and impossible as she was. The danger was worth it, for Sophie."

For the first time since Claire had started talking to herself, she thought she heard the trees whisper again. *"For Sophie . . . Sophie . . . Sophie."*

An echo of Claire's own voice.

Suddenly, as though the echoes had conjured it, Claire saw a clear footprint in the dust, then another, and another, leading toward the center of the plains—toward the great obsidian rocks.

With a triumphant shout, she put Fireblood back on her hip, and burst out of the forest. Joy mixed with hope rushed through her blood, seeming to give wings to her feet.

The squiggly lines of the footprints could only belong to a tennis shoe. And only one person in all of Arden wore tennis shoes.

Sophie was here.

CHAPTER
25

$\mathcal{T}$he sneaker prints stopped at the rocks.

Claire circled the stones, apprehension adding energy to her steps. She had missed something. It didn't make sense that there was only one set of footprints in the dust that led *to* the rocks, and none that led *away* from them. The only mark she could find was a solitary hoofprint in the dust. Did it belong to Malchain's horse? Or to something else entirely?

She wove between the monoliths, checking behind each one. Then she looked a second time. And finally a third.

Even though Claire knew now that the tale of the unicorn and the queen was only a myth, she could understand why the Royalists believed there might have been something more to these stones. Beetle-wing black, they stood defiantly in the plains, two stark gravestones for the Unicorn Massacre.

But there was no Sophie to be found.

What, she mocked herself, *did you think Sophie would just be standing here, waiting for you?*

In her heart of hearts, Claire had.

Because up until the revelation of the queen's true nature, Claire had thought that maybe Arden's magic was working with her. That it would somehow reunite her with her sister. Because that was how these stories, tales of magic, were supposed to end.

Anger crackled around her edges. How could she have been so naive? How could she have thought that Sophie would just be *here*? That Anvil Malchain hadn't already kidnapped her sister?

She threw her rucksack on the ground and its contents spilled out. Fighting the urge to kick the small jars of herbs across the plains, Claire instead whirled around and hit one of the monoliths.

"Why aren't you real?" she yelled. "Why can't you be a unicorn and find Sophie?"

Her hand smarted, and the pain made her even *more* angry.

"Where did you go?" she yelled again. "Why did you leave?"

But of course, there was no reply. She was alone. She'd come all this way to find Sophie and had failed. Somehow, she'd misunderstood. Somehow, she'd gotten it all wrong—she'd gotten *Sophie* all wrong.

Maybe she'd never really known her sister in the first place.

The weight of that notion crushed her chest, and soon, a sob shook loose. The tears came, and she let them.

After all, there was no one here to call her a baby.

Claire cried for her loneliness.

She cried for Nett, who had risked a poisonous swamp to help her. And Sena who'd not only given her Fireblood, but had taken time away from her own search to help find Sophie instead. She cried for kind old Francis, who had stood up for her at the Hearing Hall, and had just wanted everyone to be safe.

Most of all, she cried for Sophie, the sister she had nearly lost once, and now, Claire feared, had lost for good.

She cried until she was too tired to cry any more, until the dark crests of clouds loomed at the edge of the sky, dragging evening behind them like a tide.

Finally, there were no more tears to be wrung out. She felt uncomfortably exposed, and disappointment shuddered through her, pushing out the anger and leaving only exhaustion.

Claire dried her eyes with her sleeve and looked at the mess she'd made. Gingerly, she bent to repack the rucksack. She picked up Sena's warming coin and palmed it, trying to glean the same comfort she had once felt from her pencil. It wasn't the same, but she squeezed it tight, hoping Sena and Nett had made it to Dampwood.

Wondering if her next stop should be to try to meet them at the village, Claire decided to consult the map. She reached for a piece of tattered parchment, but it wasn't the map, it was her drawing of the unicorn mother and foal—the one she'd made in Chimera Fields.

Last time she'd looked, the foal in the drawing had been staring straight at her, but now its head was turned left, horn pointing somewhere in the distance, its expression grave and ears pressed flat, as though in warning. Claire turned her head left, too.

Movement skirted the outlines of the plains.

For one heart-stopping breath, Claire thought it was wraiths. But though the sun was low, it hadn't yet set. Wiping her nose with the back of her hand, she scooped up her rucksack and crouched behind one of the smaller boulders that ringed Unicorn Rock and Queen Rock. As quietly as she could, she removed Fireblood from its scabbard.

Soon, Claire could make out voices, then the soft *thud* of people walking on grass. As quietly as she could, Claire kneeled and peered from behind her rock. Ten or so cloaked figures had arrived at the center of the stone ring. They would have seen her if they had not all been so focused on Unicorn Rock and Queen Rock.

"The artifact?" a woman's voice demanded. From the volume of the speaker's voice, Claire guessed the woman was standing just in front of her boulder.

"Here," a man responded. "Where would you like it?"

"At the foot of Queen Rock," the woman replied crisply.

There were soft discussions as the hooded figures walked by, and Claire slowly slid onto her stomach. From her new vantage point, she could see about twenty pairs of booted feet and the white trim of their midnight-blue cloaks.

A hooded figure bent down, placing an object at the foot of one of the monoliths. When the figure stepped back, Claire could finally see the object: a mahogany harp with a unicorn's head arching from its pillar and pearly white strings glowing in the dimming light. *The Unicorn Harp.*

Heart beating rapidly, Claire tried to squirm a few inches back. She knew now who hid behind these cloaks: Royalists.

Her thoughts raced. Thorn had said the Royalists met each blue moon—there must be one tonight. Claire let out her breath slowly. She should have thought about this! Only last evening, she'd noticed how round the moon was, and she'd known, thanks to Thorn and Kleo, that Anvil Malchain and the Royalists were on the move.

"Are we all here?" the woman asked.

"I count only nineteen, Fray," a gruff voice said next to her.

"Then it is time to see which of us has not heeded the call. Remove your hoods."

Claire peered around the boulder to watch as the figures revealed their faces in eerie synchronicity. They were mostly old, bowed with age as though their intense hope in Queen Rock was slowly grinding them down.

From where Claire hid, she could only see the back of the woman who had spoken. Her long, white-and-gold hair tumbled down her back in a mass of braids and ribbons. A gray quill was tucked behind her ear—a quill that exactly matched the one Claire had seen Kleo use to scribble down their story.

Claire stifled a gasp. Could it be that the leader of the

Royalists was none other than Kleo's teacher, the famed story-teller Mira Fray?

No wonder she hadn't needed her boat this summer. The Spinner was busy trying to find—and steal—unicorn artifacts. But Fray wasn't the one Claire needed to see.

She shifted a few inches, desperate to catch a glimpse of another: the face of the man who had chased Sophie through the Petrified Forest and out onto the Sorrowful Plains.

But none of the figures circling Queen Rock matched the man she'd seen in the Looking Glass.

Disappointment mingled with relief. Claire was glad she didn't have to face Anvil Malchain's battle-ax quite yet, but if he wasn't here, she was no closer to locating Sophie.

Though she was itching to get away from the Royalists, Claire was trapped behind the boulder. There was no way she could dash across the plains unseen. She would just need to hide here and wait for the Royalists to do whatever they were going to do, then leave once they were gone.

She glanced toward the sky. The sun would set soon, and then the wraiths would come. Even a secret society would need to finish by then.

A Royalist pointed in the distance. "He's coming!"

Claire's drifting attention suddenly snapped into place like the last piece of a puzzle. Anvil Malchain was coming!

Sitting up as much as she dared, Claire looked to where the Royalist had pointed. Just beyond the circle of stones, she saw a hunched figure hurrying toward them.

"Francis!" Fray called out as Francis Green puffed toward the cloaked Royalists. "You're late."

Shock exploded across Claire's back in a tidal wave of pinpricks. Francis was a Royalist!

"My apologies." The old Tiller smiled weakly, then bent over, clutching his side. "I had to travel discreetly."

Fray walked over to him, and now Claire could see her face. Her eyelashes and eyebrows were translucent white, making it seem as though she had none. The overall effect was reptilian.

"Where's the girl?" Fray asked.

Claire's mouth went dry as Francis's eyebrow raised in an umbrella of surprise. "Don't *you* have Sophia?"

Fray shook her head, her ribbons and braids clacking together in disapproval.

"But"—Francis looked around the circle, as though Sophie might step out from behind one of the Royalists—"I thought one of us had taken her into safekeeping. When she disappeared, I assumed you'd taken her on your narrowboat, Fray."

"Correct me if I misunderstand," Fray said, the tone beneath her words searing, "you finally found a descendant of the royal family, *and you managed to lose her?*"

Francis took a step back, almost tripping on one of the boundary boulders. "You—you really don't have Princess Sophia?"

There was a strange ringing in Claire's ear. *Princess* Sophia?

"She is not in our possession," Fray said.

"But"—Francis pointed toward the Unicorn Harp, which

lay at the base of the stone—"you have the harp. How do you have that, but not the girl?"

Fray's unblinking eyes did not move from the old Tiller's face. "Yans bought it off-market." Her hand slowly drifted to her braids. Sena's voice came back to Claire: *Spinner's hair, beware.*

"I was warned," Fray continued as she undid a thin braid, "that you might grow attached to the girl, and compromise our centuries-long endeavor. Answer me truly: Have you hidden the princess to keep her blood from us?"

"No!" Francis said. He looked as tired and worn as a shriveled onion peel. "I swore to eradicate the wraiths. I'd do *anything* to avenge my son's death, Fray, you *know* this!"

His son's death? For a moment, Claire was confused, but then she remembered: Nett had told her Francis had raised him after his parents—Francis's son and his son's wife—had died from a wraith attack.

"And yet"—Fray's voice dangled like a thread—"the princess we need is not here. The only one who could possibly have warned her about our intentions was *you.*"

"No," Francis said. "I didn't—"

"Admit it." Fray's voice dipped in as swiftly as a needle. "You don't have the stomach to bear the girl's death on your conscience."

A high-pitched whine filled Claire's ears. The Royalists wanted Sophie *dead*? Or not Sophie, but the person they thought she was. *Princess Sophia.*

"Death?" Francis looked surprised, too. "I thought we only needed her blood!"

"We have this *one* chance," Fray lashed out, as she pulled a thin blue thread from her loosened braid and twined it through her fingers. "We cannot afford to make a mistake. What if a drop of blood is not enough? And we cannot risk you working against us. Now tell me: Where is Princess Sophia?"

Claire knew she had to do something—but what? If she ran, she would be caught. If she stayed, they might find her.

Francis spread his hands in front of him, pleading again. "I swear to you, I don't know where she is," he said.

The thread in Fray's hand looped—and pulled tight.

Francis dropped to his knees as though someone had set a bag of bricks on his shoulders. His arm flailed as he tried to push his Royalist cloak off, but as hard as he tried, he could not lift the garment from his shoulders. There were a few snaps as his ribs cracked.

Repulsed, Claire realized that Fray's tiny thread must control the Royalists' cloaks the same way Kleo's thread had controlled the Guardpet. The old woman's magic was slowly crushing Francis.

"No, please!" Francis croaked. "Mercy—"

Fray flicked her wrist, and the largest Royalist stepped forward, the last ray of the setting sun a hard glint off the spikes of his club.

A whimper escaped from Claire. It was a soft sound, but it was loud enough.

"Hold!" Fray ordered. The club stopped its descent. "Someone's behind that rock."

Heart in her throat, Claire lurched to her feet. A second later, the Royalist appeared, raising his club high, gaining momentum.

Holding Fireblood like a baseball bat, Claire swung at the club, trying to keep it away from her.

Sword and club met with a *clang* that reverberated through her. The force knocked Fireblood to the ground, and Claire followed it, her elbows slamming into hard-packed dirt.

"A spy!" Fray shrieked as the Royalists stared at the unexpected girl. "Axel!"

The large Royalist nodded, and again, his spiked club rose. Claire tried to scramble back, but her arms and legs weren't working.

For one moment, every detail stood out in sharp relief. She saw each blade of dead grass, each loose thread on the Royalist's cloak, each nick on the club's spikes as it rose again above her.

"No!" Francis cried out, voice ragged. "That's Sophia's sister! That girl is a princess of Arden, too!"

"Stop!" Fray's voice rang out, and the club curved away from Claire as the Royalist changed direction at the last second, the heavy weapon connecting with a stone in a shower of sparks.

Fray whirled on Francis. "Is this some sort of joke?"

"No joke," the old man gasped. "That's Claire Martinson. She's Sophia's sister!"

"Francis," Claire panted. "What are you saying?" She wanted

to cry, but something in her felt numb. Broken. Francis had helped her in the Hearing Hall, but now he was using her to save his own skin. Disgust and anger replaced her confusion.

"And what does it matter if I am?" Claire shouted from the ground. "The story of the queen and the unicorn isn't true. Estelle didn't save the last unicorn by turning him into stone— she killed him."

Claire didn't know what she expected this announcement to accomplish. Shocked horror, startled yells, mocking laughter, even, but definitely not the silence that settled over the circle.

"I heard the queen myself," Claire added, trying to sound confident.

"You heard the queen *yourself*?" Fray's voice arched incredulously. Her fingers flew across the thread, undoing the knot. On the ground, Francis let out a sigh of relief, his chest heaving as the cloak unbound him.

"In the Petrified Forest," Claire said. "I don't know how it works exactly, but I think the magic somehow saves echoes from the past—"

"You were in the forest?" Fray asked. When Claire nodded, the woman's thin lips curled into a smile.

"Ah, dear child," she said. "Those woods have made you mad."

"They didn't," Claire insisted. "The voices there are real— or at least, they were real once, but the legend of the Unicorn Rock and the Queen Rock was never true! If you kill my sister trying to wake the queen, nothing will happen. *The rocks are just rocks!*"

Mira Fray bent down and held Claire's chin between her thumb and forefinger. The rest of the Royalists and Francis remained quiet, waiting. Watching. Ready.

"Tell me," Fray said, her tone sickly sweet as her blue eyes drilled into Claire's, "how did you come into Arden?"

"What does that have to do with anything?" Claire asked, hating the feel of the woman's strong fingers on her face.

"Did you, or did you not, climb up a fireplace and find yourself in a water well?" Fray asked again.

In the same way that the right color brought a painting to life, that the right thought inspired art,

    things

        fell

           into

              place.

Claire had climbed from a hearth that once held fire to find herself in a well that once held water.

She'd been in a place where fire meets water. Just like the line from the old poem! The line Thorn had recited to her.

"The fireplace," Claire breathed, and as the circle of Royalists murmured, she realized too late that she should have stayed quiet. "The well!"

"Yes, indeed," Fray said, smiling triumphantly. "Through extensive studying and careful research of the past, I learned that the key to unlocking the enchantment would be found where fire meets water. Naturally, I assumed this object would be a unicorn artifact, the likes of which we had never seen before, and that would amplify our own magic enough to break the enchantment.

"But then Francis brought your sister to my attention. *He* was the one who encouraged Sophia to visit the Spinner fleet and speak with me. I began my studies with renewed vigor, even missing a month of Spinner trading to rummage through Ribbonshire's archives. I began to devise a new theory."

She paused, knowing exactly when to use silence to her advantage. "What if, as some reports claimed, the young Prince Martin had not died, but simply ran away all those years ago? And not to another country, but to another place entirely?

"What if," Fray continued, her eyes never leaving Claire's, "the 'end' the poem speaks of was not some single, all-powerful unicorn treasure hidden away in a mysterious place, but was instead a member of Arden's royal family? Or more specifically, the blood of a Gemmer princess—the same blood that once ran in Estelle's veins and that she needs in order to return."

Mira Fray released Claire's chin, though Claire could still feel her hand's pressure.

"But we're not royal," she protested. "Sophie's not a princess!"

"What is your full name, my dear?" Fray asked.

Claire opened her mouth, then abruptly stopped.

Martinson. *Martin's* son. Prince Martin.

She stared at Fray, forgetting to close her mouth. Fray

nodded in approval. "So you're not completely unintelligent, I see."

Stalling for time, Claire asked, "So what—you want to *kill* my sister for her blood?" She looked wildly around at the blue-cloaked figures. Not one turned their head away from her. Not one offered help.

"No," Fray said calmly. "We want to waken Queen Estelle, who will bring with her the knowledge lost after the Guild War. Who will know how to defeat the wraiths. Who will know how to bring unicorns back to Arden. Your sister's death would have been an unfortunate side effect. Luckily, we don't need her anymore."

Claire's body went numb and she took an instinctive step back from Fray.

"Stop!" Francis's shout made her look around.

And so Claire saw the very moment when one of the Royalists notched an arrow to his bow and fired it—straight at her heart.

CHAPTER
26

As the arrow traveled for a brief infinity, all Claire could think about was Sophie. She'd never had a chance to say good-bye. She hoped Sophie was okay—that she'd get home safely to Mom and Dad.

Her parents' faces flashed in front of Claire. Mom's eyes like Sophie's. Dad's mischievous smile, a twin to Sophie's wild grin.

Then suddenly—Sophie was there!

Her dark hair flew into Claire's face as Sophie hurtled in front of her sister—and in front of the arrow.

With a horrible sound, the arrow's head buried itself in Sophie's chest, lodging just beneath her collarbone.

A scream burst out of Claire as her sister's blood poured over her knees. Arms free, she wrapped them around Sophie, curling herself around her big sister.

Nothing made sense.

"*Sophie!*" Claire croaked as she cradled her sister. All this time, she'd been imagining this moment—but in all her dreams, it hadn't been like this. "Sophie, say something!" she pleaded.

Sophie whimpered, and though the arrow had not even scratched Claire, she exploded with pain.

"Sophie?" Fray asked sharply. She looked at Francis. "Is this the princess?"

Francis didn't say anything. He didn't need to. Claire's tears were answer enough.

Suddenly, someone was tugging Sophie away from her.

"No!" Claire yelled. "Leave her alone!"

"Claire?"

Sophie's pitiful whisper made Claire grab on to her tighter, but Claire was no match for the tall Royalist. He carried Sophie away and laid her at the foot of Queen Rock, next to the Unicorn Harp. Red seeped into the ground.

Claire lurched to her feet and staggered over to her sister. Salt burned her cheeks and coated her tongue. She expected someone to stop her, but the Royalists didn't seem to care. They had done what they needed to do, and their attention was fixed on the Unicorn Harp.

One woman lit a torch and handed it to Fray. The light illuminated her face, naked craving and longing clear in its every line.

"Are you sure you want to burn the harp, too?" the Royalist murmured.

"Yes," Fray said. "The girl is not Estelle's direct descendant, nor even her niece. She's but a many-times-great-grandniece. Her blood might be too weak to wake the queen, but with a unicorn artifact like the harp, we have a chance." Fray looked over at the Royalist. "And the only thing that amplifies magic more than a unicorn artifact is the *sacrifice* of a unicorn artifact."

Claire's stomach clenched as Fray's overbright eyes fell on Sophie again.

"We burn the harp," Fray continued, "and when the unicorn magic has reached its peak, we shall mark Queen Rock with the princess's blood—the same royal blood that once flowed through Estelle's veins. D'Astora blood shall call to d'Astora blood."

Fray lifted her arms, holding the torch high in the air. "Royalists," she called, raising her voice, "are you ready to step away from the shadows and into the light?"

The circle cheered as Fray swooped down to touch her torch to Greenwood Village's greatest treasure. Blue flames began to lick the harp's edges.

"Now is the time for thread to unwind!" Fray chanted.

The cobalt fire suddenly became yellow, twisting and turning like a cloud of hornets. Fray held up her hands, blocking her face from the heat. White pops of light danced along the woolen threads of Fray's cloak, and Claire could feel a hum in the air.

The harp began to char, becoming a blaze of orange fire.

Claire dragged Sophie away from the flames and Queen Rock, but she couldn't move far—her bones were beginning to buzz, tingling like an unbearable itch she could never scratch. Arden's magic—but it had come too late to save them.

Sophie's eyes were closed, and Claire gripped her tightly, trying to shield her from the heat of the fire. She wondered when they would add the Unicorn Tooth to the flames. The Royalists had stolen it, too . . . hadn't they?

Fray gasped with effort, but she managed to remain upright as she addressed the stone again. *"Now is the time for metal to snap!"*

A high whine drenched the air, filling Claire's ears until all she could think about was the intense ringing. It was as though a hundred Phlogiston Academies were each ringing their hundred bells.

Claire clutched Sophie to her, burying her face in Sophie's long hair, but there was no way to block out the screaming rush of magic that seemed to come from the burning harp.

If only Nett were there, she was sure he would be able to smother the fire with a random bit of Tiller knowledge and make everything awful go away. But since he wasn't, she knew the only thing she could do was wait for the sound to fade.

The Royalists had fallen onto their knees, wrapping their hands around their ears, but still Fray kept chanting, her voice perfectly pitched: *"Now is the time for green to harden!"*

Grass seed exploded into the sky. Millions and billions of seeds pinged against Claire like hail, getting into her nose and mouth and stinging her skin. She hunched over Sophie, trying to put herself between her dying sister and the bullet-hard seeds.

"*Now . . . is the time . . . for stone . . . to crumble!*" Fray shouted against the rising magic. She reached down and touched her hand to the dirt stained red by Sophie's blood, then placed her hand on Queen Rock.

The buzzing Claire had felt moments ago was no longer contained to just her. It whipped through the ring of rocks. She felt it in the back of her jaw, an energy that gnawed and gnashed around them all.

And then everything went still.

The flames flickered and died, leaving only embers and ash at the base of the rock.

And Queen Rock was still a rock. Nothing had changed. The hum, the wind, the magic—it had all been a drumroll to nowhere.

"What happened?" one of the Royalists asked. "What does it mean?"

"I told you!" The words tore from Claire's throat. The same words that Sophie had said to her not so long ago in Windemere: "The story is just that—a story!"

"No," Fray said. She shook her head and her hair clicked dangerously. "I'm not wrong. I've worked too hard—sacrificed too much!"

She whirled on Francis. "These aren't the princesses at all, are they? You've lied to protect the real girls."

Fray's hands plunged into her cloak, and she pulled out a long stick. At first, Claire thought it might be a wand, but then she saw that the twig had a wide, circular base. It was a spindle.

The other Royalists recoiled, and Francis covered his head with his arms, the heavy cloak still keeping him in place on the ground.

"If you do not tell the truth," Fray snarled, "I will have no choice but to *spin* your thoughts."

The Royalist with the club murmured something to Fray.

"What was that, Axel?" she snapped. "Speak up!"

"Fray," he said nervously, though he was twice as big as the woman, "the sun is about to set."

For a moment, Claire thought Fray would ignore Axel's warning, but then she seemed to reconsider and pocketed her spindle.

"Bind the traitor," she ordered. "We'll cross-examine him in a safe location." She pulled her hood back up, and the others followed her lead.

"What about the girls?" Axel asked.

The Royalist leader didn't even bother to look at Claire and Sophie. "Leave them for the wraiths. They're useless—and they know too much."

Claire was vaguely aware of Francis's protests as his hands were bound. But nothing, not even the sound of the Royalists shuffling away, seemed real to her, except for Sophie's ragged breathing.

"Sophie? Sophie, talk to me!" she demanded, but there was no response.

Weighing her options, Claire watched the sun tiptoe toward the horizon. Soon the plains would be stripped of light and warmth. For a moment, she was reminded of Nett's story—and she wondered if the moon would see their tears and take pity on them. Her heart squeezed at the memory of Nett. She might never know what had happened to him and fearless Sena. They might never know who Queen Estelle really was or what Francis had done, or where the Martinson sisters had gone.

"Claire?"

She looked down to see Sophie's eyes blink open.

"Oh Clairina, don't cry."

"Sophie!" Claire hiccupped and dragged her arm across her face. "I'm not."

"It kind of looks like you are." Sophie's lips twitched, but it was only the impression of a smile. She still wore the moonstone necklace, a purple shadow against her neck. "You shouldn't . . . have come."

"*I* shouldn't have come? *You* shouldn't have come!" Warm tears began to course down Claire's cheeks and her nose started to run. "What were you thinking? Where have you been? You promised you wouldn't climb up the chimney, and now—now this!"

"It's . . . okay." Sophie pushed the words from her lips. "It would have been the same ending . . . either . . . way."

"What do you mean?"

Color seemed to be draining from Sophie. Even the freckle constellations across her nose seemed to have lost their hue.

"It's back, Claire. We thought it was gone, but when we went to Dr. Silva's . . . it was there again."

And there it was so clearly, the reason for Sophie's sudden mood changes. The reason for her fight with Mom. The reason she'd been avoiding her sister. She hadn't been running away from Claire at all; she'd been trying to protect her from the truth. But even now, Claire couldn't face it.

"But you got better before!" she said. "You'll get better again. *Stop shaking your head!*"

"The doctors . . . they've never seen it." Sophie shivered. "I thought in Arden . . . I mean, there's *magic* . . . I thought . . ." She began to cough, and Claire waited quietly, though each cough felt like a slap. When she finally stopped, Sophie whispered, "I'm sorry I lied, but I . . . didn't want you . . . to worry."

Claire nodded, forgiving the lies.

Sophie's voice went in and out. "I was wrong. You didn't need protection." She smiled. "And I'm . . . so proud of you."

But even her sister's words —the words Claire had wanted to hear from her for such a long time—could not extinguish the cold creeping through Claire's body.

Sophie gave a shaky laugh, then immediately winced. "I thought . . . I could awaken . . . the stone unicorn. I should know better . . . there are no such things as unicorns, are there? Not even here."

Claire glanced at where the ashes had been at the foot of the rock. Only traces were left. Even now, a suddenly icy wind was scattering them across the Sorrowful Plains.

"I'm here, Sophie," she said. "I'm here."

Her sister's face crumpled in pain. Sophie looked less and less like her vibrant sister and more and more like a wax doll.

"We're going to be okay," Claire whispered. "You're going to be okay. This is another Experience. Just . . . just wake up!"

The silence broke her heart.

From somewhere deep within Claire came a low moan. An unarticulated word of immeasurable loss. Now the sun had finally and truly set.

At the edge of Claire's vision, something scurried.

A coldness wafted toward them, clinging where it touched her skin. Twists of darkness like the black beneath rocks began to crawl toward them. Slowly, they took shape.

The wraiths had finally come.

Claire squeezed Sophie closer to her. There would be no running this time. No mad dash to the well and the safety of a chimney. No help from Sena or from Nett, who was also grievously ill.

Claire closed her eyes. She didn't want to see the wraiths slinking closer, or the too-much-red on the ground.

She wanted to see the strong, healthy Sophie who dominated her memories.

Bossy Sophie, who tricked her into standing up to change the channels when the remote was lost.

Melodramatic Sophie, who cried dry tears when she claimed Claire had stepped on her toes.

Nurturing Sophie who had spoonfed Claire Jell-O after her tonsil surgery.

A thousand Sophies flashed through Claire's mind, followed by a thousand more.

Moody Sophie. Stubborn Sophie. Laughing, wild, kind Sophie.

Her intolerable, lovable sister.

A loud howl rent the air, and Claire's eyes flew open. Immediately, she wished they hadn't. The wraiths were approaching—not fast but slow, a stalking predator made from darkness and horror and bone.

The air was so cold that Claire could see a little puff of white each time Sophie exhaled, and she took comfort in each tiny wisp.

If only unicorns still roamed the plains, she knew they could heal her sister. But all that was left of the unicorns was a pile of smoldering ashes and a false legend.

But the legend had been partly true, Claire's thoughts whispered. Sophie and Claire might not be the princesses of Arden, but . . . a place where fire met water *did* exist.

The wraiths prowled closer.

If only Claire were a Forger, who knew how to fight with a sword. Or a Tiller, who could call sunlight from mulch. But she was just Claire, and the only thing she had ever really been good at was drawing. Noticing the small details that everyone else overlooked.

Claire tried to remember what Fray had said. The Royalists wanted Sophie because they needed royal blood, the same royal blood that flowed through Queen Estelle's veins and carried her power.

Claire's heart began to pound.

The *same* royal blood.

Sena had said that guild magic was like eye color—how sometimes, brown-eyed parents would give birth to blue-eyed children. And gray-eyed Claire knew that sometimes even sisters didn't share the same eyes. Sophie's were a warm brown.

Sophie's blood hadn't worked, but maybe that was not because she wasn't a princess. Maybe it was because she wasn't a *Gemmer* princess.

But Claire—whose drawing of unicorns seemed to have come to life, who'd pushed a pencil into rock, who'd spoken with a wyvern, who'd plucked a story from stone trees—she *was*.

She'd known, but hadn't wanted to know. She didn't want to be a member of the guild that had enslaved Sena's people and had created a rock slide that destroyed a Tiller village. The guild that Sena said was full of stubborn, hard-hearted people, the guild that only produced villains.

But as a Gemmer, Claire had a chance to save her sister.

The Unicorn Harp, though mostly ember and ash, still burned. Its magic lingered in the air, like rain before a storm. To wake the unicorn, all she needed to do was add her blood to the rock.

She slipped out from under Sophie's weight and gently lowered her sister's head to the base of Queen Rock. Then she ran toward Unicorn Rock.

Getting royal Gemmer blood would be easy enough. The wound on her knee from when she'd fallen by the narrowboats had opened when the club-swinging Royalist knocked her down.

Wiping the blood away from her knee with her thumb, she hesitated for just a moment. What if she was wrong? But then she saw the wraiths, hundreds of them, circling Sophie's pale form.

"*GET AWAY FROM HER!*" Claire screamed. "*DON'T TOUCH HER! STAY—*" Something cold and hard wrapped around her throat, cutting her off.

She had been so focused on Sophie, Claire hadn't noticed the wraith that had come for her.

As its skeletal hand, smelling of rotten flesh, tightened around her neck, Claire knew, in that horrible way one always knows, that she had made an irrevocable mistake.

She gasped for breath as the wraith dragged her slowly back, away from Unicorn Rock, and away from her sister, lying still on the ground. Sophie seemed so small as she lay there, unaware of the shadows swooping down toward her.

Dark thoughts wrapped around Claire's mind as she felt herself drowning in the wraith's cold. All she wanted to do was stop caring. Numbness might even be all right.

No.

Something turned inside Claire. She would wade through swamps, traverse a thousand tunnels, and even face a hundred wraiths—*but she would not lose her sister.*

She would *not* lose her again.

Claire lunged, swinging out with her hand. She missed the

shadowy skeleton, but the wraith had not expected her sudden movement and she felt the creature's grip slip just a hair.

She slammed herself forward once more.

Pain thrummed through her knuckles as they scraped against the Unicorn Rock.

Nothing happened.

Her blood wasn't enough. She wasn't enough. She couldn't do it. She didn't know the spell Fray knew. She didn't know how to harness magic. The wraith began to pull her away from the rock again.

How had she crafted magic before? The answer was there almost before she'd finished the question: *with her pencil.*

It was with her pencil that she had collapsed the cave. And she remembered the unicorn she'd drawn by the Rhona River—the one that had come to life. The one she'd sketched when she'd let herself imagine what it would have been like if there were still unicorns.

Try harder, Sophie's voice came from a memory. They sat at the dining room table, Sophie holding up multiplication flash cards for Claire. *Think!*

Claire had created magic before with her pencil and her thoughts. She didn't have her pencil anymore, but if she imagined what she had to do . . . If she could *shape* it . . .

Scraping the last of her strength, Claire lurched against the wraith's grasp again and slammed her bloody hand against the rock. But this time, she imagined the feel of glossy fur instead of obsidian. The warmth of a living heartbeat instead of a surface that cooled at sunset. The pounding of hooves against rock.

The tiniest tingle blossomed in her pinkie. The smallest of hums that Claire now knew wasn't a sign that something was wrong, but a sign that something was completely *right*.

Gasping for breath, she tried to focus. Storm-swift legs. Mane like a waterfall. Magic that crackled like lightning. A horn that pierced the sky.

The hum of magic zipped through Claire's bones and the rock beneath her palm warmed. Exhaustion crept toward her, threatening to drag her under, but still Claire held on.

She remembered the luminescence of the harp's strings, of the fire in Kleo's tapestry. She remembered the splintered unicorn statue that had stood alone, guarding Windemere's chimney.

A sharp blast of heat erupted from the stone, and the wraith screamed. Its clawed hand released Claire, and she fell to the ground, gasping as air rushed into her lungs. Lifting her head, she saw that the monolith had turned blazing white, the color of sun on snow.

Claire stumbled to her feet and ran back toward her sister. She threw herself next to Sophie just as there was a loud *crack*, followed by the sound of a million pebbles hitting the ground.

Scared of what she might see, she hesitated, but only for a second. There would be no more hiding from the truth. She forced herself to look.

Where the monolith had stood, there was a blinding radiance. And in the center of the brightness, she glimpsed diamond hooves, an arching neck, and eyes as clear as water, filled with such understanding that Claire wanted to sob for joy.

And between pointed ears, nestled in ribbons of silky mane, was a slender spiral that reached toward the sky.

Claire's eyes welled with tears.

The unicorn reared up, challenging the night, before it charged the sea of wraiths.

Claire clutched Sophie to her as the shadows howled their fury. And though some of the monsters tried to stand their ground, they stood no chance against the unicorn's horn, which dipped and rose, growing brighter and stronger each time.

Every strike of its hooves sent tremors through the ground, and the wraiths fled from it, like storm clouds from a spring wind.

It was beautiful, and yet even though the wraith's hand was no longer around Claire's neck, she still felt its chill pulling her away from consciousness, dragging her under. She willed herself to stay awake, but acrid thoughts, black as crude oil, were slowly eroding her away.

With misty eyes, Claire watched the last unicorn reach the edge of the plains. She wanted to call out to it. To tell the unicorn to come back and help Sophie, but her throat felt like it had been crushed.

And then, as if it had heard her thoughts—and maybe it had—the unicorn pivoted. Suddenly it was galloping back across the plains, streaking like dawn, toward the sisters.

As it drew near, the unicorn became less defined, until it looked more like a ball of light than a creature with legs and a tail—or maybe that was Claire's vision flickering out.

She thought she saw the arched neck bend low over Sophie, touching its spiral to her bleeding heart, but it was hard to know for sure.

Claire's own eyelids were closing, and something gleamed above her. But was it a spiraling horn, or the edge of a double-headed ax?

Before Claire could decide, everything—rocks and unicorn and world—extinguished like a falling star.

And then she, too, went out.

CHAPTER
27

Something wrapped around Claire's chest, keeping her trapped and still and angry. But she couldn't remember *what* it was, exactly, that she was mad about.

Sweat dampened her back. At least she was warm now, because the last thing she could remember was being cold—achingly cold.

No, that wasn't right.

The last thing she remembered was a burning harp. And rocks cracking, and a brilliant light, and ruby blood.

Her heart pounded faster.

And Francis lying, and the Royalist notching an arrow and—

"Sophie!" Claire surged awake, knocking the heavy quilt that had been tucked suffocatingly tight around her to the floor. She blinked.

Warm, white walls with scenes of golden trees and birds

surrounded her, while the ceiling above was decorated with sunbursts. A pinecone fire crackled behind a delicate lattice, filling the tiny room with the sharp, fresh smell of the mountains. The overall impression of the room was of sun and light and air.

Trying to find the memory that linked her last image of icy gloom to this merry place, Claire almost missed the soft sigh next to her.

Turning her head, her heart stopped. If this—the cozy room, the soft blankets, the sight in front of her—was a dream, it was one she never wanted to wake from.

For slipped under the heavy quilt and breathing evenly next to Claire was Sophie.

But not Sophie as Claire had last seen her, tunic crusted in dirt, hair wild, and complexion fading.

The Sophie next to her looked as though some museum restoration workers had come along with their paints and glosses, brushed away the fine tension around her lips, touched up her freckles, and added something *else* to her features that hadn't been there before.

As Claire stared at her sister, Sophie opened her eyes.

"You took all the covers again," she murmured. "*Oof!*"

The *oof* came from Claire flinging herself at Sophie. This Sophie wasn't some dream too delicate to be touched. She was warm and solid, even if she was a bit bony.

And the strength with which Sophie returned Claire's hug was the strength of a girl in full health—one who could be squeezed by her sister and be fine. A girl who could have

Experiences and scrape her knees again. A girl who had never spent a month in a hospital . . . or taken an arrow to her chest.

Claire pulled back. "Sophie, what *happened*?"

Sophie flopped back down onto the pillow. "I have no idea. The last thing I remember is looking at you, and then just kind of"—her fingers fluttered—"fading, I guess."

That wasn't exactly what Claire had meant, but before she could ask what Sophie had been doing in Arden this whole time, she needed to know one very important thing first.

"Are you okay?"

"I think so." Sophie wiggled her toes. "I'm pretty tired, but in a good way. Like after an afternoon of running around, or field day, or something." She rubbed a spot below her left collarbone, the same spot where the arrow had entered. "I'm a little sore here."

She moved her hand away to reveal a small pink scar in the shape of a crescent moon.

"The unicorn!" Claire breathed.

"Unicorn?"

And so Claire told Sophie what she thought she'd seen, never taking her eyes away from the unicorn's mark. When she'd finished, Sophie's eyes sparkled, shining with a joyful radiance that only comes after a harrowing ordeal.

"Does it hurt?" Claire asked.

Sophie brushed the crescent with the tip of her finger. "It kind of aches, but not really."

Gently, Claire placed her palm on Sophie's, and they interlocked fingers. "Can we go home now?"

"I'm afraid that is impossible," a voice said from the doorway. The tall form of Anvil Malchain stepped into the room.

He was even more terrible in person than he'd seemed in the Looking Glass. Everything about this man, from his haughty posture to the studs on his leather gloves, reminded Claire of barbed wire and sharp edges.

She lunged for the copper pitcher on the side table. "Get back," she said as she stood. "Leave us alone!"

"Please lie down; you'll exhaust yourself," Malchain said. "I mean you no harm."

"Why should we believe you?" Claire asked. The pitcher was small, but it was heavy. She could swing it if she needed to.

Malchain looked over at Sophie. "I take it you haven't told her yet?"

Sophie shook her head, her expression slightly bemused. "We just woke up."

Claire felt suddenly cold again. Maybe her sister wasn't okay after all, if she was talking to Malchain as though he were a friend and not a terrifying hunter.

"What's going on?" she demanded. "Why did you kidnap us?"

"*Claire*," Sophie said exasperatedly. "You've got it all wrong. Anvil hasn't captured us. He's helping us!"

Claire stared at her sister. She couldn't understand what Sophie was saying. "Helping us? Sophie, he's been *chasing* you! I saw you running from him in the Looking Glass!"

Malchain ran his hand over his shorn head. "Sophie, would you like to explain?"

Sophie bit her lip. "I can try." She looked at Claire and patted the quilt. "Sit."

But Claire had been quick to trust before, and that had gone badly. What if her sister was making the same mistake now? She shook her head.

"Suit yourself," Sophie said, sounding surprised. After all, Claire usually did what she asked.

Sophie sat up a little more in the bed and leaned back. "After the trip to Dr. Silva's, I knew the only thing that could fix me was magic. *Real* magic, not the coincidences that hospitals talked about at home."

Sophie brightened. "And there's such wonderful magic in Arden, Clairina! I've seen cloaks that make you invisible and shoes that help you dance and—"

Malchain cleared his throat, and Sophie quickly stopped. "Well, I'll tell you later. Anyway, I knew what I really needed was a unicorn, but everyone I asked in Arden said that that was impossible. Everyone, that is, except my friend Thorn. He's—"

"I know Thorn," Claire interrupted. "And Sena and Nett."

Sophie raised her eyebrows. "Really? Okay, then I guess you know that Thorn's Grand—that's what he calls his grandmother—was a Royalist. He told me that the only unicorn left in Arden was turned to stone. When I asked Francis about the legend of Queen Rock and Unicorn Rock, he told me to meet with Historian Mira Fray."

Sophie sighed as she wriggled deeper into her pillow nest. "I figured out the poem myself—it wasn't hard to do when all

I could think about was the well and the chimney. I wasn't sure what to do with the information, but everything at home kept getting worse and worse. That day when we were packing in the unicorn gallery it all kind of snapped into place. Even though I didn't know how to wake the unicorn, I just needed to *try*." Her mouth quirked into a smile. "You know me."

And Claire knew that she did.

"Then Thorn told me that a Forger was asking about me." Sophie looked at Anvil apologetically. "I thought you were going to force me out of Arden. I couldn't risk that! So I left Greenwood without asking Nett or Sena for help. I figured I would go to the capital and research crafting, but because of inspector raids and suspicious Tillers, I got all turned around."

Claire wanted to interrupt and ask how, exactly, she'd kept it a secret that she wasn't from Arden—and how she'd kept such a big secret from her—but now that Sophie was finally talking, Claire didn't want her to ever stop. Though she still kept one eye on Malchain, she lowered the pitcher a fraction, drinking in her sister's voice.

"I ended up in the Petrified Forest," Sophie continued. "Anvil found me there, and saved me. And that's when he explained—well"—her hands fluttered like white moths—"*everything.*"

"I see my cousin is making you do his dirty work, Princess Sophia." A new, female voice came from the doorway. "Why are you making her explain?"

Looking up, Claire saw a small woman with steel-gray

braids and a sensible dress bustle into the room, holding a tray with two steaming bowls. She looked how Claire would have imagined a fairy godmother to look: apple-round cheeks and gleaming spectacles. But when she bent over to set the tray on the nightstand, Claire saw two small axes strapped to her back.

A warrior fairy godmother, then.

"You are putting too much pressure on her, Anvil!" the woman scolded, and Claire was surprised to see the man look down at his toes. "She's still young, even if her manners are better than yours. Why haven't you introduced me to the new one yet?"

"Because you haven't stopped talking," Malchain said as Sophie hid a smile with her hand. "Claire, my cousin Aquila Malchain. This is her home."

"Pleasure." Aquila nodded to her. "Will you please put that pitcher down? It's an antique." And before Claire knew what had happened, the old woman had plucked the pitcher from her hands and replaced it with a bowl of soup. "There you go. Eat up!"

Claire looked sideways at Sophie, but her sister looked perfectly content—smug, even.

"Sophie, you still haven't told me we why we should trust them," Claire said, not bothering to lower her voice. She'd been through so much to get here, and she was tired of hiding places and hushed whispers. She just wanted to know why she shouldn't dump this soup on Malchain's head and take off running for the well. "If they aren't Royalists, why was Malchain after you?"

"You haven't told her yet?" Aquila looked at Malchain and Sophie. "Why haven't you told her?"

"Because she just woke up," Malchain said through gritted teeth. "If you would all just give me a moment. It's hard to know where to begin . . ."

"At the beginning," Aquila said.

"I suppose," Malchain said drily. He looked over at the girls, and Claire was startled to see how different he appeared than from his Looking Glass form. His eyes were not lusterless at all, but deep as a bass note and filled with something like sadness. "I'll take over the story, if that's all right with you, Princess."

Sophie nodded slightly. It was unnerving to Claire how easily her sister had adjusted to the title.

Malchain pulled a wicker chair from the corner and scooted it to the edge of the bed, while Aquila added a pinecone to the fire.

"What do you know about Queen Estelle of Arden?" he asked Claire.

"I know that people say she's a hero," Claire said, hesitating before plunging in, "but she wasn't. She wanted to kill the last unicorn, not save him."

Astonishment flicked across Malchain's face, looking as out of place as a butterfly in winter. Claire doubted the man was surprised often.

He nodded. "You're right. Queen Estelle is also responsible for the Unicorn Massacre that took place on the plains. She must never be woken from rock. Her return would mean a new reign of darkness for Arden."

"How do you know?" Claire asked, wondering if the Malchains had some secret way of making the Petrified Forest give up its secrets.

"The Gemmers were losing the war," Aquila said softly, taking a seat by the pinecone fire. "When Prince Martin defected from the Gemmers and Spinners, he went underground with some Forgers, helping them battle the royal armies. But when he heard what his sister had done, and what she was planning to do, he knew he had to do whatever it took to stop her.

"He sought the last unicorn, and together, unicorn and prince managed to trap Estelle in stone. It required a great deal of magic, though, and the consequence of this act was that the unicorn turned to stone as well. That was the price of ending the war: Arden's last unicorn."

Slowly, Claire sat down on the edge of the bed next to Sophie.

"With no more unicorns left in Arden," Aquila continued, "Prince Martin knew he must protect the Unicorn Treasure at all costs."

Claire frowned, pressing the soup bowl's warm sides against her hands. "But I thought there was no one all-powerful Unicorn Treasure that would be magic enough. I thought that the unicorn artifact the Royalists have been looking for this whole time was actually me and Sophie."

"You were right," Aquila said, smiling at Sophie who was listening intently, "she *is* smart."

Claire flushed with pleasure, as Anvil cut back in. "Prince Martin asked the most talented Forger of the time, Alloria

Malchain, for her help. Together, they created a passage between worlds, a magical place where fire meets water, and where both he and the Unicorn Treasure would be safe from Estelle's greed. Knowing that his blood would unlock his craftsmanship, he exiled himself until a time when the unicorn could be safely awoken, in a time when no one would want to kill it."

"Well, there's a unicorn out there *now*," Sophie said excitedly. "Claire woke him! He healed me."

Aquila and Malchain exchanged a look.

"Maybe, my dear," Aquila said tenderly. "But the unicorn is very old, and the power needed to heal someone so close to death must be very great indeed. I'm not sure of the . . . consequences."

Sophie's face fell a little, but Claire could tell that she hadn't let go of her hope. And maybe Sophie was right to hope. After all, Claire hadn't seen what had happened to the unicorn. In fact, she wasn't even sure if there had been one until she'd seen the thin scar on Sophie's collarbone where before there had only been a gaping wound.

The soup bowl was now cold, but Claire didn't care. "And what *is* the Unicorn Treasure?" she asked.

Malchain looked at Sophie, and Sophie nodded. She reached around her neck to unclasp Great-Aunt Diana's necklace—the moonstone one she had found in Windemere's linen closet. Carefully, Sophie laid it on top of the quilt.

The four teardrop moonstones glimmered softly, iridescent rainbows against the quilt.

Sophie nudged Claire. "Go on, pick it up."

Claire tried to read her sister's face, but it was impossible to tell what she was thinking. The necklace's weight was comforting in her palm, smooth as a marble and oddly warm to the touch. And though there was a faint magical thrum under her finger pads, something felt . . . off.

Not wrong, far from it.

But she didn't get the same sense of *rockness* she'd experienced in the wyvern's cave, or in the Petrified Forest, and then again on the Sorrowful Plains. In fact, they didn't *feel* like rocks at all . . .

Claire looked up to Malchain and Sophie, who were staring at her intently. "They're not moonstones, are they?" she asked. "They're not rock."

"You are right," Malchain said, nodding. "They are not. They're what we call 'moontears.' They each hold, within, a unicorn waiting to be born. *They* are the last hope of Arden—the unicorns' greatest treasure."

Claire gaped at him, at the wild, wondrous things he was saying. She was glad she had sat back down on the bed. She wasn't sure if her legs would have been able to support her.

"Though we're not entirely sure what must be done next," Malchain said, his gray eyes boring into hers, "we *are* certain that only a princess of Arden can waken them."

"That's why Anvil was able to track me so easily," Sophie said softly, putting her hand on Claire's. "Alloria Malchain forged a Kompass so that her descendants would know when the moontears had returned. For three hundred years, their family has watched the needle, waiting for it to spin. And finally, several months ago, when you and I first arrived at Hilltop Palace, it did."

Sophie twisted a strand of dark hair around her finger. "Malchain and Aquila took me to the Sorrowful Plains, and I tried to wake Unicorn Rock. It didn't work, obviously, but we didn't know why until now. We needed *you*, Claire."

"Me?" Claire asked, confused. "Why?"

"I'm not a Gemmer, but you are." She shrugged casually, but Claire recognized the tiniest twinge of envy in her movement.

Malchain stood up, looking ridiculously big and solid in the small, airy room. "Princess Claire, we will not keep you against your will, but we ask—no, we *beg*—you to stay, for a little longer at least."

He looked at her expectantly, waiting for her reply, but Claire was still caught on that strange word: "princess."

"What would I do?" she asked, buying time.

"We'd go to Stonehaven," Malchain said. "It's one of the few remaining Gemmer settlements, and perhaps the only place where there might be more information on how to care for moontears. You also need training."

Malchain eyed Claire as though she might turn the room to pebbles at any moment. "An unpracticed apprentice with obviously strong powers makes me nervous, even if you aren't a Forger."

Thoughts and information skidded in Claire's mind. "Can . . . can I talk to Sophie? Alone?"

Malchain hesitated, and Aquila swooped in. "Of course, my

dears. Just ring the bell when you've decided." She pointed to the little copper bell on the nightstand. Malchain looked like he wanted to say something, but Aquila opened the door and waved him out.

After the door clicked shut, the sisters were silent for a moment.

Claire kept her eyes on the quilt, tracing the embroidered leaves that curled around the edges.

"Claire, look at me."

She didn't want to, but after all they had just been through, she wasn't about to refuse her. Meeting Sophie's eyes, she was once again struck by how well she looked. Not just pretty, but healthy and strong.

"What's wrong, Claire?"

"Nothing," she said, shrugging. "It's overwhelming, the whole 'princess' thing. But—"

"No, not that," Sophie said, and her eyebrows lifted. "There's something else. I know you're mad at me. Tell me."

"You really don't know?" Claire asked.

"Just tell me, already!"

"Fine," Claire snapped in her most Sena-like way. "How's this: you *knew* I was in Arden!"

"What? No I didn't!"

"Yes, you did," she insisted. "How else did you know I was at the Sorrowful Plains? How else did you show up at *exactly* the right time?"

"Oh!" Sophie said. She gave a smug smile. "That's easy to explain. The Malchains forged different ways to keep an eye on Queen Rock without having to actually be at the Sorrowful Plains. You know how scientists use seismographs to measure earthquakes? The Malchains crafted something similar, but instead of drawing waves, it draws full scenes of what's happening there at any given moment."

She reached out and tugged one of Claire's curls that had long ago fallen from her braid. "You can't believe how scared I was when I checked it this evening and saw that it had drawn *you,* surrounded by a bunch of Royalists. Neither Anvil nor Aquila were home, so I ran to you as fast as I could."

She squeezed Claire's leg. "You have to believe me. If I had known you were in Arden earlier I would have come to you immediately!"

And by the tilt of Sophie's head and the slightest squint of the eyes, Claire knew—from the ends of her curls to the tips of her toes—that this time, Sophie was telling the truth.

Claire nodded, and Sophie opened her arms. Claire fell into them.

She could have stayed like that for ages, basking in her sister's pride and admiration. There were no words to describe what she was feeling—but she thought that if she only had a paint set, she would be able to capture its impression.

It was Claire who finally broke the hug.

"So what do you want to do?" Sophie asked.

"You're asking me?" Claire was surprised. Sophie had never before asked what Claire thought about something. She normally just did, and waited for her little sister to follow.

"Of course." She grabbed Claire's hands and squeezed. "You

came all this way to take me home, and I promise, if you say you want to leave, we will. We will go straight back to the well and never come back. Mom and Dad won't know either way because of the difference of time. It's up to you."

Claire had thought she'd known the answer, but suddenly she wasn't so sure.

A memory of blue flames turning yellow consuming the Unicorn Harp on the Sorrowful Plains darted into her mind. Arden was a place both dangerous and lovely.

Yes, there were wraiths, but there were also lonely wyverns and glories of fireflies. And unicorns.

Her heart squeezed—and friends, too. What had happened to Sena and Nett? Were they okay?

And Claire realized then what she wanted to do.

"I want to stay," she blurted out. For a heartbeat, she wished she still had her pencil's comforting point, but her sister's hand was there to squeeze instead. "I want to help."

A smile broke across Sophie's face. "Are you sure? You could always go back while I finish things here."

"No, I *want* to stay," Claire said, wrapping her thumb around Sophie's like an anchor. "We're sisters. And this time, we'll be together."

Sophie squeezed back. "Always."

Claire smiled and rang the bell.

EPILOGUE

He was too late.

The boy stood among shards of black stone, their razor-sharp edges scattered across the Sorrowful Plains like memories best forgotten.

Unicorn Rock was gone, though Queen Rock still stood.

He puzzled at it, wondering why the wraiths had chosen to destroy the first instead of the latter. Or why they had destroyed Unicorn Rock at all.

A breeze brushed his cheek, and with it came the smell of smoke, though the nearest village was a few hours' ride from the plains. Not for the first time he was glad he'd waited until morning to come. Even in sunlight, the plains were . . . ominous. Desolate. Creepy.

But it would be worth it when he'd proven himself to them all.

Setting his travel pack down, he pulled out a small bundle of sticks and a handful of straw he'd packed for just this moment. Quickly, he stacked the twigs and straw together in a small pile. He spent the next fifteen minutes rubbing two sticks together, trying to get a fire to start. He'd always been the slowest of the apprentices at these things, but not for long . . .

First there was smoke, then a spark, and finally—flame.

He reached into his pocket and withdrew a small handkerchief, careful not to touch the red flecks on it. Unfolding the fabric, he removed the pearly tooth from its center.

His heart began to pound.

Soon.

He held the Unicorn Tooth over the fire, but there he paused.

What if Grand was wrong?

But what interested him more was what if his Grand was *right*? That was why he'd come. Well, that, among other reasons.

If you stick to what people think of you, that's all you'll ever be, she had said.

He dropped the Unicorn Tooth into the fire, and the flames flared blue. He hoped that meant the pure magic trapped within the unicorn ivory was being released. He hoped that it and the drops of blood would be enough.

Holding the handkerchief by a corner, he thought how lucky he'd been that Claire—*Princess* Claire, with Gemmer blood—had scraped her knees on the banks of Rhona River. It hadn't been until later, when the three were already down the river and he was trying to fall asleep, that he'd truly realized what Nett had said: Sophie had escaped down a *well*.

So he'd stolen a Greenwood horse and hurried to join Claire in Fyrton. He'd recognized the remnants of Insta-Grow outside Phlogiston Academy, and after he'd talked his way in, he'd gone to the library. Claire hadn't been there, but he'd seen the tooth, and an idea had come to him, one that would guarantee he would find Sophie . . . he just needed magic first.

And then, just as he'd been about to set out, he'd seen Claire and the others break into Scythe's Silverorium. When he'd rescued them and learned that they were also going toward the Sorrowful Plains, he realized he did not want to share his plans.

He did not want their help.

He did not want them taking credit for what *he* had discovered.

Arden needed only one hero.

For a moment, he wondered if it was possible that Unicorn Rock hadn't actually been destroyed by wraiths. That the unicorn had been awakened. But that was impossible, because he had sent Claire on a longer route under Mount Rouge, through the mines and into the swamps, while he rode straight for the Sorrowful Plains.

And now he was here, staring at the handkerchief. Alone. Ready. Lucky. So lucky, in fact, that he thought it must be fate.

He was *destined* to wake the queen.

He was destined to finally get his magic.

Thorn Barley raised the blood-speckled handkerchief to Queen Rock, and hoped Grand had been right.

ACKNOWLEDGMENTS

Magic doesn't stop on this side of the chimney—far from it. I am incredibly lucky to have an entire academy of Forgers, Tillers, Spinners, and Gemmers who helped in the crafting of *The Unicorn Quest*.

Many thanks are owed to the story Forgers at Glasstown Entertainment: Laura Parker, Lexa Hillyer, Alexa Wejko, Adam Silvera, Emily Berge, and Lynley Bird. Their relentless enthusiasm, compassionate criticism, and limitless belief helped forge me into the writer I am today. Special thanks to Lexa, who hammered my ideas into shape and polished my words into focus, and to Alexa, for following me up the chimney time and again with boundless creativity. Thank you to Stephen Barbara, not only for his help with this book, but for taking a chance on me years ago. An author doesn't need a Kompass with him around to guide. Thank you to the rest of the Inkwell Management Literary Agency team, in particular Lyndsey Blessing and Claire Draper, for helping with the navigation.

For the Tillers at Bloomsbury, I have only endless amounts of gratitude and awe for the incredible people who have dedicated their lives to growing authors and nurturing books. To Cat Onder, thank you from the bottom of my heart for journeying into Arden with me, and to Sarah Shumway for eagerly joining and carrying on the charge. Thank you to Cindy Loh, Erica Barmash, Amanda Bartlett, Anna Bernard, Bethany Buck, Alexis Castellanos, Beth Eller, Alona Fryman, Emily Gerbner, Cristina Gilbert, Betts Greene, Courtney Griffin, Noella James, Melissa Kavonic, Emily Klopfer, Donna Mark, Elizabeth Mason, Shaelyn McDaniel, Linda Minton, Brittany Mitchell, Oona Patrick, Emily Ritter, Claire Stetzer, Ellen Whitaker, and Chandra Wohleber. I feel incredibly lucky to have Arden so beautifully depicted by Vivienne To on the American cover and Matt Saunders on the UK cover. I want to live inside your magical illustrations. And across the Atlantic, thank you to my wonderful UK team: Elise Burns, Nicholas Church, Jenny Collins, Anna de Lacey, Laura Main Ellen, Maia Fjord, Adele Lee, Fabia Ma, Lucy Mackay-Sim, and Emily Monckton-Milnes.

The first step to writing a book inevitably takes place in a classroom, and I had A+ scholars throughout my life whose lessons have remained with me even as I've graduated and moved away by miles and years. They are Maggie Cassidy, Tracy Luke, and Missy Ellis at Bishop Chatard High School, and Professor Shannon Martin and Thomas French at Indiana University.

I am grateful to be surrounded by many Spinners of tales. Thanks to the indomitable Rhoda Belleza for sharing her wisdom; Tiffany Liao for her unwavering support; Kristina Pérez for her keen eye and sharp observations; Tara Sonin for her immeasurable encouragement and ebullient spirit; Annie Stone for her generosity and expertise in fantastical worlds; Angela Velez for her empathy and ingenuity; and to the ladies of TQB for their ongoing support, particularly Melissa Albert, as we journey into the next phase together.

To my fierce and loyal Gemmers, who have given their guidance and friendship throughout the years, special thanks goes to Medea Asatiani, Catherine Bates, Kati Gyulassy, and Matt Richman. And enormous thanks to Liz Silva, D.J. Silva, Molly Silva, Katie Blacquier, Charlotte Blacquier, and Eliza Blacquier—your insights were invaluable and your reactions were exactly what every author dreams of one day hearing.

And last, but not least, my utmost gratitude to my unicorns. To Marguerite Benko who read to me every day and whose strength I one day hope to have. To Zoltán Benko, who encouraged my wild flights of fancy and pored over each draft of this novel with love and laughter. To Gabriella Benko and Matthias Benko, my sister and my brother, whose tenacity, talent, and imagination inspired me then and today. And to Andrej Ficnar— there are not enough scrolls in this world or Arden to contain my appreciation. This book would not exist without you.